"We're good together."

He plunged his long fingers through her hair. "You know I'm right."

His fingers slid from beneath her hair and trailed tenderly across her cheeks. Catherine's belly ached in repressed arousal. Her chest ached with the depth of her emotions. Her eyes and throat ached from holding back tears. Intuition nagged her soul, telling her only Easy held the power to soothe those aches.

She lifted her chin. His mouth, so perfectly shaped and sensual, weakened her resolve.

"I can't, Easy," she said, pleading more with herself than with him.

"I need you." His voice was husky with sincerity. "I'll never stop wanting you. We belong together and you know it. And I won't let you marry another man. You're mine."

D0028013

ABOUT THE AUTHOR

Sheryl Lynn lives in a pine forest atop a hill in Colorado. When not writing, she amuses herself by embarrassing her two teenagers, walking her dogs in a nearby park and feeding peanuts to the dozens of Steller's jays, scrub jays, blue jays and squirrels who live in her backyard. Her best ideas come from the newspapers, although she admits that a lot of what she reads is way too weird for fiction.

Books by Sheryl Lynn

Don't miss any of our special offers. Write to us at the following address for information on our newest releases.

Harlequin Reader Service
U.S.: 3010 Walden Ave., P.O. Box 1325, Buffalo, NY 14269
Canadian: P.O. Box 609, Fort Erie, Ont. L2A 5X3

Easy Loving
Sheryl Lynn

Harlequin Books

TORONTO • NEW YORK • LONDON
AMSTERDAM • PARIS • SYDNEY • HAMBURG
STOCKHOLM • ATHENS • TOKYO • MILAN
MADRID • WARSAW • BUDAPEST • AUCKLAND

If you purchased this book without a cover you should be aware that this book is stolen property. It was reported as "unsold and destroyed" to the publisher, and neither the author nor the publisher has received any payment for this "stripped book."

This is for John Hawk, wherever he may be.

ISBN 0-373-22467-2

EASY LOVING

Copyright © 1998 by Jaye W. Manus

All rights reserved. Except for use in any review, the reproduction or utilization of this work in whole or in part in any form by any electronic, mechanical or other means, now known or hereafter invented, including xerography, photocopying and recording, or in any information storage or retrieval system, is forbidden without the written permission of the publisher, Harlequin Enterprises Limited, 225 Duncan Mill Road, Don Mills, Ontario, Canada M3B 3K9.

All characters in this book have no existence outside the imagination of the author and have no relation whatsoever to anyone bearing the same name or names. They are not even distantly inspired by any individual known or unknown to the author, and all incidents are pure invention.

This edition published by arrangement with Harlequin Books S.A.

® and TM are trademarks of the publisher. Trademarks indicated with ® are registered in the United States Patent and Trademark Office, the Canadian Trade Marks Office and in other countries.

Printed in U.S.A.

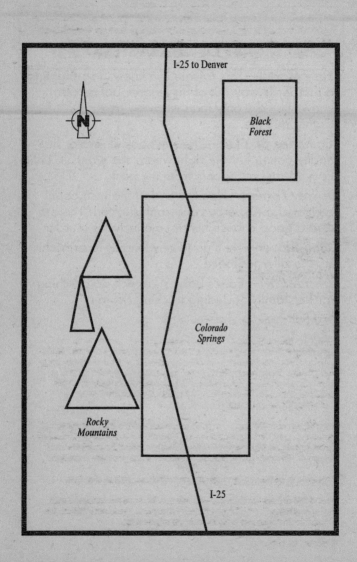

CAST OF CHARACTERS

Easy Martel—This private eye knows investigating a murder is way out of his league, but he also knows he's the only man who can save Catherine's life.

Catherine St. Clair—The shy book illustrator has finally gotten her life right where she wants it, until Easy Martel reappears from the past.

Jeffrey Livman—He's the perfect man, smooth, educated, prosperous and sophisticated. There's also a good chance his résumé includes murder.

John Tupper—He'll go to any lengths to bring his sister's killer to justice.

Trish Martel—Easy's baby sister will do anything for her family, including tracking down a lost child.

Chapter One

While hurrying across the parking lot, Easy Martel spotted his sister emerging from her Mustang. He lifted his gaze to the heavens and whispered, *"Yes."* Dumb luck, his favorite ally, came through for him again.

"Trish!" he shouted and waved her toward his Chevy. She said something to the man who accompanied her. Easy urged them both to hurry. He flung his equipment bag into the back seat of his car. He slid behind the steering wheel.

Trish opened the passenger door and peered suspiciously inside. "What—?"

"Get in, get in. Your timing is perfect. I need your help. Hurry." He glanced at his watch and prayed the traffic lights were with him. "Come on, Trish! I'm running out of time."

She told her friend to get in the back. She sat in the front passenger seat. Easy gunned the engine and squealed out of the parking lot.

"Are you crazy?" Trish fumbled with her seat belt. "Don't bother answering. You are crazy. What are we doing?"

"Going to the airport." He looked over his shoulder at the stranger. The man was around forty, slim, with thinning blond hair and bulging eyes. Not one of Trish's boyfriends, Easy surmised. She had a weakness for the tall, dark and stupid type.

"Wait a minute! I'm not helping you." Trish emphasized the words by clamping her arms over her bosom and jutting her chin. "The last time I helped, that guy sicced a dog on me and chased me with a pipe wrench. He almost killed me!"

Trish was thirteen months younger than he, but they looked so much alike with their dark hair and eyes, people often mistook them for twins. Like him, she had an adventurous streak seven miles wide. He flashed his most winning smile. "I promise, no dogs, no pipe wrenches. I need to shoot some video. My client tipped me off. She's positive her husband is taking his girlfriend on a business trip."

Trish pulled a face. "You are so sleazy!"

"Me? This dirtbag tells his wife that he has to go on an emergency trip. Ha! He set it up so she can't interrupt his fun." He met the stranger's reflection in the rearview. "Hi, I'm Easy Martel, the sleazy private eye."

The man used a handkerchief to mop at his brow. "Uh, John Tupper." He nervously eyed the passing scenery while Easy raced down Fountain Boulevard.

Trish twisted on the seat. "John, this is my brother. Easy, John works with me at the insurance company. He's an adjuster. I told him you can help him."

The majority of Easy's business dealt with insurance fraud. In the past six years he'd become an expert at ferreting out cheats who faked injuries or lied about stolen property. He kept his eyes on the road, alert for any lurking cops who might object to his speeding. "What you got?" He stomped on the gas to beat a yellow light. "Fake back injury? Phony burglary?"

Trish yelped and clutched the dashboard. "Slow down!"

He turned onto Powers and checked the time again. The

dirtbag's plane departed in thirty-nine minutes. Easy hoped to catch him playing preboarding kissy face with his honey. He goosed the speed up to sixty-five.

"Uh, actually, it's personal, Mr. Martel," John said. He held on to the back of Trish's seat with both hands.

"Call me Easy, John. We're all family here."

Trish enjoyed tagging along when he needed an extra pair of hands, and she was as good, and sometimes better than him when it came to research. Some aspects of his job repelled her, though. A hopeless romantic when it came to family matters, she'd never recommend him for a child custody case or a cheating spouse.

"How personal are we talking?"

"His sister was murdered," Trish said. "The police say it's an accident, but it's not."

Easy changed lanes to pass a semi. To his left he noted an airliner banking for final approach toward the Colorado Springs airport. "If I've told you once, I've told you a million times, I don't stick my nose in capital cases. Only TV private eyes get involved in murders."

She huffed her exasperation. "You have to hear what's going on. You can help him, Easy, I know you can. You *have* to."

He reached the airport entrance in record time. Concentrating on driving, praying for a parking spot in the usually overcrowded lot, he waved his sister into silence. He'd been after this slimeball for two weeks. His client knew her husband was cheating. Wives always knew. She wanted proof, something to shove in his face, but the dirtbag knew his wife knew and was being very careful. The spur-of-the-moment "business" trip proved it.

So as not to get hung up at the security checkpoint, he began emptying his pockets. He tossed coins, pens, a penlight, a Swiss Army knife, a pair of handcuffs, a ring of master keys and his cell phone on the floor at Trish's feet. She grimaced at the clattering collection.

"If you don't chase killers, why bother carrying handcuffs?"

"My girlfriends like them."

Dumb luck stayed with him; he found a parking spot in the first row. He grabbed his equipment bag. "We can talk inside. Hurry!" He took off at a run for the terminal with John and Trish right on his heels. Inside, he tore up the escalator. He paused at a monitor displaying departure times to find the gate he needed.

"What are you going to do?" Trish demanded breathlessly.

"Put you in the movies." He clapped a hand on John's bony shoulder and shoved him closer to Trish. He approved of the man's gray suit and her soft blue dress. Nice, but not too dressy. "You two make a great-looking couple."

Cringing away from Trish, John tugged at his jacket. "Uh, I'm married."

"It's only acting."

They met up with a crowd at the security checkpoint, but fortunately airport security hadn't limited entry to ticket holders only. Easy anxiously checked his watch while Trish peeled off her oversize earrings, necklace and an armful of bracelets before she stopped setting off the metal detector alarms.

"You wear too much junk," Easy grumbled.

"I didn't ask for a trip to the airport." She trotted to keep up while she worked the earrings back into her earlobes.

He strode down the terminal, unzipping the bag as he went. He pulled out the video camera and turned it on. He double-checked the battery and blew minuscule pieces of lint off the lens. Everything operated perfectly.

At the gate his luck continued. Seated side by side in the waiting area, Dirtbag and his honey held hands. Even better, they faced the broad bank of windows; sun glare wouldn't interfere with the taping. Easy huddled with Trish and John.

"Make like honeymooners." He handed John the equipment bag. "It's the guy over there in the checked suit sitting with the brunette. Move behind them so I can get them in the picture."

John slung the equipment bag over his shoulder. "We don't have to go to court or anything, do we?"

"Nope. You're just innocent passersby."

Trish groaned. "I can't believe I'm doing this."

"Hey, when you get married and your old man cheats on you, you'll thank me when I catch him."

Trish stiffened, arching her brows. "Any man I marry will never cheat."

"That's right, because then I'll have to kill him. Go on. Ham it up. Make me believe you're in love."

The taping went as smooth as creamy peanut butter. He even captured the dirtbag grinning at Trish's and John's antics. The brunette leaned over to give Dirtbag a big smooch on the lips.

He kept videotaping while the adulterous pair boarded the plane. Chuckling, he turned off the camera. "Thanks, Trish, John. I love it when a plan comes together." He patted the camera, knowing he'd earned yet another month's payment on his motorcycle. "I owe you lunch."

"You owe me a lot more than that." Trish grabbed his arm and steered him into a small cafeteria. "You have to listen to John. It's really important."

Forcing a sober expression he turned to his sister's friend. "I don't have access to the forensic tools the cops have. Besides, interfering with police investigations is a good way to end up in prison. I'm sorry, man, but I'm the wrong guy for the job."

Trish urged the men to sit at a small table. "Shut up and listen, Easy. It's a lot more personal than you think.

Remember Catherine St. Clair? She's back in town." She swished away to fetch coffee.

Easy gawked at his sister's back. Catherine...*his* Catherine? Never Cat or Cathy or Cee-cee or Cate—Easy had nicknamed her Tinker Bell. Even after twelve years the sound of her name turned his insides hot and cold while an odd sensation ruffled below his diaphragm.

He knew she'd moved to Arizona. Years ago, he'd traced her address and phone number—he kept them locked away in a file cabinet. Sometimes the urge to call her or appear on her doorstep grew so strong it drove him a little bit crazy. Only the still-tender shreds of his broken heart kept him from following through.

Annoyed at the way old emotions sneaked up on him, Easy cleared his throat. "How do you know Catherine?"

"I don't," John said. "I know the man she's dating. His name is Jeffrey Livman. He was my sister's husband, the man she loved. He murdered her." He smoothed a hand over the side of his fine hair and dragged in a long, shaky breath. His voice firmed up, seething with well-nourished rage. "Jeffrey didn't wait a full month after Roberta died before he began dating Miss St. Clair."

Trish returned with a red-plastic tray holding three cups of coffee. "I freaked when John showed me the pictures he took of Catherine with Jeffrey. I haven't seen her since high school when you guys broke up and she moved away."

His Catherine... "You said the cops don't think it's murder. What am I supposed to do?"

"You better figure out something," Trish said. "John and I are convinced Jeffrey is going to marry Catherine so he can murder her, too."

"WILL YOU MARRY ME, Catherine?"

Catherine St. Clair nearly choked on a spoonful of raspberry sorbet. Momentarily frightened by the sensation of her throat filled with shards of crystalline ice, she swallowed hard and followed it with a gulp of water.

Jeffrey patted between her shoulder blades. "Did I startle you? I'm sorry."

She dabbed at her lips with a napkin and cast him a look askance. "Don't make jokes when I have my mouth full."

"I'm serious. I love you and want you to be my wife. We're the perfect couple, honey. Together we'll conquer the world."

She searched for any hint of laughter in his pale blue eyes. He was serious.

She shifted on the seat and glanced nervously around the restaurant. She and Jeffrey dined often at the Grape and Olive, and always took the back corner booth. The few other diners didn't pay her and Jeffrey any attention. "I'm flattered, but we barely know each other."

He shook a finger at her. "You said we were soul mates."

"I meant because of the house." Five months ago she'd hired Jeffrey, a real-estate broker, to help her find a house to buy. He'd found the perfect property for her—a charming raised rancher, with fixer-upper potential, on ten acres in Black Forest—as if he'd magically conjured her dream into reality. Since it had been a cash sale, she'd closed quickly on the deal. To celebrate, Jeffrey had taken her to dinner. They'd been dating ever since.

She admired his energy and assertiveness. He liked being in control of any situation. In small doses his domineering personality suited her, acting as a foil for her withdrawing nature. He loved the outdoors as much as she. He was brilliant when it came to finances, so she often sought his advice about investments. They had fun together.

But marriage?

"I love you, Catherine, truly, madly, deeply. And—" He reached inside his jacket and brought out a velvet-covered box. "I am more serious about you than I've ever been about anything, or anyone, in my entire life." He opened the box. Jewels glittered in the candlelight.

An elaborate gold setting contained a large blue sapphire nestled inside a double circle of diamonds. Her breath caught in her throat. She clutched her hands into fists, wanting to touch the ring, but not daring.

"I had this custom-made to match your eyes." He inched the box closer to her, urging her to touch it. "Please, darling, do me the honor of being my wife."

Gus Neci, the restaurant owner, approached the corner booth. Catherine sat in stunned silence while Jeffrey leaned forward, his handsome face alit with eager anticipation.

"Everything is well, yes?" Gus asked. He wheeled a small cart next to the table. Atop a white linen cloth, a silver ice bucket chilled a bottle of champagne. Two slender flutes gleamed in the candlelight. A bouquet of red roses, wrapped in silvery paper, rested next to the ice bucket.

Flustered, she shoved another spoonful of sorbet in her mouth. Jeffrey had obviously planned the proposal down to the smallest detail. Annoyance tightened her forehead and chest. He had no right to spring this kind of surprise on her. "Everything is fine, Gus, thank you."

Neither man reacted to her icy tone. Jeffrey displayed the ring for Gus's admiration. With a grand flourish, Gus presented Catherine with the roses. She forced herself to accept them. She managed a gracious smile, but inside she seethed. While Gus opened the champagne, she whispered, "I haven't said yes, Jeffrey."

"You can't say no." He pulled the ring from the box and reached for her left hand.

She twisted on the seat and fussed with the roses. Jeffrey managed to snag her pinkie finger. In the midst of the ridiculous tug-and-pull match that ensued, Gus set the champagne flutes on the table.

"A toast to the happy couple! May you live happily ever after."

Catherine snatched her hand free. She struck a champagne flute and set it flying. She lifted a stricken gaze to the restaurant owner. "I'm so sorry!"

Gus snapped his fingers for the busboy. "You must be shivering with joy. Such a handsome couple you are. Both so blond and all-American. You are every person's dream, yes?" He whipped a napkin from his back pocket and began mopping up the spilled champagne.

Jeffrey offered his champagne to her. "We're like Romeo and Juliet."

"They died," she said darkly. Not only was Jeffrey the only friend she'd made since moving back to Colorado, he was the first man she'd met in years with whom she felt comfortable. If she refused to marry him, he might break off the relationship altogether.

"I have to go home," she announced and tossed the napkin on the table. "Gus, the fettuccine was superb and do tell the chef the sorbet is excellent. Thank you."

"Catherine, wait—"

"I'm sorry, I have an early morning appointment. I'll call you, okay?" She grabbed her purse and scooted out of the booth. Her gauze skirt tangled around her thighs and for a moment she feared falling flat on her face.

Jeffrey's pale eyes turned flinty in the flickering candlelight. "The champagne. It's Dom Pérignon—"

"I can't drink and drive." She swiped at her skirt, knowing she made an ass of herself, but unable to help it.

Two booths away, a slim blond woman wearing a tailored suit stood up and stared. Catherine recognized the title company closer who had processed the paperwork for Catherine's house purchase. Jeffrey claimed he and the woman were good friends, but at the closing the woman had seemed uncomfortable and not friendly in the least. At the moment, she appeared horrified.

Noreen, Catherine finally remembered. Her cheeks burned, but she forced a smile. "Well, hello, again. Noreen?"

Noreen shifted her stare to Jeffrey. "I thought I recognized your voice, Jeff. Did I hear right? You guys are engaged?" A sickly smile thinned her lips. She lowered her gaze to the cart holding the champagne. Her voice rose an octave. "You're going to get married?"

Jeffrey had said "good friends," but Noreen's reaction clearly showed they'd been closer than mere friends. Catherine had never asked Jeffrey about his past relationships—she'd never cared. All she cared about at the moment was escape.

"Nice seeing you again, Noreen. I'd love to stay and chat, but I have…" Her ability to continue the lie ran out of steam. "Goodbye, Gus." She fled the restaurant.

Jeffrey caught up to her in the parking lot while she unlocked the door of her Blazer. "Darling, what's the matter?"

"You know I'm not comfortable with public scenes. How could you do that to me? I'm so embarrassed." She stared miserably at the toes of her woven sandals. "I'm sorry, I need some time to be alone. To think."

He opened the car door for her and reached past her to place the bouquet of roses on the passenger seat. "You do love me," he said. "I know it, you know it." He pressed the ring box into her hand. She resisted, but he persisted until she closed her fingers around the box. "We can't fight fate, darling."

The velvet box seemed to weigh a hundred pounds. "I can't—we don't—you don't know me!"

He stepped back and hung his head, his sheepish smile painted gold by the parking lot lights. "I'm a fast learner. I'll never do anything to embarrass you again." He pulled his fingers across his lips in a zippering motion. "I won't pressure you either. I won't say a word about it. All I ask is that you take the ring and think about how much I love you.''

Somewhat soothed, she nodded dumbly. He pressed a tender kiss to her forehead.

''I'll make you the happiest woman in the world. I'll devote my life to making you smile. Think about it.'' He gave her room to slide behind the steering wheel. ''I love you.''

She wished she could say, ''I love you,'' back at him. Except she could not say what she did not mean. Until she trusted him enough to tell him the truth about herself, she could not love him. Unless she loved him, she could not tell him. She hoped he returned to the restaurant and shared the champagne with Noreen. They could rekindle their romance, and Catherine wouldn't have to deal with Jeffrey anymore.

Ambiguous emotions wore on her during the long drive home.

At home she set the ring box on the fireplace mantel in her studio. She tried to forget it. It was like trying to forget a sore tooth. She refused to open the box, refused to try on the ring—Mrs. Jeffrey Livman.

She didn't sleep well that night.

''WOULD MARRIAGE BE SO BAD?'' she asked Oscar and Bent, the greyhounds, when the three of them took their morning run. Up and down the hilly red graveled road she jogged, trying to regulate her breathing in the thin high-country air. The greyhounds focused straight ahead, their long legs springing in graceful motion.

The dogs liked Jeffrey. Or at least, they tolerated him with the same regal aloofness with which they tolerated most visitors. She frowned at their knobby, bobbing heads. If the greyhounds judged character, they kept it strictly to themselves.

Later, when her agent called from New York, Catherine asked, "Margaret, what do you think about marriage?"

"I think it's a hell of an expensive way for a man to get his laundry done."

A grin tugged Catherine's lips. "I forgot. You're a cynic. Never mind."

"Does this have to do with that car salesman you're dating?"

"He's a real-estate broker, and yes." She fixed her gaze on the ring box and sighed. "He asked me to marry him."

"Cars, real estate, it's all the same. Forget it."

"He gave me a ring. You ought to see it, it's beautiful. A sapphire."

"Keep the jewelry, dump the man. I need your full attention right now, sweetie."

"Lots of artists are married. In fact, all the ones I know are. So are the writers and the editors and the art directors." Catherine laughed. "Considering that my work is for children, don't you think having a few of my own would be a plus?"

Margaret groaned loudly. "Babies and diapers and nannies and preschools—don't do this to me! You are about to become very, very hot. Tabor Publishing is now talking a twenty-book series."

Catherine sobered; her hand tightened on the telephone. Her stomach suddenly felt very heavy. "Twenty?" The word emerged in a squeak. "I thought they wanted three?"

"Doc Halladay loves your work. He's renegotiating the book series. He's convinced it'll be as big, maybe bigger than his television show. He's full of crap, of course, nothing is bigger than TV, but these books are going to sell millions."

Catherine didn't doubt it. Doc Halladay, the Science Brain, had taken the media world by storm. With a winning smile, a magician's shtick and a gift for making the complicated sound easy, he'd won a bigger preadolescent audience than Barney the dinosaur and Sesame Street combined.

"If we put this together, this could make your career and set you up for life. You could end up being the hottest children's book illustrator of the century. Of two centuries! You'll win a Caldecott."

"Twenty books?"

"After Doc Halladay saw those mock-ups you did using photographs of him along with paintings, he flipped. As far as he's concerned, you're the second coming of Michelangelo."

"How much money are they talking?"

"A cool million. Of course, that's a five-year commitment, and we're still squabbling about royalties, but it's a very nice package."

Catherine had to take several deep breaths to calm her fluttering belly.

"The contract proposal needs a Rosetta stone to decipher it. I'm overnighting you an outline of the terms and payouts. It looks complicated because it is complicated, but try not to be intimidated. I'll have the whole thing vetted by an attorney before anything gets signed."

Catherine loved her work, which combined her two great passions—art and science. In college, believing there was no future in fine art, she'd earned a biology degree with the goal of going to veterinary school. Then a friend had asked her to illustrate a children's story she was trying to sell. The publisher had rejected the story, but asked Catherine if she'd submit more illustrations. Her career had been born.

After dozens of projects, she still loathed contract negotiations. She didn't understand the fine print. The money terms were convoluted with the publisher paying out in bits and pieces based upon schedules apparently created by a necromancer scrying moon signs in springwater.

"They're asking impossible deadlines, too," Margaret said.

"I can do impossible. I live for impossible."

"I know, sweetie. So don't do something stupid like get married and run off to Tahiti to paint flowers on black velvet."

"Yes, ma'am."

Margaret ended the conversation with details about the contract. Catherine tried very hard to keep her excitement under control. Contract negotiations could fall apart at any stage, and nothing was certain until everyone signed the paperwork.

After she hung up, she clasped her hands and danced around the studio. "Doc Halladay loves my work," she sang. "I'll be famous—"

Oscar and Bent lifted their narrow heads and looked toward the front of the house. Greyhounds, Catherine had discovered, were the perfect house pets. They were tidy, quiet, dignified and loved to lounge around on the furniture. They rarely barked. She'd set up an old sofa for them in her studio where they spent their days with their long legs sprawled, luxuriating in comfort.

"Is somebody coming?" she asked. "Normal dogs bark, you know."

She heard an engine, throaty, powerful, unmistakable— a Harley-Davidson motorcycle. The noise increased, approaching the house up the long, curved driveway through the pine trees. Wondering who in the world she knew who owned a Harley, she stepped out onto the deck. She blinked in the bright sunshine. Oscar and Bent joined her. They stretched their long bodies and yawned mightily.

The motorcycle appeared, a modern-day destrier of sleek black shine and glittering chrome. The rider wore a black, full-face helmet. He guided the motorcycle around potholes and ruts in the wide, but ill-maintained driveway. The bike's rear tire dropped and bounced in a pothole, and

Catherine winced. Having the driveway graded and paved was her next home-improvement project.

The rider wheeled the bike around the circular drive to park before the deck. He was a big man, his suntanned arms roped with muscle. She glanced at the dogs, now flanking her feet. They weighed eighty pounds apiece and could run down a rabbit without breathing hard, but protect her?

The rider cut off the engine. The sudden silence heightened her awareness about her seclusion, with the pine forest shielding her from the road and neighbors. She watched the man dismount. With his back to her he worked off the helmet. His hair, thick and sooty black, gleamed with bluish lights. Despite her nervousness, her artist's eye delighted in his powerful shoulders and the sinewy curves of his back.

He turned around.

He smiled and his dark eyes glittered like obsidian.

"Hello, Tink," he said. "Long time, no see."

Her brain froze. All sensations centered square in her chest where emotions long buried burst from their shell. For years she'd wondered what she would say to Easy Martel if she ever ran into him. She'd wondered what she would do, how she would act, what she might feel.

He was bigger than she remembered, his youthful slenderness grown into lean, broad-shouldered maturity. Once smooth olive cheeks now sported a definite beard shadow. He wore his black hair short rather than letting it hang shaggily down his neck. The smile remained the same, however, wry yet warm, completely focused, while those dark, dark eyes melded into hers.

Heart melting. Soul searing.

"Don't you remember me?" he asked. "It's me, Easy—"

She whipped about, raced into the house, slammed and locked the door.

Chapter Two

Easy Martel slid a hand around the back of his neck. He frowned at the half-glass door where curtains swayed gently. He stood chest level to the deck flooring, eye to eye with a pair of dogs who poked their narrow heads between the railing. They watched him with quiet curiosity. Despite the dogs' whip-thinness, they were large animals.

"Nice doggies." He sidled to the steps. Alert for a growl or other threat, he climbed the steps slowly. "Good doggies." He offered a hand for their inspection.

As one, the dogs turned and walked around the corner of the house. The clicking of their toenails on the decking faded in the distance.

Wary that this might be some canine trick, Easy hesitated. Maybe Catherine had trained her dogs in ninja tactics. He waited a few moments to see if the animals returned. When they didn't, he knocked on the door. "I didn't mean to startle you. It's me, Easy Martel. Wasson High School?"

He considered she may have forgotten him, but she'd been as madly in love with him as he'd been with her. She'd never forget him. More likely she still had that weird habit of running off when flustered. Smiling in fond remembrance, he knocked again.

The door opened an inch. He glimpsed a hostile eye glaring back at him. Memories rushed in with tidal-wave force, sweeping him back twelve years. Catherine's eyes had always fascinated him with their jewel-rich color and expressiveness. In high school she'd walked hunched over with her eyes downcast, her messy hair falling over her face. Despite her being awkward, pudgy and painfully shy, he'd looked into those sapphire depths and known she was beautiful. Cursing his own cowardice, he regretted every second they'd missed in the past twelve years.

"What are you doing here?" Her icy words startled him.

"Don't you remember—"

"I know exactly who you are. Now go away."

He retreated a step and rubbed his chin, thinking. Their breakup had been messy and acrimonious. That, however, had been when they were only kids. If he remembered correctly, she'd dumped him. "It's been a long time, Tink. Are you still mad at me?"

She threw the door wide. Chin up, feet spread, shoulders back, she faced him squarely. She wore a cropped T-shirt that clung to the rounded rise of her breasts and revealed an alluring inch of flat belly. Denim shorts showed off a pair of shapely legs. Barefoot, she sported a thin gold chain around one slim ankle. He leaned forward for a better look. Gone were the baggy black clothes and self-conscious posture.

The guys in high school who used to call her a dog ought to see her now. Their eyeballs would pop out of their skulls.

"You've got some nerve. How did you find me?"

Suspicion prickled up and down his spine. Her attitude transcended hostility—she hated his guts. "I looked you up."

"How? I'm not listed in the phone book."

He accepted that insurance cheats, disability frauds, embezzlers and adulterers took exception to his snooping around. But an old girlfriend?

"I looked you up in the public records," he said. "Your property is listed." He tried a smile and a compliment. "You look great. You got yourself in shape. Took off the baby fat."

Her mouth fell open. Color drained from her cheeks. She gasped.

Knowing he'd said something wrong, he backed up another step. "What?"

"You are so heartless, so cruel. You haven't changed a bit, Earl Zebulon Martel. Not one tiny bit!"

Call "Ripley's Believe It or Not," he'd found a woman who didn't like compliments about losing weight. He showed his palms in appeasement. "I mean you look nice. Your hair and everything. It's pretty. You're pretty."

"That gives you the right to make cracks about the baby?"

Now he was so lost he may as well be out of state. "You have a baby?"

She charged out of the doorway like a grizzly bursting from the brush. Easy scooted backward until he hit the deck railing and could go no farther. She came close enough for him to smell an intriguing mixture of paint and vanilla. Each time she waggled a finger at his face, scent wafted to his nose. Memories teased and distracted him— her scent had always intoxicated him.

"That stupid, dumb jock act worked in high school, but don't you dare pull it now. You know damn well I had a baby!"

His cheek muscles twitched. Every inner sense screamed danger, but as yet he couldn't quite identify the source. Cautiously he tried, "Congratulations?"

"Get off my property or I'm calling the police."

He half turned in automatic response, but stopped. He replayed in his head the confrontation thus far. She recognized him, she despised him, the comment about baby fat enraged her, and she accused him of knowing she'd had a baby. Logic said, since they hadn't seen each other in twelve years, then the only way he could have possibly known about a baby...

"You had a baby?" Sensing how she would reply, his words came softly, slowly. "*My* baby?"

She flipped her left hand. "Knock up your girlfriend." She flipped open her right. "She has a baby. It's biology, you idiot."

Jeffrey Livman and John Tupper faded into insignificance. Memories built, the details growing clear. It had been the night of the winter festival right before Christmas break. At the dance he'd been horsing around with his friends; they began ragging him about Catherine. His buddies hadn't understood why Easy loved her. She wasn't popular, she didn't know how to dress, she made straight As and she wasn't cheerleader pretty. At eighteen, he'd been immature enough to join his friends in making fun of her. She'd blown up at him, telling him she never wanted to see him again. During Christmas break, she refused to see him or return his phone calls. When school resumed, she'd cut him dead, pretending he didn't exist when they passed in the halls.

"You never told me you were pregnant." As the implication sank in, his temper rose. He'd loved her—maybe he still did. They'd planned a future together and she hid a baby? "You never said one word."

She clamped her arms over her chest. Her eyes blazed in heated challenge. "That's why you dropped out of school and ran away to join the army."

"I didn't drop out. I had enough credits to graduate midterm. You're the one who ran away. When I came back from basic training, you were gone. *You* dumped *me*."

"You were a creep. And irresponsible."

"You said you never wanted to see me again. You wouldn't talk to me."

"And give you a chance to not just call me a fat cow, but a fat, pregnant cow? You were cruel, Easy."

She had him there. He hung his head. "I wrote you about a hundred letters from basic training. I thought joining the army would make you miss me and—" he shrugged "—maybe scared I'd be killed. I was trying to be a hero. But you didn't answer my letters. You wouldn't take my calls. When I went to your house, your parents wouldn't let me see you. Nobody knew what happened to you."

Some of the fire drained from her face and her rigid shoulders relaxed. Her brow furrowed in an expression of uncertainty. "My parents sent me to Arizona to live with my grandmother. They couldn't stand to have me around, causing talk. I never got any letters."

Easy remembered Catherine's parents. Stiff, unsmiling people who never spoke to him and rarely said a word to their daughter. Mr. St. Clair was a hotshot lawyer—Mr. Perfect with plenty of big bucks and a high society lifestyle. Easy wondered how many of his rich clients and golfing buddies knew St. Clair had a vicious temper and a habit of smacking his daughter around. A lump lodged in his throat.

"I didn't know, Catherine. I swear."

She turned her face away, gazing distantly. A light breeze ruffled the ends of her hair. He remembered its softness and how she used to swing it in his face, tickling him.

"I tried to tell you at the dance. Do you remember? But your friends wouldn't leave us alone and then you said all those mean things and you were laughing at me. I was so scared, so ashamed, and when you laughed at me I couldn't face you anymore."

He passed a hand over his eyes. "I'm sorry. I am so sorry."

She gave herself a shake. Lifting her chin, her expression now cool and unreadable, she met his gaze. Those deep blue depths held a coldness Easy had never suspected she could reach. She inhaled deeply and the corners of her mouth tipped in a strained smile. "It was a long time ago. I'm over it now."

And he was the Pillsbury Doughboy's evil twin. "So where's the—"

"Excuse me," she interrupted. "As fun as old home week could be, I'm sure you understand why I don't feel like strolling down memory lane. I'd like you to leave. I'd appreciate it if you didn't contact me anymore."

"Where's the kid, Catherine?" He looked about, seeking bicycles, roller skates or toys. He couldn't do a thing about what happened twelve years ago, nor could he make up for the time they'd lost. Despite her accusations, though, he'd never shirked a responsibility in his life.

"There is no kid."

Horrified, he pushed away from the railing. "The baby died?"

"I put her up for adoption." Her rounded chin lifted another notch, defiant. "It was a girl. Six pounds, twelve ounces, perfectly healthy. She had hair. Black hair, just like yours. I signed the papers when she was twenty-four hours old. I held her once." Her chin trembled and her voice cracked. Unfallen tears glazed her eyes. "I named her Elizabeth, after your mom, because she was always so nice to me. On the birth certificate I listed the father as unknown."

He closed his eyes, trying to picture Catherine in labor, little more than a baby herself—alone, banished from home, deserted. He saw instead her face when they'd made love, her softly curved cheeks aglow without a trace of shyness or self-consciousness. Loving her had made him a better person. He hadn't known it then, but he knew it now. She'd never disguised her intelligence or played games or treated him with anything other than respect. He'd lived for her admiration, sought her approval, strove to measure up to her standards.

He had a child. A funny piece of information. He held it in his thoughts as if it were a strange bug he'd never seen before.

"I didn't know," he said. "I swear, I didn't know."

Her belligerence faded, leaving her face naked with pain. "Now you do. So go away. I'm not in the mood for a class reunion." She turned for the door, reaching for the handle.

"Catherine." He took a step toward her. "Tink. We need to talk about this."

She shook her head. Her blond-streaked hair shone with glimmering lights. "We have nothing to discuss."

"Wrong answer. Where's the kid? Where does she live?"

She turned about, her expression now bemused. "How am I supposed to know?"

"You're her mother."

"Her mother is the woman raising her. She isn't mine anymore, and she certainly isn't yours."

"I never gave up my parental rights."

"Rights? How dare you?" She clamped her fists on her hips and leaned forward. "The only person who had any rights was Elizabeth. She had a right to be raised by adults."

"So you gave her away like a puppy."

Catherine flinched as if he'd slapped her. Hot color flushed her cheeks and her big eyes grew bigger. So low he barely caught the words, she said, "Giving up my baby was the hardest thing I ever had to do in my life."

Her sorrow touched him. He clamped his mouth shut.

"I regret being irresponsible, for having sex without being old enough to know what I was doing. I regret not using birth control. I regret not being able to give her a home. But I made the right decision, and that I don't regret. Wherever she is, she has two parents who love her.''

At least a fourth of his cases involved missing persons. Many of those clients were adoptees seeking birth parents. A few were parents seeking children they regretted giving away. He had never understood why they couldn't leave the past alone. Now he felt a glimmer of that urgency to know.

Did his daughter hate him? Did she believe he'd discarded her like unwanted garbage?

"I can find her." He nodded eagerly. "Give me the date she was born. The hospital, the doctor and the name of the adoption agency. We can find her.''

Catherine cocked her head. "Are you nuts?"

"I'm serious. I can do it. That's how I—''

"Why would you want to? She has a family, a life, people who love her. We can't pop into her life and mess things up.''

"If," he said slowly, "I had known you were pregnant, I'd have married you. You never gave me a chance—or a choice.''

She snorted in derision. "I wouldn't have married you. Not after what you said at the dance.''

Taken aback, he glared down his nose at her. She had changed more than her appearance. Catherine St. Clair had grown a backbone. One made of pure steel, if he were any judge. His temper flared. The more he struggled to control it, the hotter his blood boiled. "So you got even with me and threw away the kid. Why didn't you just kill her?''

Bad words, fighting words. He regretted them as soon as they popped out of his mouth.

"Good grief!" She threw up her hands and turned her gaze to the heavens. "Ten minutes ago, you claim you didn't even know I was pregnant. Now you want to play daddy of the year. Get lost, Easy. Just go away.'' She entered the house and slammed the door. The clunk of a dead bolt sounded like a pistol shot.

Easy wavered. He hadn't accomplished what he set out to do. He didn't know any more about her involvement with Jeffrey Livman than when he'd arrived. He breathed hard, trying to get back to the present problem.

John Tupper had told a chilling story. After a whirlwind courtship, Roberta Tupper had married Jeffrey Livman. In the year they were married, Roberta had severed contact with her family. Six months ago Roberta had fallen from a rock formation in Garden of the Gods, and died from massive head injuries. There were no witnesses and no physical evidence of foul play. The coroner had declared Roberta's death accidental.

Except, Roberta had been asthmatic and shunned physical activity such as hiking or rock climbing.

Except, a few weeks before her death, John Tupper had confronted his sister at her place of work, demanding to know why she refused to visit him or his family. He had come away with the impression that Roberta was terrified of her husband.

Except, Livman never notified the family of her death. Livman had Roberta's body cremated without so much as a funeral or a memorial service. John had learned of the tragedy from the newspaper.

Except, Livman had collected on an insurance policy to the tune of five hundred thousand dollars. In John's words: "I sell insurance. A childless woman whose husband is young, healthy and employed does not need half a million in life insurance."

In Easy's mind, all those *excepts* added up to murder.

He had hoped, because of their former relationship, Catherine would cooperate. Through her he might obtain a confession of murder, or discover some basis for John to proceed with a wrongful-death suit against his former brother-in-law.

At the moment he considered himself lucky she didn't shoot him on sight. Stunned by how much her revelation about the baby hurt, he mounted his motorcycle and rode away.

CATHERINE RESTED with her back against the wall until the motorcycle noise faded in the distance. She breathed deeply through her mouth, her chest aching.

On wooden legs, she walked downstairs to her bedroom. From the bedside table she picked up a polished silver frame. It contained a photograph of a little girl with dark hair, dark eyes and a gap-toothed smile. Catherine had clipped the photograph from a magazine and did not know the girl's name. Over the years, she'd changed the anonymous photographs from baby pictures to this present child.

Not for the first time, she wondered if her insistence on pretending to have a photograph of Elizabeth was a sign of insanity. A means of punishing herself for a guilt she couldn't shake.

She accepted her action. She knew she'd done the right thing for Elizabeth. At the time, she'd been sixteen years old, little more than a baby herself. She had no right to destroy Elizabeth's life. Still, the hurt, guilt and shame lingered.

Catherine traced the smiling child's jawline with a fingertip. Seeing Easy again hurt most of all. The pain of learning he'd joined the army remained burned into her memory. He'd left without so much as a goodbye. He'd left her alone to deal with her pregnancy and her parents and the shame.

Closing her eyes, she remembered vividly the feel of Easy's skin. He'd been a breathtakingly beautiful boy. She'd filled notebooks with sketches of his face and hands and the alluring musculature of his arms. Tall, slender and graceful, he'd always been ready with a joke and a laugh. A smart aleck, the class clown and captain of the football team—she'd loved him desperately.

A scratching noise startled her. The greyhounds waited at the French doors leading to the lower patio. Oscar lifted a paw and patted gently at the glass.

With a trembling hand, she opened the door for the dogs. "I can't believe I yelled at him," she told them. "I never yell."

She trudged upstairs to the studio. With the shock of seeing Easy fading, she was appalled at how she'd reacted. The rage had erupted within her like a volcano lain dormant for all these years.

She glanced at the telephone. She wanted to call Jeffrey, but what could she say? She'd never told him about her high school love affair or the child she'd given up for adoption. Now that Grandma had passed away, she never talked about it at all.

As much as she longed to put the past behind her, it affected every aspect of her life. Her relationship with her parents remained strained. Although they lived in the house where she'd grown up, she saw them less than once a month. Visiting them remained a chore. She supposed she waited for them to say they were sorry for the way they had treated her.

She remained terrified of pregnancy, terrified of losing yet another child. She didn't trust birth control devices or drugs. She couldn't trust fate. No sex until marriage, she'd vowed, and stuck to it all these years.

She couldn't marry anyone, or even fall in love, unless she trusted him enough to tell him about the baby. How was she supposed to tell anyone when she could not bear to speak of it?

At a worktable, she frowned at a painting for a beginning reader's book about spiders. In painstaking detail she'd depicted hatchlings bursting from an egg sac. *Babies*. It occurred to her that the projects that excited her the most dealt with babies in one form or another.

She kept seeing the look of astonishment on Easy's face. All these years she'd assuaged some of her guilt by blaming him for deserting her. She was rotten, but she always had the comfort of knowing he was more rotten.

He hadn't known.

How could he have known? She slumped on a stool and rested her chin on her fist. The day after she told her parents about the pregnancy, they'd shipped her off to Arizona. She'd been too humiliated to tell anyone at school. No one had known.

For the first time in twelve years, she faced the hard truth that Easy wasn't to blame for Elizabeth's loss. She believed he'd written letters and called; she didn't put it past her parents to "protect" her. She also believed him impulsive enough to join the army on a romantic whim. Maybe they should talk. Maybe they—

"No!" The dogs lifted their heads to see if she was speaking to them. "I refuse. The past is over. I don't want to see him or talk to him. I won't."

As much as she wanted to drop the matter, pass it off as an unpleasant blip in an otherwise placid life, Easy wore on her mind. He lurked like a shadow while she finished the painting.

The velvet ring box perched atop the fireplace mantel kept drawing her attention. Easy was the long-ago past; Jeffrey represented the future. She called Jeffrey and reached his voice mail. At the tone, Catherine left the message that she needed to see him.

After she hung up, she marched resolutely to the fireplace and opened the ring box. The sapphire seemed to wink at her.

She had a career and a neatly ordered life. She always imagined she didn't need anything else. Easy's startling reemergence made her see the lie. She *did* want a husband and children, but she was afraid, simple as that. Afraid to love, afraid to lose again, afraid of a broken heart.

Bearing an illegitimate child didn't brand her as a fallen woman. She'd been sixteen, a child who made a mistake. She rubbed her flat belly, dismayed by the emptiness she felt inside.

She slid the ring onto her finger. It was weighty, flashy, alien.

Certainly Jeffrey would understand. What's more, she felt, he would still love her.

INSIDE THE PEAK CAFÉ, Easy looked toward the booth where he and Trish usually sat. The small café off Academy Boulevard sat halfway between his office and hers, so they often met here for lunch. Trish waggled her fingers at him. He joined her.

"I ordered you a Peak burger," she said.

"Thanks." He wondered if he'd be able to eat it.

She searched his face. "Oh God, Catherine doesn't believe you about Jeffrey Livman."

A waitress arrived with two iced teas. She smiled at Easy. He tried to smile back at her, but failed. His gut ached as if he'd been kicked.

"We never talked about Livman."

Trish's face twisted in a puzzled frown. She dumped Sweet'n Low into her iced tea. "She wasn't home?"

"She was there all right." He huffed a long breath, staring at the iced tea, repulsed. He'd been a confirmed soda drinker until Catherine introduced him to the pleasure of a glass of icy cold sun-brewed tea.

"What happened, Easy? Was Livman there? He's not supposed to see you. You'll spook him." She launched into a diatribe about how Easy was supposed to operate. John had tried to convince the police to investigate Roberta's death, but they'd found no evidence of foul play and there had been no witnesses. Romoco Insurance, which had carried the life insurance policy, had worked with John, but despite the large benefit, they had turned up nothing to suggest Roberta's death was anything other than an accident. When the coroner declared the death accidental and closed the file, the insurance company had been forced to pay out, and John's hope for a police investigation had died. They needed a confession. The only way to get it would be to lull Livman into believing he'd gotten away with his crime.

Easy waited until his sister ran out of steam. "Livman wasn't there. Remember when she left town?"

"Yeah, junior year. She moved."

"Her parents threw her out. She was pregnant."

Eyes wide, mouth opened, Trish stared at him.

"I didn't know. We had that big fight before she could tell me. I can't believe how stupid I was. I should've known."

"I'm an aunt?" A slow smile brightened Trish's face. Her eyes glowed. "Boy or girl? Name? Did—"

"She gave the baby up for adoption."

Her smile winked out like a blown lightbulb. "Oh no. How could she do that? It's your baby, too. Why didn't she ever tell you? You guys were so much in love. You'd have married her, right? I know you would have."

"Why don't you use a bullhorn? I think some of the people in the parking lot didn't hear you." Embarrassed as if he were eighteen again, caught doing something nasty, he glanced around the small restaurant to see if anyone paid attention.

"Sorry," she mumbled. She leaned over the table and lowered her voice. "I thought she was so smart. Why didn't she tell you?"

He shook his head. "I was mean to her. When I joined the army, she thought I ran out on her."

The waitress arrived with their lunch. She set a steaming

burger covered with onions, mushrooms and Jack cheese in front of Easy. The knots in his belly jerked tighter. He averted his gaze.

Trish stole the dill pickles off his plate, arranged them on her burger, then sliced the sandwich in half. "You better not tell Mom and Dad." Her voice reverberated with dire warning.

Their parents bemoaned the single status of their children. They wanted them married, and the house filled with grandchildren to spoil. News of a lost grandchild would crush them.

Trish bit into her burger, chewed and swallowed. She wiped her mouth with a paper napkin. "You can find your kid. You find adopted kids all the time. Shoot, it's so easy, I could do it."

Tempting, very tempting. He imagined his daughter looking like a miniature version of Catherine. She probably insisted on being called Elizabeth, never Lizzy or Beth or Betsy. Maybe she was artistic, she was definitely a brain, pulling straight As.

"You have to," Trish insisted.

Shaking away the images in his head, Easy grunted irritably. "Right now the problem is Livman. I did some research. Catherine paid cash for her house in Black Forest, so she's got some money of her own. Livman won't have to shell out for insurance premiums in order to turn a nice profit."

Trish shuddered. "You can't let her marry him."

He poured ketchup on the plate and swirled a french fry through it.

"What are you going to do?"

"I don't know," he snapped.

She reached across the table and placed a slim hand atop his. "She really got to you, didn't she?"

"It's weird. Seeing her again..." He pulled his hand away from hers—he deserved a good kick, not comforting.

"She hates me. She thinks it's my fault she lost the baby. She won't listen to me."

"I'll talk to her. We were friends. Sort of. She'll listen to me."

He considered the offer, but discarded it. He suspected one more blast from the past would cause Catherine to run out and buy a shotgun in order to shoot any trespassing Martel on sight. "I have to dig up some dirt on Livman."

"John already looked. There's nothing."

Easy had been impressed by the amount of information John had dug up on his former brother-in-law: schooling, job history, finances, family. None of it, unfortunately, pointed to murder. "There has to be a pattern somewhere. He didn't decide on the spur of the moment to push Roberta off that rock."

Trish scrunched her face into an expression of distaste. "You think he killed someone else?"

"Who knows? But I'm thinking Roberta isn't the first woman he abused."

Chapter Three

Easy smiled at the elderly woman who answered the door of the small brick bungalow in Arvada. This quiet neighborhood in a suburb of Denver consisted of tract homes built in the 1950s. Mature elm trees shaded the sidewalks. In this house Jeffrey Livman had grown from a boy into a man.

"Mrs. Vera Livman?" He looked up from the clipboard he carried and glanced at the metal house numbers attached to the bricks next to the door. "I'm from the utility company." He flicked a finger against the identification badge clipped to the pocket of his coveralls. A computer publishing program, a Polaroid camera and a small laminating machine made producing identification badges and cards a snap. At the moment he was Earl Spencer, employee number 187 with the gas company.

"We've got a suspected gas leak in this block. May I come in to check your lines, ma'am?" The lie slipped smoothly from his mouth—he'd used it before. It rarely failed, especially with older women who lived alone. He held up a toy laser gun. Shaped like an oversize television remote, it had an impressive array of dials, switches and lights. It made a terrific "gas detector." "It won't take five minutes, ma'am."

"Gas? I haven't smelled anything." She blinked owl-ishly from behind thick bifocals.

"With any luck, you won't. Safety first, though. It's nothing to mess around with."

She unlatched the storm door and pushed it open. "Certainly."

He walked inside. "Gas leaks are worse in the summertime. People have their windows open so they don't smell the fumes. Gas builds up in pockets. Is your husband home, ma'am? I'd like to show you both where the—"

"I'm a widow." She nervously rubbed her hands together.

He noticed the telltale swelling of arthritis in her knuckles. He noticed, too, the guileless trust in her eyes.

A pang of conscience tightened his chest. He preferred gathering information in a straightforward manner. Ask the questions, glean what answers he could, then split. He needed, however, to handle this operation as he did for the occasional bail jumpers he traced—carefully, without alarming friends and family with too many questions. He especially didn't want to alarm Livman's mother. No matter what, a mother's love won out every single time.

He'd discovered a worrisome pattern in Livman's life. The man apparently felt no qualms about dumping jobs, homes, cars or acquaintances. In the past twenty years, he'd worked for more than a dozen real-estate companies. He'd bought and sold dozens of homes and properties. Nobody seemed to know Livman well. A few people had been surprised to learn he'd been married and was now a widower. Easy suspected if the heat turned up too high, Livman wouldn't have a second thought about skipping the state. Still, sneaking around, asking covert questions and hoping nobody noticed his interest, was getting on Easy's nerves.

Mrs. Livman showed him to the basement. It had linoleum flooring, simulated wood panelling on the walls, and

that funky, old-house-basement smell. It reminded him of
the house where he'd grown up. While the woman hovered
anxiously, he played with the laser toy, sweeping it around
the gas lines, furnace and water heater. He made lights
blink and a few presses of his thumb caused dial indicators
to jump.

"Clean as a whistle," he announced.

"Oh, good! You were scaring me, young man."

"Sorry. My instrument is sensitive. But everything is
operating normally. No leaks, no problems. Thank you for
your time, ma'am, and sorry for bothering you."

She protested heartily that he was no bother at all. At
the top of the stairs, he noticed the knob was loose on the
basement door. He pretended to lose his grip on his clipboard and while catching it, he gave the doorknob an ex-
trahard shake. It rattled loudly.

"You're about to lose your doorknob, ma'am."

She sighed heavily. "Sometimes it just seems like this
old house is falling apart. Sort of like I am."

He pulled a Phillips head screwdriver from his work
belt. "Just need to tighten the screws, ma'am. Only take
a second."

Her smile beamed pure gratitude; he lowered his head
so she couldn't see his shame. He jiggled the doorknob
into place and tightened the screws. As he sensed she
might, she acted as if he'd saved her from a burning building. She offered him something to drink. He made a show
of checking his watch, but allowed her to coax him into
accepting the offer.

In the small living room he pretended to make notes on
the clipboard while she fetched him a glass of lemonade.
He sipped and declared it the best he'd ever tasted. Then
he nodded at a large, framed portrait hanging prominently
in the middle of a montage of photographs. It pictured five
girls, ranging from around ten to perhaps eighteen, all of
them blue-eyed blondes with pretty faces and big smiles.

Seated on the lap of the eldest girl was a toddler, a blond, blue-eyed boy.

"Your family?"

"My children." She practically wriggled with pride. "All grown-up now and on their own. They visit whenever they can."

"My wife and I have only one boy. He's a handful. A real little terror."

"Boys are like that. Always into one thing or another." She clucked her tongue. "Mischief and pranks and being ornery. I never had a speck of trouble with the girls, but Jeff sure gave me the devil."

"I bet it was hard," Easy said sympathetically.

"It sure was! My husband died soon after little Jeff was born, leaving me with six kids and no money. Fortunately I was a skilled legal secretary. I managed to support us. And the girls were a great help with little Jeff." She giggled. "He's not so little anymore. But he's still my baby. He would have come to fix that doorknob, but he's a very important businessman. He owns a huge real-estate company down south in Colorado Springs."

A creepy sensation crawled up Easy's spine. Livman's sisters were all blue-eyed blondes. Roberta had been a blue-eyed blonde. As was Catherine. While Mrs. Livman waxed poetic about her perfect family and how the girls all rallied to help their mother raise the baby boy, Easy began to wonder if perhaps something more than money had motivated Livman to kill his wife.

CATHERINE HOPPED onto a picnic table. She shook her ponytail and raked damp tendrils of hair off her face. Not a whiff of breeze offered a cooling touch on her hot face, but she didn't care. She loved Fox Run Park with its winding trails and pine trees. Oscar and Bent loved it, too. Mouths wide open and tongues dragging, the greyhounds lay in a patch of shade, serenely watching the small lake below.

She watched Jeffrey stretch his hamstrings. He'd been avoiding her all week. She'd hurt his feelings during the scene at the Grape and Olive. She'd acted poorly—reacted poorly. He loved her and she had treated his proposal like a personal attack. No wonder he'd been short on the telephone and "busy" all week. It surprised her somewhat that he'd agreed to meet her for a run in the park this morning.

"For an old guy," she said, "you run pretty good."

"Old, huh?" He used both hands to swipe sweat off his face. He sat on the picnic table beside her.

She admired the way he looked in his shorts and sleeveless T-shirt, his body toned and fit, his smile relaxed. He worked hard, vowing he'd be a millionaire before his fortieth birthday, but he knew how to play, too.

They liked the same music and movies. Both of them loved their work. Jeffrey enjoyed the outdoors—biking, hiking, running, camping—as much as she did. Most of the time they were so comfortable together it seemed as if she'd known him all her life.

"Can we talk?" she asked. All week she'd been working toward this conversation, seeking the perfect time and place. Now alone in the park, she knew it would never get better than this.

"Uh-oh, sounds serious."

She couldn't face him. "It's about…the other night."

"Is this a good talk? Or the kiss of death?"

She rested her forearms on her knees. This was hard. She didn't know anything about relationships. "I owe you an apology. I realize now that what you did was very special. You're romantic and impulsive, and I do want you to know I appreciate the gesture."

He snorted. "Didn't look appreciative. It was a real kick in the gut when you ran out on me."

She cringed inwardly. She'd had plenty of time to consider what he meant to her. After Easy's visit, it struck her that she could live her life on hold, or she could really live. A man as good as Jeffrey didn't come along every day. Considering how difficult it was for her to meet new people, she might never meet another man like him. "I've been doing a lot of thinking. You're right, we're good together. We could make a great life."

He lifted an eyebrow. His lips pursed. "It seems to me, that's what I told you."

"Please don't be difficult, Jeffrey. I'm trying to apologize. To explain. There's something I have to tell you, but it's hard."

"Sounds ominous."

Maybe it was. She watched crows wheeling lazy circles over the pine trees. Did she love Jeffrey? If love meant respect, affection and a desire for his approval, then she did. It felt far, far different than what she'd felt for Easy. That, she reasoned, had been infatuation, not true, mature love.

"Cath—"

"Give me a minute. This is hard. I've never talked about it before." She licked her lips and swiped sweat off her brow. The only way to say it was to just say it. "When I was sixteen, a junior in high school, I fell in love with a boy. I got pregnant. I gave the baby up for adoption." She closed her eyes, waiting.

"That's it?" he asked.

"That's it." She made herself look at him, seeking clues to his reaction.

"You've never told anybody?"

Bemused by his nonreaction, she lifted a shoulder. "Nowadays, the talk shows and magazines make out-of-wedlock babies seem like no big deal. But it was a big deal to me, and still is." She stretched out her legs and flexed her feet. "It still hurts."

"Are you scared I'll call you damaged goods and stomp off?"

It startled her to discover that was exactly what she feared. At hearing it said aloud, it seemed ridiculous. She forced a smile. "I don't know. Will you?"

He laughed and picked up her hand. "I should have known it was something like this. You're too sensitive. I'm glad you told me, Catherine. Honest. It explains a lot."

"Like what?"

"Like why it's so hard getting close to you." He scowled in mock ferocity and leaned his face close to hers. "Why you ran out on me when I proposed. I felt like a jerk. Not to mention wasting a bottle of very expensive champagne."

"I said I'm sorry."

"And I forgive you." His scowl transformed into a smile. "Does this mean you love me?"

She opened her mouth to answer, but hesitated. She'd loved Easy Martel, passionately, desperately, painfully, joyfully. One of his smiles could leave her floating on air all day long. His touch had set her on fire. She'd placed her heart at his feet and invited him, without reservations, to do with it what he would.

That was a long, long time ago.

With Jeffrey there was no pain, but no mindless joy either. She enjoyed talking to him, but the sound of his voice didn't set her heart racing. When she imagined a life with him, her visions made practical sense. Jeffrey could do repairs on the house and maintain the cars. He could give her financial advice. She could make sure his laundry was done and he ate properly. They'd keep each other company and make babies. He seemed very safe. Very sensible.

"Yes, I love you, Jeffrey."

His smile rivaled the sun. He caught her shoulders and planted an exuberant kiss on her lips. "You'll marry me?

Say yes, Catherine. Say yes or I'll die right here as we speak.''

"Wait a minute! Wait!" She struggled out of his embrace and half turned to put her back to him. From inside her damp sports bra she worked loose a chain where she carried the engagement ring. The sapphire and diamonds flashed and sparkled with cold fire. She pulled the chain over her head and unfastened the clasp, freeing the ring. For a long moment she stared at the shiny piece of jewelry. Once she committed, there was no turning back. She closed her eyes and envisioned a yard full of laughing children. She handed him the ring.

She offered him her left hand, her fingers extended.

With great solemnity, he slipped the ring onto her finger. It was a perfect fit. "So when are we getting married? Tomorrow?"

She hopped off the table. "No quickies." She waved her left hand slowly, admiring the beautiful ring. "I want plenty of time to savor my status as a fiancée." She pointed at the gazebo perched on a rock pile that jutted into the lake. "We're doing this right. I want to get married there."

His features tightened. "In the park? Like hippies?"

His reaction dismayed her, but she quickly recovered. He was a special guy, but still a guy, and she doubted if wedding plans interested him in the least. "It'll be beautiful, and dignified."

He loosed a martyred sigh. "Let's run off to Vegas. We don't need a dog and pony show."

"I only intend to get married once. I'm not doing it in a cheesy chapel officiated by an Elvis impersonator. We'll have a proper wedding. If you really object to holding it outdoors, then we'll do it in church."

"Whatever you want," he grumbled.

She poked his chin playfully. "Countless men have survived weddings. You will, too." She laughed, whirling in a dreamy circle. Oscar and Bent leaped to their feet and posed ready to run. She ruffled their floppy ears. She did love Jeffrey and this was the right decision and they'd live happily ever after—

She spotted Easy Martel.

She stopped so quickly, she stumbled and stared open-mouthed toward the other, smaller lake. Only Easy's head was visible, his hair as black and glossy as the wings of crows flying overhead. He wore dark sunglasses, but she knew. He spied on her!

She confessed her youthful indiscretion to her fiancé, and then lo and behold, there's the daddy. Easy's timing couldn't be more appalling.

"Catherine?"

"I have to get home. Oscar, Bent, come." The dogs crowded her legs and she gathered their leashes.

Jeffrey put a restraining hand on her shoulder. "What in the world is wrong with you?"

She sneaked a peek toward Easy. He'd ducked out of sight. The Front Range, encompassing Colorado Springs, stretching from Fountain to the far south and Monument to the north, covered an area more than forty miles long. In the eight months she'd been living here, she hadn't run into a single person she knew from her childhood. That Easy Martel chose this particular day to be in Fox Run Park was not a coincidence.

"Nothing, nothing," she said weakly. "I have a million things to do."

He glowered at his wristwatch. "I cancelled two appointments to run with you this morning. Don't jerk me around."

She scuffed her running shoe through a pile of pine straw. "See what happens when I get frazzled? I turn into a flaky artist." She fished in her fanny pack for her Blazer keys. She tossed them to him. "You drive."

He eyed her suspiciously, but acted amiably enough as

she herded him and the dogs to her Blazer parked above the lake. She began to wonder if she'd conjured Easy out of her guilty conscience.

By the time they reached the park entrance, she convinced herself she hadn't seen Easy. When she adjusted the air-conditioner vent to blow on her hot face, she noticed in the side mirror a white car pulling out of the park behind them. She thought little of it until they reached Roller Coaster Road and turned right, and the car turned right behind them. The car continued following them south, all the way to Shoup Road where she felt certain it would continue toward the Springs, but it turned after them.

"You haven't heard a word I said," Jeffrey complained.

"What?" She clenched her hands on her lap, resisting the urge to turn on the seat to see better the driver behind them. She hadn't a clue as to why Easy had appeared on her doorstep last week, as she hadn't a clue as to why he followed her now. A sinking sensation, however, said telling him about the baby they'd made twelve years ago had been a major mistake. He'd been a quick-tempered, impulsive boy with far more energy than good sense. For all she knew, he hadn't changed. She wouldn't put it past him to pester her until she told him what happened to Elizabeth.

"What is the matter with you, Catherine?"

She should tell him about Easy. After all, it had been Easy's surprise visit which had clinched her decision to marry Jeffrey. As her official fiancé, Jeffrey had a right to know about any unresolved issues from her past.

He slowed to turn into her driveway. The white car slowed behind them. Anger boiled up like bubbling soup, infusing her blood, tightening her jaw.

"Don't talk to me then." Jeffrey turned the wheel sharply. In the back seat, Oscar and Bent lost their balance. Jeffrey managed to hit every pothole and rut in the driveway. The dogs bounced around, unable to get their feet under them. Bent fell onto the floor.

"Quit driving like a maniac!" Catherine yelled.

He slammed on the brakes and gawked at her.

She covered her mouth with a hand. The dogs grumbled as they rearranged themselves in the back seat. She stared at the side mirror, expecting to see Easy pull in behind them. Clouds of dust hovered like haze over the driveway.

"You were happy and practically singing, then all the sudden you're acting like a lunatic. You won't talk to me, then you're yelling. Is it hormones or something?"

His sexist comment earned him a dark glower.

He drove forward. "I will not have you yelling at me."

Tell him, she urged herself, but could not find the words. "I guess my nerves are… I don't know… I'm sorry, okay? Please forgive me."

He pulled into the garage and shut off the Blazer's engine.

"I'm so sorry. I desperately need a shower and a cup of coffee and a chance to pull myself together." She pushed open the door and went around to the side door to let the dogs out. They gave Jeffrey canine equivalents of filthy looks before hopping out of the Blazer and stalking toward the house.

"You can't treat me like this."

For a moment he sounded so much like her father—cold and authoritarian—she froze, her mind gone blank. Ridiculous, she told herself. Jeffrey was nothing like her father.

She forced a smile and used her left hand to smooth hair off her face, exaggerating her movements so he noticed the engagement ring. With no sign of Easy or even the sound of a car engine, her agitation faded. Maybe she'd dreamed him up after all. "You're wonderful and perfect and I do love you."

He held out her car keys. When she opened her hand, he dropped them onto her palm. "And you're nuts, lady.

What am I going to do with you?'' His voice was calm, but lines strained his brow and cheeks.

Catherine swallowed hard. His quiet fury frightened her in a way she couldn't quite define. ''I'm so sorry. Please say you forgive me and kiss me?''

He caught her shoulders in both hands and kissed her.

EASY RAN THROUGH his repertoire of dirty words—after spending four years as a military policeman, he knew plenty. None served to describe how he felt watching Catherine St. Clair kiss a killer.

He crouched at the base of a towering ponderosa pine, and peered through the thick foliage of a scrub oak. He watched Livman grasp Catherine's shoulders and pull her close. She slid her arms around his waist and her right foot raised until only the toe of her running shoe rested on the ground. Intimate, familiar, comfortable—the sight turned Easy's stomach.

Catherine patted Livman's cheek and said something that caused the man to laugh. Easy tensed, wondering if they'd go inside now. Perhaps to shower together, to…

Catherine hopped lightly onto the deck. She wore satin running shorts, electric blue under the sun. Her ponytail bounced around her shoulders. Livman strode to a black BMW parked in the shade of the house. She waved and went inside.

Easy watched Livman guide the BMW carefully around potholes. Livman's face was taut, angry-looking as he drove past. Easy waited until he was sure the man wasn't coming back.

Catherine had spotted Easy at the park. That much he knew for certain. What he did not know was if she'd told Livman. And if she had, what she'd told him. Easy considered how she might react when he told her why he'd been tailing them. He suspected she wouldn't clasp her hands and say, "My goodness, Jeffrey is a killer? Thank you for telling me. I'll break up with him right away."

He hefted the envelope he carried. The man was a creep. Other than his mother, few people seemed to like him. Some people acted afraid of him. Former employers all had the same thing to say: Livman talked a good line and had a gift for salesmanship, but he was unethical, dishonest and lazy. He didn't get along with men, but actively cultivated relationships with women. Livman had been arrested twice, both times for beating girlfriends. Both times, the women dropped the charges.

Catherine could blow this investigation with a single phone call. Easy walked a fine line between protecting her and catching Livman.

The way they'd been kissing decided him. Livman moved fast; Easy had to move faster. He walked up to the house. Guessing she might slam the door in his face, he prepared himself for her anger. He rang the bell.

Catherine surprised him with a smile. A cold smile, true, but it beat having her yell at him. "Are you a stalker? Do I need to get a restraining order against you?"

She hadn't lost her sense of humor. Her attitude gave him hope. "I'm not stalking you."

"I see. You just happened to be at the park, and you just happened to follow me home. Coincidence?"

"No coincidence. I was tailing you."

She laughed softly and swung her head side to side, so her ponytail curled like a lover's hand around her slender neck. Her laughter pierced his heart, drumming up old emotions. Impulsively, he touched his fingertips to her cheek. He knew his mistake as soon as he felt warm silky skin and her eyes widened. She jerked her head away. She clamped her arms over her breasts, her shoulders hunched.

He crammed his hand in his back pocket. "Can I have five minutes of your time? Please?" He turned on his most winning smile. "It's important."

Her eyes narrowed and she backed a step into the house. He seized upon what most courts would interpret as an invitation and walked inside. She huffed about his trespass, but didn't throw him out. His hope flourished. At age sixteen she'd been different from any other girl he knew. Now a grown woman, perhaps she'd prove different than most women when presented with distressing news about a boyfriend.

The skinny dogs hopped off a sofa, ears pricked and eyes suspicious. The slightly larger brown-and-white male raised his hackles. Keeping a wary eye on the dogs, Easy paused by the door.

Catherine sized up her escape routes. Easy blocked the door, but she could reach the sliding glass doors in the adjoining wall, or make it down the stairs. She didn't sense anything dangerous about him. While they dated he'd always been gentle with her, but a man could change in twelve years.

"I brought something for you." He held up a white, nine-by-twelve-inch envelope.

Her mouth felt sticky. She'd seen the recent news stories about adoptions gone sour. Courts were favoring parental rights over the rights of children. She'd erred twelve years ago in not telling Easy about the child. She'd lied on the birth certificate about not knowing the father's name. If he pressed the issue by taking her to court, he could learn what happened to Elizabeth. Or worse, he could fight for custody. Whether or not he successfully contested the adoption was moot. No matter what happened, he would destroy Elizabeth's life.

He approached. She forced herself to stand fast. She tried not to notice his graceful, loose-hipped walk. She tried not to notice her own pounding heart. "The past is history, Easy. I did the right thing for our baby. Let it rest. Please."

Her reference to his lost child stabbed through his heart.

He clutched the envelope so tightly that paper crunched. He wanted to know what had happened to his daughter. He *needed* to know. He realized it with a certainty that infused his very bones and laid bare the massive hole in his life created when he lost Catherine.

"Even if you had known, it wouldn't have made any difference." Her eyes went soft and pleading. "We were too young to get married and too young to raise a child. I did the right thing. Please accept it."

He pulled his attention away from her. The spacious front room had been turned into an art studio. The walls were covered with anatomical posters. Easels held partially finished paintings. Old cups, mismatched vases and cans held arrangements of dried weeds and flowers. Cork boards were covered with photographs of animals. Plastic models ranging from dinosaurs to whales perched upon shelves. Bookshelves and tables overflowed with books and magazines. The place smelled of paint and chemicals, overlaid with an odor of something spicy cooking in the small kitchen off the studio.

"You're an artist?" A stack of children's books caught his attention. Elizabeth probably adored books.

"I illustrate children's books."

"You always did draw good pictures." He glanced at the dogs. "I thought you were going to be a veterinarian. You were always taking care of sick birds and stuff. Remember the baby magpie?"

He placed the envelope carefully on a table, making certain she noticed it. He wanted to trace the fine sheen of sweat on her flushed skin, and rub her hair between his fingers. He wanted to kiss away all traces of Livman's kiss from her mouth. He made himself stand in place; his joints ached with the effort.

Her gaze went distant, softening the tense muscles of her face. A trace of a smile curved her lips. "You named it Bosco. That was a dumb name for a bird."

"Mom almost had a heart attack when she found it in my room. But we saved its life."

She fussed with a messy stack of magazines. When she finally turned to him, all traces of fear had left her face. Even if Livman weren't a stone-cold killer, Easy didn't want the man touching her.

"I'm sorry for how I acted the other day. I don't usually lose my temper like that. Please forgive me."

Humbled by her apology, he remembered vividly why he'd loved her so much. Around her, he'd always felt like a man. Even at sixteen, she'd had class. Drawn by her shining eyes, he leaned closer to her, catching a whiff of sweet womanly scent heightened by her exercise-warmed skin. He stared into her eyes, mesmerized by their sparkling azure shadowed by lush brown lashes. Her pupils swelled and her eyelids lowered, darkening her eyes into mysterious pools. He drowned gladly.

Don't, she thought. *Don't look at him, don't stand so close, don't remember....*

The warnings in her head proved no defense against the burning intensity of his eyes. He cupped her chin in a gentle hand, lifting her face, and she was powerless, trapped as if in a dream from which her desire to escape was as weak as wisps of fog. His hand was cool against her skin. His breath was warm.

His lips were velvet.

She sprang away, gasping. "Who do you think you are?" In her haste to escape, she struck a table with her hip. Several cans of fixative clattered to the floor. She grabbed blindly for them.

He looked dazed. He raked a hand through his hair, mussing it into spikes.

"It's over!" She thrust out her left hand, showing him the ring. "I'm engaged. I have a life. You can't interfere. I won't let you."

His mouth fell open. "You can't marry Jeffrey Livman!"

"I can and I will—" Now she realized the danger. Easy had been doing a lot more than merely following her around. For all she knew his impulsive nature had evolved into an obsessive-compulsive disorder. "How in the world do you know about Jeffrey?"

"I'm a private investigator." He spoke in a rush, his voice harsh. "I'm not interfering in your life, I'm trying to save it. Jeffrey Livman murdered his wife, and now he's targeted you. I knew you wouldn't take my word for it, so I put together some hard information. It's in the envelope. Read it."

She wished she knew as much about mental disorders as she did about animal anatomy. She hadn't the faintest idea how to handle his delusions. She clamped down on the urge to shout and threaten. If she angered him, he'd eventually get around to figuring out how to destroy her in court. "Okay, I'll read it."

The dogs crowded her legs. Oscar growled, an ominous rumbling from deep in his chest. She rested a hand on his head.

"I have a lot to do," she said. "Is there a number where I can reach you?"

"Don't blow me off, Tink. This isn't a joke. Jeffrey Livman is a stone-cold killer. He collected half a million dollars from his wife's death. He'll do the same thing to you."

"I'm sure you only mean the best for me." She nodded, hoping to impress him with a show of credulity. "I'll read your stuff. But I do have a lot to do and I really can't ask you to stay. I'll call you. I promise." *After* she called her attorney and found out what kind of options she'd have in a legal battle. "I promise, Easy. I will call you."

She held her breath, waiting. The look he gave her

ripped at her heart and made her mouth burn where his kiss had touched her. But he left her home.

She sprang after him and threw the dead bolt. She eyed the envelope he'd left behind. If he'd turned into a deranged stalker intent on destroying her life, she didn't know what she'd do.

Chapter Four

Catherine glared at the envelope Easy had left behind. She scrubbed at her lips where his touch lingered, taunting her with old memories and hurts. She refused to remember how much she'd loved him—how much he'd loved her.

Oscar and Bent eyed her curiously.

"I don't know what his game is," she told the dogs, "but I'm not playing. He's crazy. Completely out of his mind."

Jeffrey murdered his wife. The accusation hung in the air like an odor.

He'd collected proof her fiancé was a murderer—ridiculous! Easy must consider her a complete dummy if he thought for a moment he could march in here and disrupt her life. She snatched up the envelope. A string looped around a paper button held the flap shut.

She stomped into the kitchen. She opened the cabinet under the sink and dropped the envelope into the garbage can. With her foot, she closed the cabinet and swiped her hands in good riddance.

She hummed old show tunes, the notes fierce in her attempt to not think about Easy, while she showered. Once clean, she used a towel to scrub at her wet hair while she sat on the edge of the bed. Her attention wandered to the framed photograph of Elizabeth's substitute. The anonymous child's dark eyes seemed to mock her: *He never lied to you.*

"I never caught him in a lie," she whispered in rebuttal. "There's a big difference."

Scrubbing her hair, she wandered restlessly around the bedroom and out to the lower-level family room. The room was stark, far too large for the lone recliner and television set that furnished it. Old-fashioned panelling on the walls reminded her of the rumpus room in the basement of Easy's parents' home.

This house wasn't pretty and it needed extensive re-modeling, but it was home. She liked it fifty times better than the pristine, overdressed, oversize showplace where her parents lived. Catherine wondered if this house had appealed so much to her because it reminded her of the Martels' place over on Uintah Street.

Troubled, she dried her hair and left it loose. After slathering moisturizing lotion on her hands and arms, she slid on her engagement ring.

She frowned at the flashy ring. Jeffrey murdered his wife.

Easy didn't even know Jeffrey, who had never been married much less murdered anyone. Easy couldn't know Jeffrey. The two men were as different as fire and water, and had nothing in common. Except he did know Jeffrey— somehow.

She went upstairs to the kitchen and jerked open the cabinet under the sink. Easy claimed to be a private eye. She found it difficult to reconcile the memory of a sports-crazy, impulsive, restless boy with a methodical, dogged investigator. It made as little sense as his insistence that her fiancé had murdered a woman.

Easy wanted Elizabeth. Now that made sense. She wondered how far he'd go to find their daughter.

She slammed the cabinet shut and studied the kitchen. The old cabinets showed their age. The walls had been painted an odd shade of blue-green by the previous owners. When her next royalty check came in, she intended to redo the kitchen. She had plans for this house, plans for her life. Easy threatened her future, her happiness and her hard-won peace.

The telephone rang, startling her. Fearing it might be Easy, she waited for the answering machine to screen the call. Margaret's brash voice insisted Catherine pick up the line.

Catherine snatched up the telephone. "I'm here! What's up?" She noticed the light blinking on the answering machine, indicating she had other messages.

"I'm glad I caught you. We have a problem."

Catherine chuckled, partly in relief because it was Margaret and not Easy, but mostly because Margaret thrived on crises and problems. "As long as you don't make me speak in front of a crowd, I can handle it."

"Does a press conference qualify as a crowd?"

It took a few seconds for her agent's meaning to sink in. Catherine nearly choked. "Margaret! You know I hate publicity. I can't do tours and press things. They make me crazy." The mere idea of having to speak to a group of strangers filled her belly with ice.

"Settle down. You won't actually have to say anything. All you have to do is stand there and look cute. You are cute, aren't you? Do your publicity photos do you justice?"

Catherine groaned and sank onto a chair. "Spill it, Margaret. What's going on?"

"I've been on the phone with Doc Halladay's publicist. The good doctor wants to meet you."

Catherine had illustrated stories, books and articles for dozens of writers, none of whom she'd met face-to-face. She'd spoken to many of them on the telephone or via fax transmissions, but she'd never done a job that required personal contact. "Whatever for?"

"We're dealing with television people. They spend the majority of their lives in meetings and at lunch. They like personal contact."

"Do I have to go to New York? Or Los Angeles?"

"Actually…Halladay is coming to you. He wants to see you in your natural environment, so to speak." Margaret paused, dramatically. "He wants to do a segment for his show. Your studio, where you live, blah-de-blah."

"No." Catherine shook her head vehemently.

"You don't have a choice, sweetie. Publicity is part of the deal, and since Doc Halladay is the star, he calls the shots." Another dramatic pause. "If you don't do this, the deal is off."

Catherine gazed haplessly at her studio. Filled with secondhand furniture and found treasures, it seemed amateurish and messy, more like a child's playroom than the workplace of a serious artist. A *real* artist had handcrafted beechwood worktables, custom lighting, overhead projectors and chaise longues. Catherine kept brushes in old coffee cups and used pushpins to hang photographs on the walls. As soon as Doc Halladay saw her home, he'd know Catherine was a fraud.

"Doc Halladay is rich. He probably has servants. I don't even have good china. How can I let him in my house?"

"You don't have to impress the man with furs and feather boas. You've already impressed the hell out of him with your work. Trust me, he's not going to do anything to make you look bad. It'll be fun, sweetie. He's a good sport and his people are total professionals."

Fun… Compared to displaying herself in public, breaking her fingers with a hammer would be fun. "Does this mean I have to do a book tour, too?"

"Mmm. In a word, yes."

Catherine groaned again. "This is getting totally out of hand. I don't know if I can do this. I'm so stupid around strangers. My hands sweat and my face breaks out. I stutter!''

"Relax. Think about the money. Tons and tons of money. Think about awards and prestige and how this will establish you as the artist of the decade. This could be your life's work."

Catherine pressed a hand flat between her breasts. "My heart is pounding already. I feel sick. You don't know how terrified I am of public speaking. I can't do it, Margaret."

"Yes, you can and you will. Even the best actors get stage fright. Tell you what, I'll come out to Colorado. I'll hold your hand. We'll find you a hypnotist or some drugs. Whatever it takes."

"There's no way to get out of it?"

"I'm afraid not. You'll do fine. I'll make sure you do fine. Just keep thinking about the money."

Feeling as if she'd been handed down a sentence of execution, Catherine closed her eyes and rubbed her aching temples. "We'll figure out something," she said weakly.

"That's my girl!"

"When does Doc Halladay want to meet me?"

"Nothing firm yet. I got the impression it'll be sometime next month. Don't worry, you'll have plenty of time to prepare. You'll be all right with this, sweetie, trust me. Who knows, you might find out you're a ham at heart and you love it."

"That'll take more than hypnotism, it'll take a miracle." She wondered if it were possible to hire a stand-in to impersonate her.

After she hung up the telephone, she realized she hadn't told Margaret about her engagement to Jeffrey. Nor had she mentioned Easy Martel—

She gasped and caught the base of her throat with both hands. Easy! She envisioned him embroiling her in a court case over parental rights. Tying her up with lawyers and depositions. The story would show up in the newspapers. Or in the tabloids! Doc Halladay's sole purpose in life was teaching children. He didn't preach religion, but he did set a good example of respect, clean living and character. He wouldn't like his book illustrator publicly unmasked as a liar who denied a man his parental rights.

Oscar nudged her knee with his nose. He eyed her with an expression of concern. She ruffled his silky ears.

"What do I do? I can't ruin Elizabeth's life just to keep Easy off my back."

She wanted advice, someone to talk to. Her parents might be interested in her news about getting married and her major book contract, but they always refused to listen to anything about the baby she'd given up. She wished desperately that her grandmother were still alive. She'd been able to tell Grandma everything and anything.

That left only Jeffrey.

She cupped Oscar's muzzle in her hand. "What's your gut feeling, old boy? Will Jeffrey have a fit if he finds out about Easy?"

Oscar's skinny tail whipped against a table leg with a loud whup-whup-whup.

"Dogs have it so easy. No moral dilemmas. Just eat, sleep and chase bunnies." She turned her attention to the answering machine.

The message was from Jeffrey. He told her he had a big deal about to fall apart and he had to meet with his clients and the finance officer. He said the negotiations would probably run late, so he could not see her this evening. He promised to make reservations at a fine restaurant for a proper engagement celebration. "I love you!" he announced cheerfully before he rang off.

"Love you, too," she muttered. He'd been so accepting about her revelation. She asked too much for her fiancé to be so accepting about an old love shaking up her life.

Grandma had told her often: "You can't hide from life,

honey. Life always finds you." Grandma knew Catherine's first response to most crises was to bury her head in the sand and hope the problem went away.

Easy wasn't going away.

Knowing she'd have to deal with him, and sooner was better than later, she returned to the kitchen. She retrieved the envelope from the trash. Feeling like Bluebeard's wife, she opened the envelope and spilled its contents onto the countertop.

TELEVISION AND MOVIES portrayed private eyes living fast-paced, adventure-filled existences, with an endless parade of sexy dames, car chases and gun battles. In reality, Easy didn't own a gun and didn't want to; he spent the majority of his time either on the computer researching databases or waiting. Waiting for subjects to do something interesting; waiting for bureaucrats to decide if he had a right to public information; waiting for clients to pay their bills.

At the moment he waited for Catherine. In the shade under a stand of ancient cottonwood trees, he sat in his car, watching the entrance to her driveway. He toyed with a pair of handcuffs, his only memento from his stint as a military cop. He hadn't particularly liked the military—too many jokers telling him what to do—but he'd loved law enforcement. Despite the constant scramble for jobs and uncertain paychecks, he loved investigative work, too. He supposed if he had to support a wife and kid, he could always join the sheriff's department. Or go to work for the district attorney's office. For the sake of a family, he'd tolerate a boss.

Uneasy with the direction of his thoughts, he tossed the handcuffs in the glove box.

What are you doing, Tink? he thought. *Isn't it clear enough for you?*

He'd taken a monumental risk in giving her that envelope. She could go to Livman, blowing Easy's cover and John's chances for justice.

Engaged! He slammed the heel of his hand against the steering wheel. She'd known Livman only a few months. How could she agree to marry him?

He vowed that no matter what, even if he had to kidnap her, she wasn't marrying Livman. No way, no how, no time. He pictured himself doing an Errol Flynn number, swinging by a rope into a church and crashing the wedding. Now that would be exciting.

His telephone rang, a birdlike trill. Hoping to hear Catherine's musical voice, he flipped open the small unit. A woman with a raspy, rushed voice identified herself as a billing clerk for an insurance company. She needed information about an invoice Easy had submitted for services. About time, he thought. He'd done the job weeks ago.

Movement caught his eye. The nose of Catherine's Blazer appeared in the driveway. He interrupted the clerk. "I'll have to call you back." He snapped the telephone closed and reached for the ignition key. Catherine turned right, away from him. He waited a few seconds before pulling out of the shadows.

Tailing Catherine on a rural road with light traffic was no simple task. So he lagged behind, relying on instinct. Where the road ended at the highway, the Blazer had disappeared. Easy guessed she headed toward town. He drove south. Past the hills, he spotted her white Blazer about a mile ahead.

"Don't go to Livman," he whispered through clenched teeth. "Use your brains, Tinker Bell. I know you have smarts to spare."

She surprised him by turning left on Research Parkway. He goosed the accelerator to catch up to her, but remained in the left lane to take advantage of her blind spot. She turned right on Lexington. Cursing the traffic, knowing fancy maneuvers would alert Catherine to the tail, he drove to the next opening in the median and made an illegal U-turn. He swung onto Lexington and resisted the urge to speed. Because of a school, cops liked to nab speeders on this road. He reached Union, dismayed to have lost sight of the Blazer.

From the corner of his eye, he spotted a white Blazer headed west on Union. Praying it was Catherine—and not one of the zillion other sport-utility vehicles in this mountain town—he thanked his lucky stars no other cars were close by as he swung into a wide right turn.

Her mysterious journey drove him wild with curiosity. She couldn't be going to Livman's office. She might be meeting him for lunch, but he couldn't think of any restaurant Livman would frequent in this part of town. The man preferred white-linen table service or yuppie chain joints with trendy menus.

He caught up to her at a traffic signal. Three cars behind her, he hunched down low on the seat on the off chance she glimpsed him in her rearview mirror. When she turned toward the library, he felt a moment of triumph.

He parked on the street leading to the library parking lot. His position gave him a view of the main entrance. She could have noticed him tailing her and had pulled into the lot to shake him. He waited to make sure she went inside. Even from a distance he recognized her bouncing blond hair and determined stride. She wore a pale blue sweater and a gauzy skirt that swung nearly to her ankles. He admired her pretty clothes.

He settled his dark glasses more firmly on his face and pulled on a baseball cap and a light jacket. Not much of a disguise, but it helped him blend. He wandered to the library entrance. He dug through the jacket pockets and found an ancient invoice. It was big enough to look like something, so he pretended to read. Head down, he looked for her Blazer and finally spotted it parked along the north edge of the lot. He hung out until he felt certain she wasn't coming out by another exit to give him the slip.

He found her in the microfiche reading room. The envelope he'd given her lay on the table beside her. Newspaper clippings littered the table. From the doorway, he watched her scroll through files. She snatched up a clipping and appeared to compare it to whatever she saw illuminated on the screen.

He slipped silently into the room to stand behind her. Over her shoulder he saw she'd pulled up a newspaper article about Roberta Livman's death.

"Now do you believe me?" he asked.

Her entire body stiffened. She met the reflection of his face on the reading screen.

"I could never make up something like this." He snagged a nearby chair. He straddled it and folded his forearms over the backrest.

"This isn't my Jeffrey. You're mistaken." She kept her eyes on the screen. Her profile appeared carved from fine marble. "He's never been married."

If her voice held a trace of conviction, he would have despaired. Weary resignation, however, gave him hope.

"You have a copy of the marriage license and her death certificate. Look at the date on her obituary. It's more than a month after she died. Her brother had to put in the obit because Livman couldn't bother. He didn't even bother telling her brother she had died. He had to read about it in the newspaper. You don't know about Roberta, do you?"

She turned her head slowly to face him. Her mouth set in a tense, unhappy line. Sorrow marked her eyes. "Why are you doing this to me, Easy?"

"I'm not doing it to you, it's for you." He wanted to touch her so badly he had to clench his fists to control himself. "I don't normally do this kind of stuff. I investigate insurance cheats. I find missing persons or dig around for hidden assets in divorce cases. But John is a friend of my sister's, and you're…a friend of mine.''

She picked up the copy of Roberta's death certificate. "It says here she died accidentally. Even if Jeffrey was married to her, it doesn't mean he murdered her.''

"She died six months ago.'' He carefully touched her finger where that big blue rock glittered, looking far too large and gaudy for her delicately boned hand. "Now you're engaged. Doesn't that tell you something?''

She jerked her hand away from his. Her chin jutted stubbornly.

"I don't know any authorities who are willing to say I have a case. I don't have hard evidence. If I did, I'd show it to you.''

"Then why are you doing this?''

"Did Livman tell you about his wife?''

She closed her eyes. "No.''

"They were only married a year. Maybe it slipped his mind.''

She shot him a hard glance. "I *know* Jeffrey. He is not a killer. He loves me.''

He could almost feel her walls going up. Believing him meant believing the absolute worst about the man she loved. "Let me buy you lunch. Give me an hour to fill you in.''

"Give me one good reason why I should? You appear out of nowhere. You make horrible accusations against the man I'm going to spend the rest of my life with. Why? What's in it for you?''

Good question. He stared at his hands, doubting if she'd appreciate knowing he'd begun dreaming about her every night. Every song on the radio reminded him of her. Every time he saw a blond woman, his heart lurched. He wanted the chance to kiss her again and hold her in his arms and make love to her to see if she still purred deep in her throat when she was happy. He wanted them to hold hands and make dumb jokes and play footsie underneath tables. None of the women he'd dated in the past twelve years had held his interest for more than a few weeks. He knew now that in the back of his mind—and his heart—he'd been waiting for Catherine. He wanted a second chance with her.

"This isn't a whim," he said. "When John first told me about his sister, I didn't see where he had a case either. He had no evidence. And he hates Livman. But he convinced me that he wants justice, not revenge. I can't force you to help me. I can only—"

"Help?" She straightened on the chair. "What do you mean, *help* you?"

"You're close to him. Maybe he'll talk to you. If I can get a confession, it'll mean opening up an official case."

She blinked slowly and touched her lower lip with the tip of a finger. A frown lowered her eyebrows. "You want me to spy on my fiancé?"

"I'm not asking you to do anything except listen to me. One hour, okay?" He stood and extended a hand. "I know where we can get the best burgers in town. My treat."

"I don't eat meat." She stared past his proffered hand as if it were invisible.

"A salad then. Or pancakes. Or coffee. Please, Tink, I really need you to listen to me."

She turned off the viewer and placed the microfiche sheets back in their envelope. She gathered the papers he'd given her. Her silence wore on Easy's nerves. Repressing the urge to crack jokes or otherwise fill the void made his belly ache. Even as a teenager he'd never fooled himself into thinking he could tell what she was thinking. She'd been a delightful mystery, a puzzle to patiently work his way through. She'd been honest, though, and as straightforward as a shy girl could stand to be.

"All right," she finally said. "An hour. But you have to promise me something first."

He pulled her chair out for her. "Sure, anything."

"Promise me this doesn't have anything to do with Elizabeth. You won't pump me for information. You won't try to find her."

Quick pain caught him unawares. Their lost child was another matter altogether, one he hadn't fully processed beyond raw emotion. In the past few days, the prospect of finding Elizabeth had nagged like a low-level white noise in the back of his mind. It wouldn't be too hard. He knew where Catherine had lived in Arizona. He could reason out which hospital Elizabeth had been born in, and figure out the date of her birth. From there he could probably trace the adoption as he'd traced dozens of others.

She backed a step. "Please, Easy, don't do this to me. Don't do it to her. If you care anything about her at all—"

He displayed his palms in appeasement. "I promise! This isn't about her or the past or even about us. I swear, Tink, on a stack of Bibles, I swear."

She backed another step and clutched the envelope over her bosom. "I don't know if I can believe you."

"I never lied to you. I'm not lying now."

For a long time she stared into his eyes, seeming to seek the depths of his soul. "If you say one word about her, I'll get a restraining order and have you arrested if you ever try to contact me again."

Chapter Five

Catherine sat uneasily in the booth inside the coffee shop. Easy removed his baseball cap. A funny yearning came over her to finger comb his thick strands of hair into place. She pulled her attention away from his hair and looked around at the cheerful decor. She rarely frequented coffee shops or pancake houses these days, though once upon a time she and Easy had spent a lot of time in places like these. They had done their homework, talked, drank copious amounts of coffee and iced tea, and she watched him eat. In high school, she'd been self-conscious about her plump figure, so she never ate in public. Instead, she'd vicariously enjoyed his meals, amused and amazed by the sheer quantities of food he could scarf down.

"Horse-boy," she said softly.

He arched his eyebrows, startling her with the realization that she'd spoken her thoughts aloud. Abashed at being caught reminiscing, she covered her grin with a hand.

"I still eat like a horse." He opened a plastic menu.

"Lucky you. You always had a great metabolism." *No, no, no,* she thought. Not old home week. None of this awkward inanity and wandering around a dreamy past. She pushed her menu away. "I'll have coffee."

"They tore down Willie's Pancake House. They're widening the freeway. It closed two years ago."

Willie's... They'd been sitting in a corner booth in that tacky little coffee shop the first time Easy had told her he loved her. She knew she'd made a big mistake coming here. Especially as the inanities continued while the waitress took their order and brought coffee. Easy asked about where she'd gone to college and why she'd decided to move back to Colorado Springs. A million questions bubbled in her throat. She wanted to know about his parents and his sister, and what he'd done in the army and if he had gone to college and where he lived. His claim to be a private investigator roused her curiosity. She told herself she didn't want to know, she didn't want to care.

He had not known she was pregnant. After spending twelve years blaming him for her loss, she had no idea how to feel about him now. On one level, he frightened her. He held the power to ruin her career and her engagement. He angered her. He had no right to make accusations about Jeffrey. Yet, his half smile enchanted her. Each time she met his obsidian eyes, her heart did a little skip. Under the table, thankfully out of view, her knees trembled.

The waitress served Easy a cheeseburger and fries with a side of coleslaw. Catherine noticed the besotted smile the young woman focused on Easy. His charm hadn't subsided in the least. If anything, he was more attractive than ever.

Easy dumped ketchup on his plate. "So you don't eat meat. What about fish?"

She shook her head. "I eat eggs and cheese, but no meat of any kind."

"Maybe I'll try it. You look great."

"Thanks." She dumped artificial sweetener in her coffee.

He swallowed and wiped his mouth with a napkin. "So, how did you manage to pay cash for your house?"

She jerked. The coffee spoon dropped from her suddenly numb fingers. The spoon clattered on the tabletop. "How in the world do you know that?"

"It's public information, Tink. Anyone can go to the courthouse and look up property transactions. You're the titleholder, no liens against the deed. Where did you get the money? Your parents?"

"How dare you snoop around in my private—"

"It isn't private. It's public. And I'm not snooping. I'm trying to figure out why Livman is interested in you." The words hung between them. He rolled his eyes and thumped his forehead with the heel of his hand. "I didn't mean it to come out like that."

"How did you mean it?"

He rolled a hand in a gesture to indicate he was starting over. "Roberta Livman was only twenty-six years old when she died. She had no children, no business debt, no major medical bills. Livman was only thirty-nine, no children, employed and perfectly healthy. Yet, he took out an insurance policy on her for half a million dollars. Romoco Insurance fought the claim, but they finally had to pay off."

Catherine chewed her lower lip, unwilling to grasp his meaning. She latched instead onto Jeffrey's age. "He isn't thirty-nine, he's thirty-six."

"Thirty-nine last year. He's forty now."

"You're wrong. He's thirty-six."

Easy made a disgusted sounding snort and turned his attention to the cheeseburger.

"Why would he lie about his age? Men don't do that."

"This one does. He's forty. And compared to killing his wife, it's not that big a deal."

She slumped against the seat and folded her arms over her bosom. At the moment she hated knowing Easy so well. Born August fourteenth, he was a Leo—always as graceful, powerful and arrogant as his lion star sign. He'd grown up on Uintah Street in a three-bedroom, one-bath bungalow. His heroes in high school had been astronauts and mountain climbers. He hated his middle name, Zebulon. The only person who'd ever called him by his given name, Earl, had been an English teacher—even his parents called him Easy. He had a diamond-shaped birthmark on his right hip and in the summer the sun caused freckles on his back. His first car had been a Volkswagen Rabbit, and he'd nicknamed it Bugs.

"The big deal is," Easy continued, "Livman collected five hundred thousand dollars when Roberta died. That's not a bad payoff for a year of marriage."

She frantically sought a rebuttal. "You can't know that! My father has sued a lot of insurance companies. I know for a fact that policies and payouts are definitely not public information. Father has to use subpoenas to make insurance companies tell him anything. Even then it's a hassle."

"Roberta's brother is an insurance adjuster. He has contacts. A half-million payout on a woman who shouldn't be insured for more than burial costs caused a lot of noise in the industry."

Suspicion prickled at her no matter how hard she tried to ignore it. Jeffrey liked money, no question about it. He lived in a luxurious condo, wore the best clothes and ate at the best restaurants. He denied himself nothing. She fingered her ring, guessing its value around ten thousand dollars, maybe more. "That proves nothing. Some people think insurance is a sound investment plan. They collect policies like other people collect stamps. That doesn't mean he killed her."

Resenting Easy for rousing suspicion, she tried to imagine any reason why Jeffrey wouldn't have told her about Roberta. Any reason, that is, except murder.

"I spoke to the cop who investigated the death. He said there's nothing at the scene to indicate foul play. Several people saw the Livmans in the park that day, but nobody saw anything unusual."

"Then it's a tragic accident. Leave it alone."

"*But,* the cop has a bad feeling anyway. He said Livman was carrying a cell phone. Some people arrived a few minutes after Roberta fell. They say Livman was staring at his wife, but not making any move to help her. They gave Roberta first aid for ten or fifteen minutes before one of them noticed he had a phone. That's when Livman called the paramedics."

"He—he—he panicked. It's understandable. I forget things when I'm excited."

"He was waiting to make sure she was dead. And guess who the grieving husband called after the paramedics told him his wife was dead on the scene?"

Catherine's stomach roiled; she had a bad feeling he was about to tell her something horrible.

"He called his insurance agent." Easy waggled his eyebrows. "Witnesses heard him. Paramedics are loading Roberta's body into an ambulance, and he's arguing with his insurance agent."

Nauseated, Catherine averted her face. "If murder is so obvious, then the police should investigate."

"That's the trouble with a fall. Roberta's injuries match Livman's statement about what happened. Nobody other than Livman saw her fall. Unless a witness comes forward or a piece of hard evidence surfaces, the cops don't have a case to investigate. That's why I need your help. If Livman confesses—"

"No!" She recoiled in revulsion. "I will not spy on my fiancé. Besides, how do I know any of what you say is true?"

"I gave you all I have. You verified the newspaper stories yourself. Look, John Tupper, Roberta's brother, hired me. He loved his sister as much as I love mine, and I'm his last chance to find justice."

"Maybe he isn't telling you the whole story. Maybe he has a grudge against Jeffrey."

Easy leaned back on the bench seat and nodded thought-fully. "It occurred to me. Grieving relative can't let it go, needs a scapegoat. Trust me, I didn't take the man at face value."

"So why are you involved when the police won't do anything?"

"Livman is a liar, and he uses people. The only thing he cares about is a fast buck. He isolated Roberta from her friends and family. She was afraid of him."

"Jeffrey is the gentlest, kindest, most patient man I've ever met."

"Melissa Meyers and Joan Black might disagree with you."

She didn't like the challenging look he gave her. She also didn't like the sinking suspicion that she stood on the wrong side of this argument. "Who are they?"

"Former girlfriends. Both of them called the cops when Livman beat them up."

His matter-of-factness pricked at her. The sky is blue, horses eat hay, Jeffrey beats up women—all of them plain old facts. "Show me his criminal record."

"Both women refused to press charges. Unfortunately the calls occurred before the law changed. Nowadays, someone would go to jail after a domestic call, but back then the cops couldn't do anything."

Catherine opened her mouth to refute his assertions, but nothing came out.

"I asked Melissa and Joan if they would talk to you. They refused. It's been years since either has had contact with Livman, but both of them are terrified he'll find out they've spoken to me."

"Jeffrey likes women! Most of his friends are women. He's charming. He's gentle. He's never hurt me and he never will."

"He hates women, Tink."

She sipped her coffee, denying his accusation by ignoring it. Get up and walk out, she told herself. Do it now. Don't listen to this garbage, especially from a man with a reason to carry a huge grudge.

"Not even his sisters want anything to do with him—"

"He's an only child." She thumped her fist against the tabletop. She wished it were Easy's head so she could pound some sense into him and make him stop telling lies. "He doesn't have brothers or sisters."

Easy lowered his face onto his hand. His shoulders shook. Catherine soon realized he laughed at her.

"We're not even talking about the same man, Easy. This is all some bizarre scheme to drive me crazy!"

"Tink," he said in an infuriatingly reasonable tone, "how can you marry this clown if you don't know anything about him?"

She opened her mouth, closed it, then grabbed the coffee cup to occupy her hands and mouth. The coffee had turned tepid. She warmed the cup from the carafe the waitress had left on the table. "He's an only child, and his parents are dead. Why would he lie about something like that?"

Easy lifted his shoulders in a lazy shrug. Catherine remembered that gesture well—and she hated it. It meant, he was right, she was wrong, so why act like a twit and argue?

"Can't you see he's playing you? Setting you up, telling you what you want to hear. So how much money do you have? Enough that he doesn't have to alert the insurance companies again?"

"I don't have to listen to this." She grabbed her purse. He lunged across the table and caught her arm. His touch seemed to burn through her light cotton sweater. Her insides constricted. "Turn me loose."

"Stay, please."

So angry she quivered, she glared at him. Her muscles burned in her upper arm as she tensed against his hold. He slowly, reluctantly loosened his grip and settled back on the seat.

"If I had more, I'd give it to you. All I have is her brother, who loved her very much, and a five-hundred-thousand-dollar motive." He slowly pushed his plate out of the way and leaned his forearms on the table.

"And a good reason to get even with me."

He shook his head in denial. "I could lie and say how I feel about you has nothing to do with this. Truth is, if you weren't involved, I wouldn't be either. I'm way out of my league investigating a murder. I need all the help I can get."

She searched his face, dismayed by the tugging of her credulous heart. His beautiful dark eyes were earnest; his very posture begged her to heed the truth. "I'm the reason you're involved?"

"You remember my sister, Trish. She and John work for the same company. They're friends. When she found out from him that you were dating Livman, she told me. Things didn't work out for us, but I always…wished you well."

His poignant note touched her. His tender smile arced straight to her soul.

"I just…I can't…there's so much going on in my life right now. I *know* Jeffrey. What you're saying about him is so outrageous, how can I believe a word you're saying?"

"I'm taking a humongous risk telling you all this. You can go to Livman, tell him John is after him and tell him about me. Then he'll clam up. If any evidence exists, he'll destroy it." His eyes narrowed to flinty slits. "You can blow me off completely and marry him."

She sensed he withheld something, but what she couldn't imagine. All she knew was that sitting here with him was a mistake. His presence roused too many memories, carried too many risks. The girl in her heart still soared at the sight of him.

"I need some time to think." She gathered her belongings and stood. This time he made no attempt to stop her. She left the restaurant.

She knew he followed even before she heard him. She *felt* him. For an instant she was back in high school when he'd suddenly materialize behind her while she opened her locker. The game had been that he'd whisper something stupid, and she'd have to resist bursting into laughter. If she laughed, he won. She opened her car door. Only then did she look over her shoulder.

He smiled at her.

Her insides did a slow melt. "What?" she asked. She looked beyond the parking lot. Clouds ringed the horizon and partially blotted the view of Pikes Peak, but the day seemed spotlight bright. Traffic whizzed by on Academy Boulevard. Jeffrey's office was less than a quarter mile away. She had a sickening sensation that all her fiancé needed to do was glance out his office window and he'd see her with Easy.

It struck her like a pail of water in the face: she didn't even know if Jeffrey was the jealous type. He didn't expect her to be jealous. He talked to women on the telephone all the time; in his business he dealt with female closers, lenders and agents.

Easy, on the other hand, used to have a jealous streak a mile wide. Other males who dared trespass had learned quickly to get out of his way.

"Remember *Fantasia?*" he asked.

Drawn back to the present, she peered curiously at him.

"You talked me into taking you to see *Fantasia.* The movie. Remember?"

Fantasia had been, and still was, her favorite Disney animated feature. The music, artistry and colors, even after countless viewings, held the power to entrance her. "You didn't want to go, but then you liked it."

"When I started the car, the radio was playing some rock and roll song."

She smiled before remembering she did not want to encourage him. Still, the image crystallized as vividly as if it had happened yesterday. She and Easy sitting in his Volkswagen, parked in the dark theater lot after the movie let out. For once, he'd been silent, thoughtful—he'd been in awe.

"You turned the radio off," she said. "I think that's the only time you ever drove anywhere without music playing."

"I didn't appreciate you enough. You were good for me. You showed me a world past the old neighborhood and the football field."

She fought the softening within her, but lost the battle before it began. She remembered too much. And she missed him. At least, she missed being in love and being surrounded by a world so bright it filled her with joy merely to breathe. She longed to believe her love for Jeffrey was mature and responsible. In her heart she mourned, knowing what she'd felt for Easy Martel was once in a lifetime, never to be felt again.

"That was a long time ago." She slid onto the driver's seat. He stepped forward before she could close the door. "I have to go."

"Whatever you do, whatever you feel, don't go to Livman with what I've told you. If I'm wrong, then no harm done. But if I'm right, he'll spook and I'll lose him."

"I'm supposed to keep secrets from my fiancé? I don't know about that." She tugged the door and he stepped out of the way.

It was only when she almost reached home that she realized that not once had she declared to Easy how much she loved Jeffrey Livman.

INSIDE DONELLO'S restaurant, Catherine paused near the cash register. For a day and a half she'd been brooding about Jeffrey. At the moment her heart pounded and her stomach ached. Damn that Easy Martel! He hadn't proved Jeffrey was a murderer, but he'd proved several times over that her fiancé was a compulsive liar.

Armed with Easy's information, Catherine had called Vera Livman. Catherine had asked to speak to Jeffrey, and Mrs. Livman had laughed, saying, "Oh my, Jeff doesn't live with me anymore! He owns a real-estate company down in Colorado Springs. I can give you the telephone number."

Catherine had called the real-estate company where Jeffrey worked. In the hopes of learning Jeffrey's true age, she had come up with a lame story about not knowing if his birthday was the fourteenth or the fifteenth of the month. The broker had gone stone cold on her. Jeffrey Livman, he'd informed her, did not work for the company any longer. The man hung up on her. Jeffrey had never once mentioned leaving the company. Nor had he ever offered a clue as to why the mention of his name would so anger the broker.

The very worst call had been when, desperate for any confirmation that Jeffrey told the truth about something, she'd called Noreen. Uncertain how to put the question innocuously, Catherine had asked flat out: "I heard a rumor that Jeffrey has been married. Since you're his friend, maybe you—"

"I am not his friend," Noreen had said. "I don't have anything to do with him."

"I'm not accusing you of anything, I just want—" Noreen, too, had hung up on her.

After all that, she had to face him. Her fiancé, the liar.

The hostess approached. Catherine said she was meeting Jeffrey. The woman guided her through the dimly lit restaurant.

"It's my beautiful bride-to-be." Jeffrey stood when she approached the table.

The only lighting came from tracks over the corner bar and a line of wall sconces. Fresh flowers added an under-tone of sweetness to the heady aroma of olive oil, garlic and freshly baked bread coming from the kitchen. Claus-trophobia squeezed Catherine. A person could die in here and no one would notice for hours.

"This is a nice place." When Jeffrey pressed a kiss toward her mouth, she turned her head so he grazed her cheek.

She forced a broad smile she didn't feel. What idiocy had ever possessed her to listen to a word out of Easy Martel's mouth? This was the man she'd pledged to spend the rest of her life with. The soon-to-be father of her children.

He murdered his wife.

She eased onto a chair and set her purse on the floor next to her.

"What's wrong, Catherine?" Jeffrey peered suspi-ciously at her face.

Lying had never come easily to her. She did better by ignoring the sore subject altogether. Focusing on a bread basket rather than his face, she shook her head. "I'm sorry I'm late. I had trouble finding this place. I never knew it was back here."

"I forgot to warn you. All the streets have the same name. Compton Court, Compton Drive, Compton Circle. Typical Colorado Springs. But you're here and you look gorgeous. I love it when you wear blue. Have I told you lately how beautiful you are?"

She smiled, though she ached inside. "Flattery will get you everywhere, big boy." She placed her hand atop his. His broad smile deepened the crow's-feet at the corners of his eyes—not bad-looking for a forty-year-old man.

A waiter arrived. Jeffrey ordered a whiskey and soda for

himself and a glass of chardonnay for her. That he hadn't consulted her bothered her. He always picked the restaurants where they ate. He ordered for her. If she failed to fully show her appreciation for his taste, he pouted.

Damn that Easy Martel!

In an expansive mood, Jeffrey told her about his hectic day. He filled her in on how his buyers had forgotten to mention some incidents of bad credit, so the underwriter wanted to reject the loan, but Jeffrey and his lender managed to save the day and the deal. A disturbing thought occurred to Catherine. Although she'd paid cash for her home, the transaction had required a full financial report. Jeffrey knew exactly how much money she'd inherited from her grandmother and how it was invested and how much debt she had and her earnings. Jeffrey also knew she was all but estranged from her parents. If she were to disappear, her parents wouldn't find out about it for weeks or possibly months.

Realizing Jeffrey had asked her a question, she snapped her attention to him. "What?"

He exchanged an amused glance with the waiter. "My fiancée is an artist," he said. "She's always lost in fantasyland."

Catherine's cheeks warmed. "I'm sorry. Are we ready to order?" She hadn't seen the menu yet.

"Caesar salad and pasta primavera? Or do you want to try the fajoli soup? It's vegetarian."

"Soup, please."

After the waiter had left them, Jeffrey leaned closer to her. "Where are you tonight? You're acting like a space case."

"It's the engagement." She fingered her ring. "I've got so much on my mind, I can't think straight. We need to set a date. You haven't met my parents yet. That's an ordeal we might as well get over and done with. The wedding! I've only been to one wedding in my life and I barely recall the details.'' She made herself smile when she looked at him. A warning voice in her head told her not to ask what she was going to ask, but Easy had planted the seed of doubt. It insisted on sprouting. ''I've never asked you before…I realize…I mean, have you ever been married?''

Despite the low lighting, she watched a shadow cloud his expression. Then he laughed, reverting quickly to his usual sunniness. ''Why do you ask that?''

His lack of denial made her want to run away. She lifted a shoulder. ''There's so much about you I want to know. I mean, you're handsome and successful, it's strange to think you've never been married. You are forty.''

He pulled a comical face. ''Pshaw, dear lady! I have years to go before I wear the mantle of middle age. I'm thirty-six, just a kid.''

Don't do this to me, Jeffrey, she thought wearily. ''Even so, how have you managed to remain single? I can't believe you haven't had lots of girlfriends.''

''Do I sense the green-eyed monster raising its perky little head?'' He plucked a bread stick from the basket and waggled it at her. ''Don't tell me you're the jealous type?''

''I don't know, Jeffrey.'' She cocked her head. ''Am I?''

''I'm flattered if you are. But I'm telling you, darling, you'll make yourself crazy.'' He handed her a bread stick with the aplomb of a gallant handing her a flower. ''You have to get used to women calling me at all hours.''

She nibbled the end of the crunchy bread stick. He had evaded her question, simple as that. She straightened her back and tossed her hair. ''Well, if you insist on playing coy, I'll go digging. Marriage licenses and divorces are public records. I can find out your sordid past easily enough.''

She expected laughter to meet her haughtiness—she

hoped for laughter. She prayed for him to dare her to go ahead and dig her way to China.

He flung the bread stick on the table with such force it bounced and broke in half. One piece fell to the floor. His eyes blazed. His entire body seemed to swell. "Who the hell do you think you are in threatening me?"

Catherine cringed. "I'm not! It—it—it was a joke."

"If you don't trust me, then let's call the whole thing off. Just walk away, baby. I won't stop you." His words grated like steel against steel.

"Jeffrey!" She looked about, hoping no one overheard his icy, angry words. "I'm teasing. I don't mean anything." She reached for him, but fearfully, afraid he'd pull away. When he didn't, she rested her hand on his wrist. "You're angry. Why?"

His shoulders relaxed slightly. He lowered his face and covered his eyes with a hand. Beneath her light touch, his skin seemed to quiver. "I should have told you." He spoke so softly she had to lean closer to hear him.

"Tell me what?" she whispered.

"I'm sorry. I can't do this." He tossed his napkin on the table, pushed back his chair and rose. He gazed down his nose at her, his air aggrieved. "I thought you loved me, Catherine."

"I do! Please, sit down. Don't walk away. Whatever is wrong? You can tell me anything, Jeffrey. Please."

Their waiter approached. "Is something the matter, sir? Can I get you something?"

Catherine tugged on Jeffrey's hand. "Darling, would you care for another drink?" People were looking at them. She shriveled beneath their curious stares.

He dropped onto his chair as if his legs weren't strong enough to support him. He pointed at his empty highball glass. "Get me another." The waiter rushed away.

"Please, what's wrong? What did I say that's so terrible?"

"This is so painful for me." He shook his head wearily. "Have you ever done something so awful, so…shameful, you just wish you could erase it from your mind?"

His pain wove a net around her heart. She added Easy Martel and his histrionics to the list of items she wished to forget. "It can't be that terrible."

"I was married." The words emerged laboriously, as if it hurt merely to speak. "It ended tragically." He cut a glance at her. "I should have told you about…her."

"Tell me now. What happened?"

"I don't know if I can. You'll hate me when you find out what I did."

Her breath caught in her throat. If he confessed to murder, then what? Call Easy? The police? She swallowed hard. "I won't hate you."

The waiter brought Jeffrey's drink, fresh bread sticks, soup and salad. Appetite gone, Catherine poked a spoon through the chunks of vegetables, pasta and beans.

"Her name was Roberta. We were friends. I thought I knew her." Moaning softly, he shook his head. "I know it sounds terrible, but I didn't love her. I thought I did, but now that I've met you and found out what love is, I know I never loved Roberta."

He'd told so many lies, but his pain and emotions felt genuine. "Why did you marry her?"

"Weakness. I was going through a bad time. The real-estate market dropped, I had debts. Every time I made a deal, it fell through. A customer was suing me and everyone in the office was getting mean. Roberta offered comfort." He lifted his head and a wan smile tugged the corners of his mouth. "She was the only one who could make me laugh. At the time, I really needed to laugh."

She sipped her wine. Her cheeks tightened at the sourness. "I see."

"I know it sounds crazy, but I can't even remember which one of us suggested getting married. It was, let's run off to Vegas and get hitched. It made sense back then.'' His chin quivered; tears glazed his eyes. ''It was wrong, all wrong, right from the start.''

''So you got a divorce?''

He passed a hand over his eyes. ''I wish to God I had.'' He took a deep breath and drank from his water glass. He looked her straight in the eyes. ''Roberta was an alcoholic and a compulsive liar. The day after we returned from Vegas, she announced she was going to be a housewife. A few weeks later I found out she had heavier debts than I did plus problems with the IRS. She'd been fired from her job on suspicion of embezzlement. She only married me because it meant changing her name and getting out of her debts.''

Catherine pressed her fingers to her lips.

''I knew there wasn't a chance we could have a real marriage. I wanted a divorce, but Roberta went nuts. She tore up the house and hit me with a chair. When she cooled off, she promised to enter treatment. She begged for a chance to clean up. I didn't feel right deserting her.''

''Did she stop drinking?''

''She tried. She would clean up, stay sober a few weeks, then go on a bender. She couldn't hold a job. She'd steal my credit cards and take out cash advances. Strange men brought her home from bars.''

No wonder John Tupper needed someone to blame for his sister's death—he couldn't accept the truth about her life. ''She was sleeping around?''

''I guess. I didn't really care. I only wanted her sober enough to take care of herself. Finally I had enough and I gave her an ultimatum. Either she entered a structured program at a center, or she was gone. Forever. She said I was trying to lock her up and she walked out. I didn't think much of it when she didn't come back. I didn't hear from her for almost six weeks.'' His chest and shoulders hitched. "That's when she asked me to meet her at Garden of the Gods."

The short hairs lifted on the back of Catherine's neck. "Why would she do that?"

"It was a special place for us. We'd have picnics there. She loved to watch birds. Anyway, she told me she wouldn't fight a divorce. She said she'd go to Vegas with me and we'd get a quickie. I thought she'd been in a treatment center, but when I got there she'd been drinking." His voice cracked and he dropped his face onto his hands. His shoulders lurched as if in a sob.

Catherine patted his back and rubbed his shoulders, murmuring, "There, there. It's okay. You don't have to tell me any more. There, there."

"I don't think she meant to kill herself. She was trying to scare me, make me promise to take her back. But she kept getting closer and closer to the edge and weaving around.... She slipped. I tried to catch her, but it happened too fast." The words trailed into a low moan.

She soothed him as best she could, assuring him over and over that she understood why he hadn't told her about Roberta. She promised him it didn't matter. What mattered to her was how much she hated herself for causing him pain. It was as if someone forced her to talk about Elizabeth—she knew how such wounds easily tore and bled.

Most of all she hated Easy Martel. He was going to pay for this.

Chapter Six

Catherine ran an extra two miles. She pushed her body to the limits by running as hard as she could up the hills and sprinting on the flat stretches. She sucked in huge gasps of thin mountain air, each cool breath burning in her hot lungs. The greyhounds kept pace, loping gracefully on either side of her. By the time she reached her driveway entrance her chest ached, sweat coated her face and dampened her T-shirt and her legs felt like jelly.

The exercise didn't help—her life had dropped into the toilet and she didn't feel one bit better about it. Dinner with Jeffrey had been a disaster. After he told her about Roberta's tragic death, there had been nothing left to say. The evening had ended early. When Jeffrey kissed her good-night, she knew he'd forced himself to touch her. The aftermath proved worse. He hadn't called her once in three days. She'd called him several times, usually reaching his voice mail. The one time she'd gotten through to him at home, he'd been cold, weary-sounding and noncommittal about seeing her again. He said she'd shaken him, and he needed time to think.

Time to think was the last thing she desired. Jeffrey had lied about his age, his family and his work history. All that she could forgive, or pass off as a quirk, or even insist he see a therapist about his compulsion to lie—but she could not pass off his story about Roberta. At the restaurant, she'd been drawn by his powerful grief. With time to ponder, she realized his story didn't match what the newspapers reported. According to the newspaper article, Jeffrey claimed Roberta had been posing for photographs when the rock beneath her feet crumbled and she slipped.

She could not decide if Jeffrey lied to the reporter in order to protect his mentally ill wife, or if Jeffrey lied to her in order to rouse her sympathy.

She wanted to get married, raise a family and live a quiet life. That wasn't too much to ask. But no, Easy had to come blowing in like a hurricane with his crazy talk about murder. He ruined everything.

On top of all that, she'd been dreaming about him. Last night, she and he had been married, living in a cabin in the mountains. They'd talked about bears and how to dig a fishing hole. Then at some point, the dream had turned sexual and she'd been sixteen again, madly in love and hotly in heat.

Tension lingered despite the killer run, infusing her lower abdomen with frustrating heaviness, a reminder of what she may never feel again. Intermittent cramps taunted her.

She slumped along the driveway, kicking at gravel and reddish dirt.

When she rounded the curve and the house came into view, her resentment burned a few degrees hotter. A deadline loomed for the spider book artwork, but she'd been so restless and out of sorts she could barely concentrate. Her beloved house felt like a cage. That was Easy's fault, too.

She unhooked the dogs from the leashes and let them run ahead. Thinking she should stick to dogs and avoid men, she followed them to the house. She worked the house key out of the small pouch she wore inside her shorts. Eager for water, the dogs jostled her legs.

"Wait a minute," she chided them as she fitted the key in the lock and turned it. The door didn't budge. Frowning, she turned the key the other way and heard the lock mechanism clack. The door opened easily. She'd left the door unlocked. She closed her eyes in self-disgust.

The dogs trotted to the water bowls and slurped noisily. Catherine showed more prudence, sipping from a glass of cool, not cold water. A chill rippled through her. It wasn't more than sixty or sixty-five degrees this morning and the house seemed freezing cold. She started a pot of coffee.

The message indicator blinked on her answering machine. Catherine scowled. Easy called several times a day, leaving impassioned messages which she ignored. She pushed the play button.

Margaret's voice crackled with indignation. "What in the world do you do at this time of the morning? Anyway, just to keep you up to speed. The producers for Halladay's show decided they needed a hand in the book deal. They've tossed another lawyer into the mix to review the contract. I know he can't possibly object to anything, but he'll delay the finalization for a week or two. Hang in there. This deal is definitely going through!"

"Yeah, yeah," Catherine muttered. "Just like everything else in my life is turning out so swell."

Oscar suddenly skittered a side step and then froze, his ears pricked. Bent startled, too. Bent crowded the male greyhound and whined anxiously, low in her throat. Both dogs swiveled their narrow heads as if attempting to pinpoint the source of some threat.

"What's the matter?" Catherine went to a window where she could see the driveway. She didn't hear an approaching vehicle or see anybody walking on the property. "Is it Easy?" she asked the dogs. "Is that jerk following me again?" She stomped outside onto the deck. Leaning on the deck rail, she peered intently at the shadows beneath the trees.

If Easy showed up, she determined, she'd call the law. She'd have him arrested for trespassing.

Oscar barked. Catherine jumped. A mule deer trotted across the driveway. Huge ears twisting like radar dishes, the doe paused and stared at the house. Catherine lunged to the side and managed to snag Oscar's and Bent's collars. The deer leaped vertically, all four feet off the ground, and bounded back the way she'd come. The greyhounds howled in excitement.

"What would you do if you caught it, you silly things?" Their tails beat in furious unison while they begged her with expressive eyes and whimpers to let them chase the deer. The normally placid dogs strained and struggled while she wrestled them inside the house. She used her foot to close the door. As soon as she turned the dogs loose, they ran from window to window.

Tickled by their excitement, Catherine had her first good laugh in days. She pictured herself chasing through the woods after a pair of dogs who could run nearly forty miles an hour. If allowed, they'd pursue the deer for as long as they could see or hear it. They were magnificent dogs, but rather lacking in the brains department.

Chuckling, she went downstairs. The good humor faded while she showered. Today, she realized, she had to talk to Jeffrey. She had to confront him with what she knew. She refused to believe him a murderer, but had no choice except to concede he was a liar. She scrubbed hard at her body, wishing she could wash away the inner turmoil.

She turned off the water; the cloud of rising steam echoed her fog of lonely dismay. Even if Jeffrey explained why he lied, she doubted if she'd ever trust him again. A man who'd lie about his age might lie about anything. She had a moment of horrible clarity, foreseeing a future of gazing at her husband across the breakfast table while wondering where he'd *really* been the night before.

"Damn you, Easy Martel," she mouthed. This particular can of worms would never close again. She ought to run off to Vegas and marry Jeffrey just to spite Easy and ruin his stupid game.

A thump vibrated in the ceiling directly over her head. Startled, she stared upward. Gooseflesh broke over her entire dripping body.

The kitchen was above the bathroom. She reasoned that one of the dogs grew bored waiting for her to come upstairs and serve breakfast. One of them had explored a counter, then dropped back to the floor. She almost convinced herself—until she heard the footsteps. Stealthy and quick, they reverberated softly through the ceiling.

Her heart leaped into her throat. She clutched a towel to her breasts.

It must be the dogs, she told herself reasonably. She strained to listen, hoping for confirmation that the dogs romped, perhaps tussling with each other, or else they'd spotted another deer.

Those were footsteps, human footsteps.

The door from the deck had been unlocked. No matter how much she thought about it, she couldn't recall if she'd locked the door when she came inside. She slid a step across the cold tiles and caught the bathroom door with both hands. She pushed it closed and winced at the faint clunk of wood against wood. She fingered the steam-damaged finish and gaps around the frame. A cheap door, hollow and flimsy, with only a simple push-button lock on the knob. She jammed her thumb against the push button. The dogs weren't barking, but they rarely barked. If threatened by a stranger, they'd probably hide.

A telephone sat on the table next to her bed. Reaching it meant opening the door and exposing herself. A sob choked her throat.

Another thump jerked every muscle in her body tight. She turned her head from side to side, trying to locate the exact source of the sound. She feared it came from the top of the stairs. Cautiously she pressed her ear to the door.

Her thumb pressed so tightly against the lock button, bands of white and pink appeared on her nail. The door felt as substantial as cardboard. If the intruder kicked his way into the bathroom, she had no window to escape through, no place to hide.

She looked around for a weapon. No aerosol cans, only environmentally friendly spray bottles of hair spray and roll-on deodorant. Her feminine razor would be about as useful as a safety pin against an attacker. The blow-dryer might do some damage, but in the close quarters of the bathroom, she doubted if she could swing it hard enough to help. Rising tears filled her eyes with grit.

She dashed impatiently at her eyes, then pressed her ear to the door again. The wooden stair steps had dried over the years, so all of them squeaked. She heard nothing.

She risked taking her hand off the doorknob long enough to wrap the towel securely around her nakedness. Then she jammed her thumb on the lock again.

Think.

Her gaze fell on the towel bar. With one side of the holder improperly attached, the bar hung loosely. Several times she'd almost accidentally torn it off the wall. Keeping her thumb securely against the lock, she stretched to reach the bar. She missed by a scant inch.

Another sound thudded overhead. It was more of a clunk than a thud. A cabinet door had closed. No matter how hungry the dogs were, they would never in a bazillion years open a cabinet. Worst fears confirmed, she stretched across the bathroom, straining to reach the bar and still hold the door. Another sob ruffled her chest. Her erratic heartbeat echoed the water drip-drip-dripping down the drain. Surely the intruder could hear the drumming of her heart.

Distinctive footsteps hurried across the floor. Light, quick, purposeful.

Catherine lunged at the towel bar and wrenched it. Screws ripped from the drywall. The end holder fell and flakes of gypsum trickled to the floor. The noise thundered like crashing crockery.

Resigned calm filled her. She backed away from the door, but never took her eyes off it. If he burst through the wood, she'd brain him. Her arm muscles quivered; her hands ached with the ferocity of her grip on the metal bar. She pictured herself hitting and hitting and hitting until she could hit no more. No matter his size or strength, no matter what his evil intent, she was going down fighting. He'd find no timid victim. If he hurt her, he'd get hurt, too.

Scritch-scritch-scritch.

Catherine screamed at the top of her lungs. "Get away!" she screeched. "I have a weapon! I'll kill you!" She shifted her weight to the balls of her feet and gripped the slick tiles with her toes. She gave the bar a short practice swing. "I'm warning you! I have a deadly weapon!"

The scratching sounded again on the door. Its familiarity penetrated her panic. She lowered the bar and leaned forward, staring as if she'd somehow see through the wood.

Scritch-scritch, and then a whine. One of the dogs scratched at the door.

"Oscar?" The husky whisper hurt her throat, which felt as if iron bands held it in a vise. "Bent?"

A low, coughlike bark answered.

Perhaps it had been the dogs after all. She turned the doorknob a fraction of an inch at a time. The lock popped with a snap that made her muscles twitch. She opened the door, but with her shoulder toward it so she could slam it shut in an instant.

Oscar and Bent waited outside the door. They peered up at her with anxious eyes. She felt positive that if an intruder were in the house, they'd be hiding under the bed. Keeping a two-handed grip on the towel bar, she crept out of the bathroom.

"Is anybody here?"

Oscar and Bent wagged their tails in reply.

She snatched her robe off the bed and jammed her arms in the sleeves. Gulping, she stared through the open bedroom door to the sliding glass doors leading outside to the lower garden. Filmy lace panels covered the glass. She saw no sign of movement outside. She picked up the cordless telephone from the bedside table. After pressing nine, she paused.

Oscar leaped gracefully onto the bed, putting himself nearly eye-to-eye with her. With his silky ears flattened against his skull, he gave her his most pitiful, starving-to-death hound look.

"What were you guys doing up there? Trying to give me a heart attack? Do you think if I kick off, you get to inherit this place?"

Bent sat on Catherine's foot. She leaned her full weight against her mistress's leg and sighed mournfully. The dogs acted so clownishly normal, Catherine couldn't conceive that anything odd had been going on in the house.

Holding the towel bar in her right hand and the telephone in her left, she sneaked up the stairs. No matter how lightly she tried to step, each time she put her weight down, a loud squeal echoed in the stairwell. The house sounded right. It felt normal. The dogs snaked past her, racing each other up the stairs.

"Hello?" The word emerged in a croak. She cleared her throat. "Is anybody here?"

Oscar gave her an impatient look from the top of the stairs. Silence answered Catherine's call. She trotted up the stairs and hurried to the front door. As she'd feared, it was unlocked. She threw the dead bolt.

The telephone rang.

Screaming, she dropped the telephone. It bounced on the throw rug in front of the door. Shrill ringing told her she hadn't broken the unit. She snatched it off the floor and answered.

"Hey, Tink," Easy said cheerfully. "I can't believe you actually answered. Is it too early for a visit?"

"You just scared me half to death! What are you doing?"

"Whoa, it's just a phone call. What's the matter?"

She eased back the curtain over the window in the upper half of the door. A tiny junco perched on the deck railing. It pecked at the wood. "Were you just inside my house?" She prayed he had been. Then she could yell at him and put another black mark against his list of deficiencies, but there wouldn't be any reason for terror.

"What?" The line crackled with static. "I'm losing the connection in the hills. Hold on. I'll be right there."

Before she could say a word, he disconnected.

Clutching the towel bar, she crept into the kitchen. The coffeemaker gurgled. The aroma of coffee filled the air. Even though the sun had come up over the trees, she turned on the lights. Towel bar ready to strike, she jerked open the tall pantry door. Canned fruits and vegetables, boxes of cereal and bags of bulky beans and rice lined the shelves. A fifty-pound bag of dog food sat open on the floor.

No bogeyman.

Both dogs grumbled when she left the kitchen without feeding them. She sneaked into the back bedroom she'd converted into a combined office and storeroom. She turned on the light. Again, ready to defend herself with the towel bar, she jerked open the closet door. Winter clothes, ski equipment and linens were exactly as she'd left them.

In the other bedroom, in which she'd used her grandmother's antique sofa, secretary and china hutch to convert the room into a Victorian-style parlor, she turned on the lights. The room was undisturbed, down to the dust she'd been neglecting on the furniture.

Perhaps it had been the dogs after all. On occasion they played in the house. The deer might have roused their spirits.

A car crunched gravel in the driveway. Through the window, she recognized Easy's nondescript white sedan. She wondered if he were sneaky enough to break into her house then pretend he *happened* to be in the neighborhood.

She watched him walk across the driveway and onto the deck. Despite her tension, she admired the fit of his blue jeans and the way sunlight sparked against his hair. The old thrill swept through her. Long ago, whenever he arrived for a visit or to pick her up for a date, the sight of him filled her with wonder that this beautiful wild boy chose her to love.

He knocked on the front door. If, she determined, he played some sick game and had broken into her house, she'd beat him to death with the towel bar. She answered the door. Too late she remembered that she wore only a terry-cloth robe and her uncombed hair dripped water down her back and shoulders.

He looked her up and down, his dark eyes warm with concern. His eyebrows knit in a worried frown. "Are you all right?"

Glad for company, even his, she invited him inside. "I was taking a shower when I heard somebody walking around up here."

He glanced at the dogs. "Somebody?"

"It could have been the dogs, I guess. But I was never so scared in my life! Sheesh, it was like being in *Psycho*."

A faint smile pulled his supple lips. She followed his gaze to the towel bar in her hand. Knowing she'd ripped a hole in her bathroom wall, she barely suppressed a groan. She set the bar on a table.

Easy glided around the room, his athletic shoes barely making a sound on the wooden floor. "Any sign of a break-in? Anything missing?"

"Everything is okay. But I forgot to lock the door." She'd left the door unlocked while she'd been out running, too. The intruder could have been in one of the back rooms, listening to her, watching her, when she returned. A shivering shudder rippled down her back.

"Catherine?" Easy rushed to her side. Only then did she feel her buckling knees. "Hey, hey, it's okay. Easy's here to protect you." He helped her onto a chair. She had enough mental facility remaining to tug her robe closed over her thighs. He crouched next to the chair. "Have you had problems around here? Prowlers? Peeping Toms?"

"It's safe here. You can't even see my house from the road." She glared at the dogs. "You two are no help. You'd hold a burglar's flashlight for him."

"They aren't watchdogs?" Easy asked. "They're big enough."

Catherine rolled her eyes. "They don't have a ferocious bone in their bodies. They're retired racing dogs. I adopted them through the greyhound rescue project so they're used to having strangers around. The only things they get excited about are rabbits, squirrels and deer."

"I know a guy with a rottweiler mix that needs a home." He petted Oscar's sleek head.

Tempted, she murmured that she'd think about it. She hugged her shoulders, repressing another shudder. "I need to feed them."

"So tell me what happened. Exactly."

While she fed the dogs, she told him what she'd heard. Easy wandered through the small kitchen, his eyes busy while his hands trailed over cabinets, counters and appliances. Catherine bristled over the way he acted as if he owned the place.

"Are you sure nothing is missing?" he asked.

She opened her mouth to assure him that nothing had been touched, but realized something was missing. She turned in a circle, but could not recall exactly what had been in the kitchen when she left this morning for her run. She kept a clean house, but not a particularly tidy house. She had a bad habit of misplacing items. "I don't know. Something…"

"Who has keys to your house?" he asked, his tone neutral.

"No one—wait. My mother has a key, but that's only for emergencies. My parents never drop in unannounced." The missing item nagged at her. She checked her purse. She always left it on the kitchen counter next to the refrigerator. Her wallet was intact, containing ten dollars in cash, her lone credit card and ATM card. Her checkbook was still there, with all checks accounted for. She glanced at the wall next to the doorway. Her spare car keys hung from a small wooden hook. In its place above a cabinet, Grandma's silver tea service gleamed.

"Did you change the locks when you moved in?"

"No." Growing scared again, she swiped at her wet hair.

"Then you don't know for certain how many keys are floating around."

"The former owners moved to Texas. I got all the keys at the closing. Jeffrey gave them to me."

He made an *mmm-mmm* noise, reminiscent of a car mechanic peering under a hood while preparing to impart expensive news. "So you don't know for certain how many keys are floating around."

"Jeffrey doesn't have a key to this house. Nor does he need one. I resent what you're implying. He has no reason to come in here and sneak around." She clutched the neck of her robe closed. "Excuse me. I need to get dressed."

She stomped downstairs. Jeffrey most certainly did not

have a key to this house and he didn't need one and he'd never asked for one. Why would he?

The answer came in a nasty little scared voice—*because if he's a killer, then why not make a copy?* It made killing her all the easier.

She dressed quickly in jeans and a T-shirt. Easy had a good motive to snoop around her house. He wanted to find Elizabeth, so maybe thought he'd find a clue in her personal papers. He could have arrived while she was running and happened to find the door unlocked. Then, when she returned, he hid and slipped out while she showered.

With indignation replacing the fear, she marched upstairs.

Easy stood before her worktable, studying a nearly finished painting for the spider book.

"Easy."

He turned his head. He raked her with an impudently admiring glance. "What?"

"Look me straight in the eye and tell me you didn't break into my house."

"I didn't break in." His steady gaze never wavered.

Believing him frustrated her. "Then why are you here?"

He followed her to the kitchen. He crossed his arms and leaned a shoulder against the doorframe. "You know how much I hate being ignored." He graced her with a smug smile. "You don't return my calls."

She poured two cups of coffee. "I have nothing to say to you." She met his grin with a sweet smile of her own. "Nothing nice anyway." She handed him a cup of coffee.

"So nothing I said about your boyfriend got through to you? I don't buy it, Tink. You just won't admit I'm right."

She jerked a carton of nonfat milk from the refrigerator. "Fine! I admit it. Jeffrey is a liar." She added a generous dollop of milk to her coffee. "Happy now?"

"What happened?" He sipped the coffee and made an approving sound. "What did he tell you?"

She cringed inwardly over the prospect of discussing her disintegrating relationship with Jeffrey. It had taken her years to find a man she found attractive and trustworthy, then with a few words Easy Martel proved her judgment was as poor now as it had been back when they were dating.

"What difference does it make? He's probably going to break up with me anyway. He won't see me. He barely speaks to me on the phone."

"Did you tell him about me? Or John Tupper?"

"Your little undercover operation is safe. I didn't tell him about you." She faced him. "We talked about Roberta. You didn't tell me she was an alcoholic with mental problems."

"Really? I didn't know that."

She caught the edge of sarcasm. "Really. Has it ever occurred to you that it's a lot easier for her brother to believe Jeffrey killed Roberta, than it is for him to think she killed herself?"

"No kidding." He cocked one eyebrow, his smile undiminished. "So what did he say about the insurance policy?"

"All I have is your word that he profited from her death. And I'm not at all convinced your word is worth anything."

He lifted a shoulder in a lazy shrug. "So he fed you a story and you swallowed it."

Knowing he deliberately goaded her, she advanced on him. He stood his ground, sipping coffee as if he had absolutely nothing better to do than hang out in her kitchen. She grabbed a paper towel off a roll. Then, needing something to do with the towel, she put down her coffee and began wiping the counter.

She caught a whiff of him, an alluring mixture of sunshine and maleness that was exclusively his. With rising panic, she realized he'd been imbedded permanently in her brain. She'd never be rid of him, ever. Her eyes glazed.

"I didn't think you were that dumb, Tink."

"I didn't say I believed what Jeffrey told me. But I don't believe you either."

"How about if you meet John Tupper? You'll find out he isn't delusional about his sister."

"Everybody is delusional." She picked up her coffee and stepped around him. "Nobody knows anyone else."

"I know you."

She stopped in her tracks. Cradling the heavy coffee mug in both hands, feeling the heat in her palms, her entire body seemed to go on alert.

"I know you're as sensitive as a wild bird." His voice dropped and softened, flowing like honey around her ears. "You hold the hurts inside. You're smart, smarter than anyone I've ever known. You don't make friends easily, but when you do, you're friends for life." He placed a hand on her shoulder. "You're more likely to cry when something touches your heart than if you're hurt. You don't know how beautiful you are and you probably never will. Somehow that makes you even more beautiful."

Her restless dreams of him came back to her, tormenting her with memories and loss. "I've changed, Easy." She hated how weak she sounded. Her voice was positively breathless. "I'm not a shy little girl overly impressed by your words anymore."

"I'm not trying to impress you." He tugged on her shoulder until she turned around to face him.

She knew better than to look at his eyes. His beautiful, expressive dark eyes had always been her downfall. She stared at the stitched-on pocket on the front of his dark green T-shirt.

"John is paying me good money for this investigation. I'm duty-bound to do the best job I can. But I'm in no way trying to earn my keep at your expense."

"If you say, 'but I don't want to hurt you,' I will slap you." She risked a peek at his now-solemn face. "My whole life is falling apart because of you."

"I'm trying to save your life."

"You always were given to dramatics." She stalked out of the kitchen. "I have a lot of work to do. I have to finish these illustrations. My bills and files need updating. The house is a mess. Thanks for stopping by."

"Damn it, Catherine! You're being stubborn."

She flinched at his passionate outcry. He loved to argue, to debate an issue for hours, or even days or weeks. Hoping he'd meekly leave her alone was foolishness on her part.

"I can be stubborn, too." To emphasize the words, he flopped onto a chair.

Finished eating, Oscar and Bent wandered into the studio. They hopped onto the sofa and stretched out their long legs. They looked between the humans as if watching a play.

Frustrated as much by her own inability to get ugly by throwing him out as by his stubbornness, she huffed her displeasure. She perched on a stool.

"Let's get something straight," he said. "Twelve years ago I screwed up. You screwed up. We mutually screwed things up. You were scared, I was a jerk. I swear, Tink, if I could go back and do things over, I would. The last thing I ever wanted to do was hurt you. I'm not trying to hurt you now."

Every fiber in her being yearned to hear—truly hear— what he said. She picked up a watercolor pen and toyed with the plastic cap.

"Tell me the truth. If you hadn't been pregnant, would you have gotten so mad at me?"

She opened her mouth to state that she most assuredly would have. What he did had been unforgivable. But…had it been? Teenage boys, she remembered too well, were crude, lewd and none too bright. Even those with the best manners and best intentions had lapses of utter idiocy.

Unable to lie to him, she shook her head. "We'd have fought, but I would have gotten over it."

"I didn't know about the baby. I didn't have a clue. If I did know, it wouldn't have mattered if your parents sent you to Siberia, I'd have gone after you."

She called herself a weak ninny for believing that, too. For wanting so much to believe. Her empty arms ached for the baby she'd never been able to mother. Her empty heart ached for Easy and what could never be.

"I'd like to know where Elizabeth is. I want to see for myself that she's okay." His shoulders tensed, a brief flexing of distress. "But that's another matter. Another day. Right now the problem is Livman."

Livman—she hated the way he spoke Jeffrey's name, as if it were some sort of disease. Some plague to wipe off the face of the earth.

"You're wasting your time. Jeffrey told me about his wife. He admits the marriage was a mistake. He doesn't want anyone knowing, or even thinking, she killed herself. It's Mr. Tupper you need to convince, not me."

"Roberta wasn't an alcoholic."

"You knew her personally?"

"I've spoken to a lot of people who did. Her family, former friends, her employer."

A frisson chilled her. "What employer?"

"Roberta was a loan originator. She worked for a mortgage company. Made good money, too."

Loan originator…Catherine knew relatively little about financial matters or institutions, but she intuited a mortgage company needed to trust its employees. "She couldn't hold a job. She was fired for embezzlement."

Those thick eyebrows lifted skeptically. "I can get her employment records. I can back up everything I'm saying."

Somehow Catherine didn't doubt it for a second. She also felt little surprise that Jeffrey would have lied about Roberta's character, too.

"So he says she was an unemployed, dishonest, unstable drunk. What kind of man slanders a dead woman?" He let the question dangle.

Catherine squirmed on the stool. Jeffrey's tale of the doomed marriage, so poignant and heart-wrenching in the telling, now seemed self-serving. He'd made himself out to be a tragic hero, attempting to save the worthless life of a wretch. A sour taste filled her mouth.

She swallowed hard. "Are you sure she wasn't drinking when she fell?"

"They checked during the autopsy. She hadn't been drinking."

Defeated, she worked the arches of her bare feet on the stool rung, her skin squeaking against the wood.

"Everybody I talked to says the same thing. Roberta was quiet, kind of shy and very sweet. She loved children. John could always count on her as a baby-sitter. She never dated much. Her shyness came out around attractive men. Livman swept her off her feet. Everyone was surprised when she married him. They'd only known each other a short time."

In a twisted way, Easy sounded as if he described Catherine. Short hairs raised on her nape and gooseflesh rose on her arms.

"After she married Livman, she changed. She grew quieter. She made mistakes she hadn't made before. She called in sick to work a lot. She refused to talk about her husband. She stopped socializing with anyone in the office."

Easy rested his forearms on his thighs. His earnest expression held her rapt. "I'm no shrink, but I notice things about people. I see patterns. Roberta displayed all the symptoms of an abused wife. She was afraid of her husband and afraid to get anyone else involved.''

''Jeffrey would never hurt a fly.''

''Abusers aren't all brutes with loud mouths and dirty habits. A lot of them are respectable men with good jobs and high positions. Your own father is a good example.''

She gasped. ''Father never abused me.'' Her back and shoulders ached with phantom bruises.

''Then you lied all those times I found you crying?''

Rapid blinking stopped the rise of tears, but no amount of swallowing could stop the thickening in her throat or the quivering of her chin. ''It was different back then,'' she whispered. ''Parents used corporal punishment.''

Easy raised his hands, showing his palms. His eyes widened. ''Fine, fine, I won't go there.''

She hated him for knowing her so well, for being privy to all her secrets. Mumbling an excuse about freshening her coffee, she hurried to the kitchen. She wanted Easy gone, out of her life forever. He represented a period of her life as terrible as it was wonderful. She rested with her hands on the countertop, her head hanging, frightened by the pounding of her heart and how much it hurt to breathe.

''I'm sorry,'' Easy said. He rested a hand between her shoulder blades. ''That was a low blow.''

He began rubbing her back with slow, sensual circles. She knew he must stop, she must stop him. He shouldn't touch her, but no matter how much she tried, she could not make herself speak.

''Let's run off and be cowboys.''

A smile caught her unawares. That had been their private joke. Back then, their big plan was to run away to Wyoming and own a cattle ranch. Whenever she had the blues or had fought with her parents, Easy would urge her to run off with him to Wyoming.

She turned around. His hand trailed over her shoulder.

His thumb barely grazed her neck. His expression grew troubled.

"I won't let you marry Livman."

She mustered all the strength she had remaining. "He is not a murderer."

"I don't care if he's president of the USA. You aren't marrying him. You're mine." He grasped her shoulders, lowered his mouth to hers and kissed her.

Chapter Seven

She knew he shouldn't kiss her, but his hands soothed her; his lips warmed her. The wrongness of the situation tangled her thoughts, but still she held her face toward his, like a flower toward the sun, and reveled in the nurturing sweetness of his caress. A touch without pressure, without demand—a touch promising only heartache. Smooth lips, a teasing tongue, the slick fresh taste of him and his intoxicating scent swirling through her blood filled her with exquisite agony.

He held her shoulders. His hands were right, they belonged. Her body knew the rightness even while her mind protested. The voice of reason grew fainter, muffled by the soft press of flesh against flesh, then, finally, silenced by the tidal wave of memory.

She slid her hands around his waist, tentatively at first, then more boldly. She explored the lean muscularity of his back, so solid and so shockingly familiar. She reached for his face. Coarse beard stubble excited her. Deep pulsations of desire, thrumming through her veins, held her captive in his arms.

He broke the kiss with a gentle tugging at her lower lip, suckling for a moment as if loath to let her go. Tingling pleasure rippled low in her abdomen, alien and familiar at the same time.

"I can't help it," he said, his voice raw.

She swallowed hard. Forcing her eyelids open seemed as difficult as running up a steep hill. His face, his beautiful, expressive face, so quick to change, once upon a time so simple to read. Now an adult, he no longer wore his emotions on the surface for all the world to see. She recognized desire, though. She recognized torment.

"I am not yours," she whispered. "You don't know me. I'm not the same."

She wanted to hate him. His crimes were many and severe. He threatened her happiness, he threatened her future. He roused memories best left buried. He ripped open her chest and brought into the light the emotions she no longer wished to feel.

"You're mine. Always."

He kissed her again, his urgency barely controlled. Her heartbeat echoed the desperation in his declaration. He tightened his hold around her body, nearly lifting her off the floor. She melted against him, wanting him…needing him.

Mustering all her strength, she broke the kiss and pushed him away. When he released her, she wanted to weep. From fear of needing him so much or from disappointment that he let her go, she did not know.

He plunged his hands into his pockets. Heat darkened his dusky cheeks. "I won't let you marry Livman. I won't let him hurt you."

He'd accomplished at least part of his mission. Even if every single thing Easy had told her about Jeffrey were a lie, she knew she could never marry him. She could not spend the rest of her life with one man while yearning for another.

She stared miserably at the floor. "Please leave."

"I'm not finished—"

"Go!" Her yell brought the dogs into the kitchen. She covered her mouth with a hand, appalled that this man could so easily rip away her peaceful facade. "Get out, Easy."

He reached for her and she scrambled away. She flung up a hand, her palm flat and rigid. "You have to go. I can't talk to you anymore. Just go."

"I can't let things drop."

Fighting a rising panic, she pressed her lips stubbornly together. Finally, to her relief, he nodded, his eyes downcast, his posture subdued. He turned away. On his way out of the kitchen, he petted Oscar. His footsteps thudded softly on the wooden floor. Belly aching, eyes closed, she listened to the front door shut.

He wanted her...she wanted him. She hated him most of all for that.

TWENTY-FOUR HOURS after leaving Catherine, Easy hadn't finished kicking himself. Sure, he had unconventional methods and a weird sense of humor. Some of his clients thought he acted bizarrely at times, but he was, and remained, a pro. He did whatever jobs clients hired him to do, all the while remaining emotionally uninvolved. He found missing persons, checked criminal backgrounds and finances and staked out crooked employees. Except for that competitive thrill he enjoyed whenever he outsmarted the bad guys, he didn't give a rat's behind about them personally.

You're mine...

"Idiot," he grumbled. He stomped around the small office, glowering at the stacks of folders he needed to file, the pile of invoices he needed to complete and mail and the bills he needed to pay. He hated paperwork, but other than paperwork he had nothing to do. He'd cleared all his business, except for John Tupper, so he couldn't dump the case no matter how much he wanted to. Without John paying for this investigation, he'd lose his motorcycle. As if fate conspired to keep him on the case, he hadn't had a job lead in days. Nobody needed him—except Catherine.

The telephone rang. He didn't feel like talking to anyone, but he needed work. He answered with a gruff hello.

Trish said, "Haven't you had your coffee yet?"

He settled onto a chair, kicked his feet up on the desk and rubbed his eyes with the pads of his fingers. "Oh, it's you."

"I'm happy to hear your voice, too. What's up?"

"Nothing. What's up with you?"

"Since you're such a bear, I'll keep it short. John doesn't want to bug you, but he's dying to know what's going on. So I'll bug you. Have you learned anything new?"

The only thing he'd learned was what he'd known all along. Catherine St. Clair was the only woman he'd ever loved and the only woman he ever would. "Since yesterday? Nada."

"Boy, you sound as though somebody shaved your head while you slept."

He wished it were that simple. He sighed heavily. "I'm in over my head, sweet pea. That's the bottom line. I don't know squat about a murder investigation."

"You're the best at digging up dirt," she protested. "You're so shameless, I'm proud of you."

"Thanks a lot."

"And you're the sleaziest private eye I know. You—"

"Quit while you're ahead." Despite his mood, Trish's teasing made him feel better. He swung his feet to the floor. "I'm out of my league. I never even investigated a homicide while I was in the army. Con artists are my gig."

"Jeffrey Livman *is* a con artist. *Duh.* He conned Roberta before he killed her."

Her comment set off a *ping* deep in his chest. He'd been trying to dig up a corpus delicti—proving a crime had been committed. He'd concentrated all his energies and resources on trying to accomplish what trained, experienced investigators had failed to do. No wonder he beat himself against a wall.

"Easy?"

"You're brilliant. We don't have to prove beyond a reasonable doubt that he killed her. All we need is evidence that he set her up to take advantage of her death. Any civil jury will accept that."

Trish cleared her throat. "I thought that was what you were doing?"

He thumped his head. "I might have gotten Catherine into trouble. She thinks someone broke into her house. I'm betting it's Livman."

"Oh my God! Did he hurt her?"

"No. I don't know if he'll hurt her unless he can profit, but I'm not taking the chance. Can you and John swing by my office today? Lunch?"

"It'll have to be a late lunch. I have a meeting, but sure. What have you got in mind?"

"We need to rethink our strategy. Instead of focusing on what happened in the park, we need to figure out what happened up until then. How would you like to do some intelligence gathering? Some of Livman's former co-workers are reluctant to speak to me, but they might talk to you."

"Guys, right?"

"You got it, Mata Hari. Do you think John's contacts will give him the details about the insurance policy?"

"Those kinds of files are highly confidential. You can't—"

"Find out the name of the agent who sold the original policy," Easy interrupted. "We don't have to actually see the files. If this goes to court, subpoenas will take care of that."

"I hate it when you suck me in," Trish muttered.

Easy took that as a yes. "Great. I'll be in my office most of the day. See you at lunch."

Energized, his mind roiling with a fresh strategy, he moved to the filing cabinet. With his hands working on autopilot and his brain racing at warp speed, he filed papers. If the pros couldn't find hard evidence, it would take a lot more than dumb luck for Easy to find proof capable of standing up in a criminal case. A civil case, now, that was a different matter altogether. In a criminal case, the full burden of proof rested on the state. The defendant didn't have to do anything except show up and demand fair legal procedure. In a civil case, however, both sides had to present evidence. Both sides had to defend and argue their case. Easy nearly salivated at the thought of Livman explaining his lies and conflicting stories.

John was willing to sue Livman for wrongful death. If he won, he'd make sure Livman didn't keep a penny of the insurance money. Livman would be publicly exposed as a liar and an abuser of women. John, however, was not willing—and Easy didn't blame him—to file suit unless he had a winnable case. As much as John loved Roberta, he wasn't wealthy and he had a wife and children to consider. He couldn't afford frivolity.

The insurance policy, Easy suspected, was the key.

Two men walked into the office. Startled, Easy straightened from a file drawer and automatically reached for the loosened knot of his tie. On office days he wore button-down shirts and ties—his one concession to being a businessman.

Walk-ins were as rare as whooping cranes. His nerves prickled in alarm. "May I help you?" he asked.

The taller of the two men smiled. Easy didn't like that smile, it held grim secrets. For that matter, he didn't like the looks of either man. The tall man wore a suit with a pale blue shirt and a striped tie, but the jacket shoulders bunched at the seams and the sleeves were too short. The tie was clumsily knotted as if he'd never tied one before and had to take instructions from a book. Suede shoes spoiled the power-suit effect. The other man wore jeans and a pullover shirt. The jeans had greasy smudges on the thighs, like wipe marks. Massive arms and a neck so thick it appeared his head rested directly on his shoulders, coupled with a lumpish expression, said he probably spent far more time at the gym than inside bookstores.

The tall man stepped aside. No-neck moved in, effectively blocking the door. Easy's back muscles tightened and twitched.

"You Earl Z. Martel, private investigator?"

Easy knew a few tricks, but in these close quarters, especially against that muscle-bound dirtbag, he doubted if tricks would do much good. He needed a bazooka. Determined to brazen it out, he extended a hand and moved away from the filing cabinet. "I'm Martel. What can I do for you gentlemen today?"

He didn't see the punch. He didn't realize he'd been hit until he was on the floor, stupidly looking up at the lazily circling ceiling tiles. Heat swallowed Easy's face and his right eye clouded. He blinked and wished he hadn't. White shards exploded in his head.

No-neck rubbed the knuckles of his right hand. Brassy metal gleamed on his finger.

"That's a wake-up call, Martel," the tall man said. "You won't see the next one coming."

"Didn't see that one coming," Easy muttered and gingerly touched his right eye. His fingers came away slickly red. A glance showed his shirt splattered with crimson flowers. He put a hand under himself to get up.

No-neck kicked him. The blow caught Easy squarely on the hip. His hand slipped on the flat carpet and he fell on his side, ending up clumsily twisted.

Years of football and years as a military cop had taught Easy that the first man to lose his temper, lost the game.

He struggled against the hot rush of fury rising in his chest. No-neck stood too close. If Easy's throbbing hip were any judge, he wore steel-toed boots.

"You stay away from Jeff Livman. Stay away from Catherine St. Clair, too. We'll be watching you, Martel. You get anywhere close to our friends, and we'll turn more than your face into hamburger." The tall man turned toward the door.

No-neck waited until his companion walked out of the office before he followed. He closed the door behind him.

Hurting too much to curse, Easy labored to his feet. He swayed unsteadily and ended up lurching against the desk. A bout of dizziness made him wobble; he held onto the desk for dear life. Fat drops of blood spattered silently on the desk. His lack of depth perception told him his right eye had swollen shut. He made his unsteady way to the bathroom.

He glared at his reflection in the mirror over the sink. No-neck had opened an inch-long gash above Easy's eyebrow. Not to mention ruining his favorite tie. Blood had stopped pumping from the wound and now congealed in thick gobs in his eyebrow. His right eye looked as if he'd stuffed marbles under the lids.

He ran cold water in the sink and jerked paper towels from the holder. He needed stitches. The thought churned his already queasy gut. He hated needles.

The office door opened with a faint squeal of dry hinges. Easy jumped, his heart in his throat. He snatched up a small metal waste can. Used paper towels fell like clumps of snow. Brandishing the can, he charged out of the bathroom.

Catherine St. Clair gasped and clapped her hands over her mouth.

Easy skidded to a stop. He froze with the waste can clutched over his head, his feet widespread. "Oh, it's you," he said. "How's it going?"

"Easy?"

He lowered the can and set it on the floor. He smiled weakly. "Sorry, I thought you were someone else."

"Oh my God, what happened to you? You're bleeding!"

"No kidding." He dropped onto a chair and flinched at the pain in his hip. He could feel a bruise spreading across his pelvis.

Catherine flung her purse on the desk. She rushed into the bathroom where water continued to run in the sink. She emerged a few seconds later, trailing water drops on the carpet.

Easy peered up at her through his good eye. Even wide-eyed and pale-faced, she looked incredible. A light green knit shirt clung to her curvaceous figure, and her green-and-fawn striped skirt floated around her legs like a gauzy cloud. A nice sight for sore eyes.

She pressed a wad of wet towels to his bloody eye. "What happened?"

"I whistled at the wrong lady," he said, deadpan. Her look of sheer horror made him regret his flippancy. "Some joker sucker punched me."

"With what? A crowbar?"

"His fist. He was wearing a ring. How bad is it?"

"It's terrible. I have to get you to a doctor. You're covered in blood. Your poor eye! Where else are you hurt?" She raked her anxious gaze over him head to toe.

"He kicked me, but no big deal." That revelation had a nice bonus effect. She held the compress on his eye with one hand while she ran her other hand gently, but firmly over his chest. He resisted the urge to tell her where he'd been kicked. When she began poking and prodding his thighs, he figured he'd had enough comforting. For now. He nudged her hand away. "I'll live."

"You don't look good." She returned to the bathroom for fresh towels.

Now that the pounding throb in his head had receded to a bearable ache, he grew curious about Catherine's presence. When she returned, he asked, "What are you doing here?"

She replaced the bloodied towel with a fresh cold compress. The cold water felt good against the hot swelling. Her light vanilla perfume had even greater therapeutic results. Once upon a time, he'd told her his favorite scent in the whole world was vanilla. She'd begun wearing vanilla after that. That she still wore it did funny things to his insides. Having her so near almost made getting socked worthwhile.

She smoothed hair off his forehead. "I think you're right about Jeffrey breaking into my house."

Of course. Livman had seen the information—complete with reports typed on letterhead—Easy had given Catherine. "Is it the packet I gave you? Did Livman take it?"

Her wondering gaze seemed to ask, How did you know? "It's gone. I looked for it this morning, but it's missing. I didn't realize it was gone until I looked for it. Jeffrey is the only person who could have any interest in those papers."

Total lack of surprise fended off Easy's dismay. His cover had been blown before, and he'd survived. He'd survive this, too. He cautiously touched a fingertip to his swollen eye. "Yep. He sent a couple friends over this morning to tell me to back off. He plays rough."

She cocked her head first one way than the other. Her eyes flashed with blue fire. "Jeffrey hit you?"

"Not personally. The thugs he sent told me to stay away from Livman and from you. He knows I'm after him, Tink. The real question is, does he know whose side you're on?"

"I CANNOT BELIEVE Jeffrey sent men to hurt you." Catherine paused inside the door of Easy's apartment. She clutched her purse to her chest. Her expression revealed nothing about her reaction to the small apartment filled with more computer equipment, paperwork, maps and books than with furniture.

Easy headed for the bedroom. Catherine's comment annoyed him. Her actions of the past few hours had convinced him she knew Livman was a murderer. She'd driven Easy to the emergency room, sat with him while he waited, and held his hand while the doctor put two stitches in his eyebrow. She hadn't said much, but her concern for him had blared through loud and clear.

Now she couldn't believe Livman hired thugs.

"Women," he muttered. He worked off his tie and shirt. Rusty blotches marred the purple, gold and blue pattern on the silk tie. No-neck would pay for it somehow, that's for certain. He carried the ruined tie and bloodstained shirt to the kitchen.

"Do you know how to get blood off silk?"

Catherine turned from the sink where she prepared an ice pack. She glanced at him, did a double take and stiffened. Hot spots flared on her cheeks. The blush spread until her entire face burned bright red. She abruptly turned back to the sink.

Easy glanced at his bare chest. She'd seen him naked before, so there was no big deal about him not wearing a shirt. Still, despite hitting the big three-oh, he stayed in pretty good shape. He guessed she thought he looked good, maybe too good. He slid in closer, his shoulder grazing hers.

"I don't want to trash the tie. Know how to fix it?"

Pointedly not looking at him, she took the tie and shirt.

"Is something wrong?" he asked innocently.

She thrust at him a pack made from ice cubes in a plastic sandwich bag. "Put that on your eye. It looks awful."

"Feels awful," he said pitifully. He maneuvered until she had to look at his face. "Kiss it and make it feel better?"

She scrambled backward. "Go put a shirt on. And use the ice."

He obediently pressed the ice pack to his eye gingerly, but remained where he was. She breathed hard, her bosom rising and falling in erratic hitches. The green knit shirt complemented her suntan and showed off her curves. He wondered when she'd turned into a fitness fanatic. Her throat worked in a convulsive swallow. She clutched his shirt and tie so tightly her knuckles turned white.

Contrition replaced his urge to torment her. "Thanks for taking me to the hospital."

She lowered her gaze. "Somebody had to."

"I'm glad it was you. I hate doctors."

The corners of her mouth twitched. "You always were a big baby." She pressed the tips of her fingers to her mouth. Her engagement ring sparkled. Traces of humor beginning to blossom withered away into a stricken expression that struck Easy straight in the gut. Her fear brought him no satisfaction at all.

"Jeffrey sent those men, didn't he?"

"Yep." He idly pressed his hip where the bruise from the kick darkened an area nearly eight inches in diameter. The doctor had claimed no permanent damage, but his hip ached all the way to the bone. The flesh covering the bruise felt tight enough to split like ripe fruit. "What did you say to him, Tink? What made him suspicious enough to snoop around your house?"

Shaking her head, she returned to the sink and began running cold water. She trailed her fingers under the stream. "I asked him if he'd been married before. He tried to pass it off, so I told him I could check public records. That made him furious. I calmed him down, and he told me about Roberta. Do you have any prewash?"

"What's that?"

She shot him a look askance. "Never mind." She

plugged the sink and reached for the dishwashing detergent.

"What do you mean by furious?"

She chewed her lower lip a moment before answering. "He was angry, as if I had no right to know about his past. He was terribly unhappy about having to speak of Roberta. I thought he was going to cry. Uh, I think I teased him about his age, too. I tried to get him to admit he's forty. He laughed it off." She squirted detergent on the shirt. "Everything he said that night was a lie. Everything."

"So you made some direct hits."

She scrubbed hard at the blood stains on the shirt, working up copious pink-tinged lather. "It still doesn't prove he's a killer. He could be...jealous. Maybe he thinks you're trying to break us up."

"Did you tell him about us?"

A light shudder racked her body. "No."

"So he had to see the papers to know about me. If I found out my fiancée hired a snoop to check me out, I'd talk to her."

Her lips thinned into an unyielding line. She scrubbed harder at the shirt.

"It's the big fad of the nineties to investigate the one you love. Every once in a while, a subject finds out about me, but he doesn't come to me. I'm just a tool."

She stilled with both hands in the water and her head hanging. "He's angry. When I discovered the packet missing, I realized he's angry and he's punishing me."

"Uh-uh. He's worried," Easy said. "Maybe he's scared."

"I'm the one who's scared. He's showing a cold—cruel!—side of himself I never expected. He won't talk to me. He won't return calls."

"Sounds like he's playing on your guilt. If he gets you worked up enough, you'll forget the lies."

She snorted in derision. "It won't work. I can't marry him anyway."

The sheer joy leaping through his heart shamed him. Here she suffered a broken heart, and all he could think about was that now he had a chance with her. He forced a frown to keep from smiling. "I'm sorry. Not that you won't marry him, but that you're hurt. I don't want you hurting."

She swished the shirt in the water. The soapy water had turned pink. "I thought Jeffrey was the real thing. I thought he loved me. I thought he was honest! I'd have a family of my own and children. I don't want to live alone all my life, drawing pictures for kids I don't know."

His shame deepened. "You've always got me."

She slumped and closed her eyes. "Oh, please. Whatever we had once is long over. We're not kids anymore. I don't even know if I can be friends with you."

"Yes, you can!" he exclaimed. "We were best friends once. We still care about each other." He placed a hand on her shoulder.

She knocked his hand away. Water splashed his bare chest. "You ruined my life once. Now you've done it again. You still haven't shown me one shred of proof Jeffrey ever hurt his wife. Not that it matters! He doesn't trust me, I don't trust him, and now we'll never get married."

Easy's anger simmered near the surface, but her trembling lower lip and glazed eyes tamped that emotion. He steeled his jaw, prepared to take whatever abuse her wounded feelings deemed necessary.

"Then you have to go and get hurt! Look at you! Your eye could be permanently damaged. You could go blind because you can't leave well enough alone!"

He lowered the ice pack. "Sounds like you care about me."

With a frustrated groan squeezing through clenched teeth, she pushed his chest with both hands. He stumbled a step. "How can I possibly care about you? You're thick-headed and stubborn and stupid and you don't have an ounce of common sense. You come roaring into my life and wreck everything! And now you got beat up."

"I'm not hurt that bad," he said cautiously.

She slammed her small fist against his chest. The blow shocked him. He dropped the ice pack and caught her wrists before she thought about aiming for his bad eye. She jerked up her head, and her furious expression crumpled.

Appalled at seeing her so close to tears, he pulled her hands against his chest. She sagged against him and he cradled her the way he'd hold a child. "I'm sorry."

"I thought I could love Jeffrey. I really thought I could and then—then—then you show up. And I know I don't love him and I probably won't ever love anybody. Nobody will ever love me. I'll end up alone and childless and living with—with—*cats!*"

Her icy, damp hands clutched at his upper arms. She sniffled.

He stroked her silky hair, wanting to soothe her but uncertain how. A million words clogged his throat, but all of them had to do with how much he loved her. He suspected in her state of mind, a declaration of love would earn him a matching black eye.

So he kissed her. Her lips were as soft as warm taffy. He told himself he merely wanted to make her feel better. She kissed him back and her fingers dug into his biceps. Her hands were cold, but her mouth was hot and eager, questing with sweet silky thrusts of her tongue. He kissed her deeply, wanting to drown within her, losing himself in the heated mindlessness of loving her.

She dragged her lips from his, so he kissed her cheeks and chin and she let her head fall back so he could kiss the tender line of her throat. She purred, a tiny, luxurious sound from deep inside her breast, and desire maddened him. Nothing else mattered except her. Her fingers worked convulsively against his back and she pressed her body against his.

She moaned and whispered what sounded very much like, ''I hate you, Easy Martel,'' then found his mouth for another kiss. He knew she didn't hate him at all.

Chapter Eight

"Stop...please, stop," Catherine whispered. This was wrong, all wrong. She shouldn't be embracing Easy, touching him, kissing him. Wanting him. She weakly pushed against his arms until he lifted his head.

Desire marked his good eye, turning it as black as midnight, smoldering with sultry heat. All her resistance against other men, she now knew, had been a sham. She had always resisted sexual advances, not because of a moral high ground or depth of character or even from fear, but because she did not want those men. She had never desired any man except Easy Martel. Fluttering anxiety in her chest told her she never would.

"We're good together, Tink." He plunged his long fingers through her hair, deliciously pulling her scalp. "No one can ever make me feel the way you do. And you feel it, too. You know I'm right."

Her knees threatened to buckle. Using the countertop next to her side for balance, she backed unsteadily away from him. His fingers slid from beneath her hair and trailed tenderly across her cheeks. Her belly ached in repressed arousal. Her chest ached with the depth of her emotions. Her eyes and throat ached from holding back tears. Intuition nagged her soul, telling her only Easy held the power to soothe those aches.

"We've changed. I've changed." She spoke with all the conviction she could muster, but still the words tasted like a lie. In light of the facts that his kisses sent her soaring and his smile reduced her to quivering weakness, it seemed precious little had changed.

"Twelve years, a hundred, it doesn't matter. I'll never stop wanting you. We belong together and you know it. You wouldn't be so mad at me if you didn't care."

Would one time hurt? she wondered, gazing helplessly at him, trapped by the truths in his impassioned speech. Seeing him bloodied and bruised caused her physical pain—she did care. Perhaps sex—*not lovemaking!*—would clear him out of her system. Her memories of him had been colored by time, most likely enhanced. The man standing before her now could not live up to the fantasies created by adolescent passion.

"I don't love you anymore." She noted no change in his expression, no flicker of dismay or flash of anger. Instead, he grinned crookedly, his calm demeanor at odds with the harshness of his breathing.

Now was the time to walk away. Sex was highly overrated anyway; she didn't need it. A twelve-year dry spell hadn't done her any harm. In fact, a celibate life enhanced her creativity. She steeled herself to march past him, pick up her purse and leave his cluttered apartment. She would erase him from her memory banks. She wouldn't think about him or dream about him or sit staring into space, lost in the memories of what used to be. No more.

She lifted her chin. His fetching mouth, so perfectly shaped and sensual hammered at her resolve.

A goodbye kiss, just one, and it would be the last one. The final kiss, the final farewell. She'd walk out of his life and that would be that.

She walked boldly into his arms. His eyebrows lifted and even his swollen eye seemed to glint with anticipation. She opened her mouth to say farewell forever, but he covered her mouth with his and she was lost again, swept away by the enveloping sensuality of his touch.

He felt so good. His skin was smooth and supple. She kissed and kissed him, delighting in the powerful thrusts of his tongue and the contrasting textures of his slick teeth and soft lips. He worked her shirt free of her skirt. His hot hands shocked her back. She arched her spine as a groan slipped from her throat.

Frightened anew by her lack of control, she twisted her face from his. "I can't do this. No...I can't... I don't have any birth control."

He nuzzled her ear. "I'm not a stupid kid anymore, Tink." He urged her to follow him out of the kitchen. As if a massive short circuit had occurred between her reasonable mind and her treacherous body, she stumbled along behind him through the living room and into the bedroom.

"I can't, Easy," she said, pleading more with herself than with him. "It isn't right."

He left her standing at the foot of the bed. It had been neatly made and covered with a cotton throw striped in blue, orange and red. He'd grown tidy, no longer flinging clothes into piles on the floor or ignoring overflowing waste cans. He entered the bathroom and soon returned. He showed her a box of condoms.

"I won't hurt you," he said. "Never again."

She met his earnest gaze and knew she'd been undone. She swiped the back of her hand over her hot face. Breathing hurt; her joints ached. Only his touch could soothe her. He offered the sexual protection as if it were a gift, straight from his heart to hers. She licked her lips, noting how hungrily he followed the path of her tongue. The flames of desire flickered hotter.

"I need you, Tink." His voice husked in urgent sincerity. "I didn't know how much I missed you until I found you again. Let's start over, you and me. I promise, I swear I'll never hurt you again.''

She rested her knee on the bed. Catercorner from her, he mimicked her action. The mattress dipped with his weight. She hated wanting him so much.

Needing him.

Knock him out of your system, that wicked inner voice taunted. Go ahead, squash the fantasy and make him go away. Bed him and forget him, or he'll be like a splinter in your thumb you just can't reach.

She reached for him and he reached for her. Entwined in each other's arms they fell onto the mattress. Easy sucked in a sharp gasp, harsh with pain.

Horrified, she knew she'd forgotten his wounds. ''I'm sorry!''

He grinned, his good eye sparkling. ''Kiss it and make me feel better.''

She tentatively, cautiously kissed his swollen eyelid. He quivered beneath her. ''You need that ice pack.'' She needed him, skin to skin, out of her increasingly uncomfortable clothing. Her bra felt as if it had shrunk two cup sizes in the past few minutes. Her panties threatened to cut her in half.

''Later.'' He snaked a hand beneath her shirt. As if reading her mind, he deftly unhooked her bra. Freed of restraint, her breasts burned with heaviness, her nipples tantalized by the loosened lace rubbing against their hardness. ''You're so beautiful,'' he murmured and caught her throat in a wet, lusty kiss that drove her wild.

Twelve years dropped away, vanished as if they'd never happened. As he peeled away her clothing and she peeled away his, the thick weave of the cotton throw against her bare skin swept her back in time to a plaid blanket on a cushion of pine needles. To a time of innocent love when she believed her passion was the first passion, the only passion to have ever existed. His warm, heady scent curled throughout her body, touching and igniting every nerve fiber. She came up for air and stared in wonder at the naked length of him, his dusky skin barely dusted with body hair, his muscles taut in alluring relief. Sunlight through the curtains striped him in gold, highlighting his purely masculine shapeliness.

A single thought whirled through her brain, driving coherency away, *He's mine.*

In wonder, she brushed her fingertip over the diamond-shaped birthmark on his hip. He'd grown, his chest had deepened, but his belly was flat and his hips were lean. Recognition tingled through her. In turn, he laid a hand flat on her belly where pale stretch marks scarred her flesh. She cringed in embarrassment and pushed his hand away. She suddenly wanted to be under the covers, away from his eyes.

"Don't hide from me, baby," he whispered. He held her down gently with one arm and pressed a sweet kiss to her scarred belly. Her embarrassment faded.

When he came to her, covered her, embraced her with the full measure of his love, she met him thrust for thrust, movement for movement, knowing without thinking how to please him and please herself. He spoke to her of love and longing and forever, and every whispered word she believed with all her heart. Then he shuddered, a delicious rippling from head to toe. A surprised groan slipped from his lips. She opened her eyes, and saw his clenched jaw and the cords standing out on his neck, knowing he could not wait and not wanting him to wait. She arched her back, straining to meet him, urging him on. Her own release caught her completely off guard. She cried out and dug her heels so roughly into his thighs, he squirmed in discomfort.

"Damn." He stared down at her face, managing to look both stunned and supremely pleased. He panted through his mouth. His arms trembled.

"Oh, Easy," she murmured, but could say no more. Waves of receding pleasure occupied her. Feminine fullness held her fast, pinned beneath his weight, reveling in the feel of him, the smell of him, the taste of him filling her soul. The sweet release of emotion weighted her limbs.

From a distance, a telephone rang. The noise seemed to increase with each insistent ring. Finally Easy turned a baleful glare on the bedside table. He made no move to answer, and the telephone stopped ringing. She touched his face, tracing the lines of maturity around his mouth and the hard edges along cheek and chin that had replaced his youthful beauty. A fainter ringing began, muffled as if from beneath a pile of cloth.

He muttered a colorful obscenity and eased away from her. Their skin clung, melded by sweaty heat. She wanted to roll with him, keeping the contact, but failed to muster the energy necessary to hold him. Sighing, she watched from beneath languid eyelids as he struggled upright to sit on the edge of the bed. She admired his back. She could happily spend the rest of her life doing nothing but sketching pictures of his beautiful back.

"Oops," he said.

Alarmed by his soft uttering, she forced her eyes all the way open. "Oops? Oops, what?"

He glanced over his shoulder. "Uh…" He held up the used prophylactic. It hung limply, shredded like a popped balloon. "It broke."

She stared at his hand, refusing to believe this was happening. "This is a joke, right? *Right?*"

He grimaced, holding the broken condom as if it burned his fingers. "Well, I guess it's kind of old."

"Old!" She jerked into a sitting position. She snatched up a pillow to cover her naked breasts. "What do you mean it's old? How could you?"

"Hey, it's not like I catch fast action every weekend."

She noticed then the stickiness between her thighs, the

hot melting of their mingled fluids. An unmistakable scent wafted to her nose. Salty and erotic, the scent of life.

Her belly clenched into a tight little knot. On her knees, she doubled over, her fists clenched to her abdomen. She rocked against the pillow. "If I'm pregnant, Earl Zebulon Martel, I will kill you. I will chop you into tiny little chunks and feed you to my dogs."

He drew away from her and stood, shoving the evidence of his irresponsibility behind him. "You've turned bloodthirsty in your old age, Tink."

His lame joke infuriated her. "This isn't funny!"

"It's not the end of the world. Come on, you must have had some whoopsies before and nothing happened."

"Only with you, you idiot. I've never slept with anyone else."

His eyebrows reached for the ceiling. She could swear his chest puffed up with pride. A faint smile confirmed his arrogant male posturing. "Just me?" he asked. "Really?"

Growling, she threw the pillow with all her might. He ducked in time to keep it from hitting his wounded eye.

Tinny ringing from the other room distracted them both. "It's my cell phone. I have to get that. Don't go anywhere." He hurried out of the room.

She gaped at his bare behind, furious at herself for daring to find those high, tight buttocks sexy. Clutching her hair in both hands, she pulled until it hurt. "Stupid, idiot, dumb, *stupid!*"

"WHERE IN THE WORLD are you?" Trish demanded. Her voice rang high-pitched with concern.

Remembering his appointment with his sister and John Tupper, Easy winced. "I'm at home."

"I called your place. You didn't answer. John and I are waiting for you. What's going on?"

"I had a little...run-in with some unsavory types. I'll tell you all about it in person." With the reminder, his side ached. He glared down at the swollen bruise on his hip. He could make out the shape of a steel-reinforced work-boot toe. No-neck, he determined, had better grow eyes in the back of his head.

Carrying the phone, he returned to the bedroom only to find Catherine jerking on her clothing. Her clumsy agitation and her refusal to look at him alarmed him. He'd lost her once because of stupidity, he wasn't about to make the same mistake twice. He waggled a hand at her, warning her not to go. "Go to the Denny's across from my office," he told Trish. "I'll be there as quick as I can."

"What kind of run-in? What are you talking about?"

"I'll tell you when I see you. I won't be long. I promise. I gotta go." Without waiting for her reply, he closed the unit, disconnecting the telephone. "Tink, hold on." With her almost dressed and him buck naked, he felt at a disadvantage. He found his briefs on the floor.

"I have to go home." Her filmy skirt tangled around her feet and she fell heavily back on the bed.

"You are not running away from me."

At that her head snapped up and she froze with the skirt halfway up her legs. "I have to go home," she repeated, each icy word clipped.

He pulled up his underwear. Keeping an eye on her to make sure she didn't bolt, he opened the closet and reached for a pair of jeans. "We have a lot to discuss."

"We have nothing to discuss. It's over. You accomplished your mission. Jeffrey and I are through. Even if I could forgive his lies, I can't forgive myself for cheating on him. But you and I are through, too. You—"

"Chicken! You're scared."

She flinched as if he slapped her. Hot spots marked her cheeks. "I am not scared of you." She leaped to her feet and jerked the skirt up to her waist. With short, awkward jabs, she tucked in her shirt.

"You're scared of something. Me, you, who the hell

knows. All I know is, you're not running out on me again.''

Her chin and lower lip trembled. His heart ached for her as he imagined the terrors of being sixteen, alone, pregnant and feeling as if no one loved her, no one cared. Of having to live each day of the past twelve years with the knowledge of losing a child.

''I never ran out on you,'' she said in a small, uncertain voice. ''You ran out on me. You disappeared. You ran away to join the army and left me all alone.''

''Damn it, Tink, you know I loved you. You know I would have gone to the moon for you. But you wouldn't take my calls, you refused to see me. You never gave me a chance to say I was sorry. You never gave me the chance to take responsibility for the baby. What did you want me to do? Commit hari-kari on your front lawn?''

She pressed the back of a hand hard against her mouth. Rapid blinking showed her fighting tears.

''I didn't run away. In my letters, I was trying to show you I was man enough to love you. When I came home from basic training, I was going to ask you to marry me.'' He turned toward the dresser and jerked open the top drawer. Beneath his underwear lay a tiny box he'd been carrying around for twelve years. He tossed it to her.

Her movements uncertain, she opened the box, revealing a thin gold band decorated with a diamond chip. It had cost him three months' pay.

''I got that for you. I thought you'd realize I was grown-up and could take care of you. It backfired. I'm sorry as hell that it did, but I'm not sorry about my intentions.''

She covered her face with both hands and bent over, her elbows on her knees. Fearing if he said anything else, she'd burst into tears, he focused on getting dressed. His chest ached with unaccustomed emotions. No wonder he'd never fallen in love with another woman—it hurt too much. He took a chance and entered the bathroom. When he finished cleaning up and combing his hair, he hesitated with his hand on the doorknob. He felt certain Catherine would be gone.

To his relief, she still sat on the bed. Now calm, her expression neutral, she brushed her shining hair. "You're right," she said simply.

He transferred his wallet and keys from his trousers to his jeans. "Right about what?"

"About me...running away." She slid a melancholy glance at the messy bed behind her and the now-closed jewelry box. "I don't know what's happening with me anymore. I think I'm losing my mind. I'm scared."

He offered his hand.

She ignored it as she stood. Head down, avoiding looking at him, she sighed. "It's not your fault about the condom. Accidents happen. You're right, probably no harm will come of this."

Dread prickled his neck and spine. "Wait..."

"I can't see you anymore, Easy. What just happened...happened. It was a fluke, a moment of weakness." She finally lifted her gaze to him. Her beautiful blue eyes held a galaxy of sorrow. "I'm not the kind of person who cheats. But I run into you again, and bam, I'm an adulteress."

"You're being ridiculous—"

"I am not! I didn't think I was so weak, but apparently I am." She shook her head so hard she set her hair swinging like a golden curtain. "I'm breaking off my engagement with Jeffrey. I'll give him back his ring and that will be that. You won't have to worry about me anymore." She fished her car keys out of her purse. "Goodbye, Easy."

He caught her arm, then like the man who held the tiger by the tail, wondered what to do next. She glowered up at him. He sought arguments to make her stay, to convince her to reconsider and be reasonable. He offered his best, for now. "You have to give me a ride. My car is at the office."

"Turn me loose."

He dropped his hand. "Trish is waiting for me. That was her on the phone. I need to go."

She wavered, her brow furrowed. "Oh, all right."

He curled his lips over his teeth, biting back further speech. Until he knew exactly the right words to say, he couldn't risk setting her off.

Not speaking tortured him during the long, silent ride back to his office. She handled the Blazer as if she were a ship's captain caught in a treacherous storm. She focused straight ahead, kept both hands on the wheel and never spared him so much as a glance.

Before she reached the parking lot entrance, he pointed across the street. "I'm meeting Trish at Denny's."

Without a word, she maneuvered into the left lane. In the restaurant parking lot, she put the transmission in Park and sat in stony silence, waiting for him to leave.

"Come in with me, Tink. Trish has John Tupper with her. You should meet him."

"No."

"He can give you some insights about Livman."

"I don't need insights. Jeffrey and I are through."

He shoved open the door. "At least come in and say hello to Trish. You two were friends in high school. Do you want her thinking you're a snob?"

She turned her head slowly. Her glower was deep and dark, burning so fiercely his skin itched. "I know your tricks, Easy. You push and push and push until you get what you want. Not this time. I mean it, I don't want to see you again. I don't want you calling me. You stay away from my house."

He grunted. "I can't believe you'd let a murderer walk just because you're mad at me."

She slammed the heels of her hands against the steering wheel. "I don't believe Jeffrey is a murderer."

"That's because you won't listen." He glanced at the restaurant, knowing Trish would be counting the seconds she had to wait for him. He also knew she would pitch a fit when he turned up with a battered face. "Look, I'll make you a deal. Talk to John, listen to what he has to say. Then I swear, I will leave you alone."

"I don't believe you."

He spit on his right palm and thrust his hand toward her. "Spit oath."

She recoiled, wrinkling her nose. "Gross!"

"You didn't think it was gross back in high school."

"I didn't know as much about germs back then." Her hands curled into knots.

He laughed. "We just swapped a lot more than spit and now you worry about germs? When did you turn squeamish?"

"You are impossible!" She jerked the transmission into Drive and stomped the gas pedal. Easy whooped, grabbing the door. She whipped into a parking space. "All right, this is it, the final deal. I will listen to what Mr. Tupper has to say. I'll keep an open mind. Then it's over. Everything is over. Me, Jeffrey, you. We will all go our separate ways. You won't bother me anymore."

He plucked a tissue from a small dispenser on the console. Wiping saliva off his hand, he nodded agreement. Of course, as in any contract, there were loopholes and he'd find a way to continue courting her. Once Livman was completely out of her system, that is.

When they reached the restaurant door, Easy paused and rested a hand on the small of Catherine's back. "Let me explain what happened to my face. If Trish freaks, she'll tell my parents and then Mom will flip."

Her eyes sparkled and her soft mouth worked slightly as if restraining a smile. "Still scared of your mother?"

His anxiety faded as he remembered their old joke. His mother had a solid-gold heart as soft as a marshmallow. She adored without reservation all animals and children—she'd all but adopted Catherine. Easy had loved teasing Mom, showing off when Catherine was around. Mom would bluster and threaten him with an oversize wooden spoon, never failing to take part in the game. Catherine had lapped it up like a cat after cream.

She'd named their child after his mother. A great swelling of warmth and aching pain filled his chest.

"Anyone with half a brain is terrified of Mom." He opened the door for her.

As he expected and feared, Trish practically screamed. "Oh my God! What happened to your face?" Diners and the wait staff swiveled about to follow her cry. Easy hushed her as best he could and urged her to slide back into the booth. He caught Catherine's hand and brought her around to the fore. John Tupper stood while Easy made the introductions.

"Wow," Trish said, "you really look great, Catherine. You were pretty in high school, but now you're gorgeous." She touched her dark, curly locks and added, "I'd kill for your hair."

A blush trailed Catherine's cheeks. Her discomfiture gave Easy an opportunity to arrange the seating to his liking. He maneuvered John into the booth next to Trish so Easy could sit next to Catherine.

"So," Trish said, leaning forward to peer critically at his face. "What happened? Those are stitches."

"Yep." He pushed John's plate of food across the table. "Livman sent a pair of thugs to tell me to back off."

Trish gasped and John paled. Trish demanded to know what weapon the thugs had used on him. A baseball bat? Billy club? Brass knuckles?

"His fist. He kicked me, too. You ought to see my side."

"You should carry a gun." Trish's flashing eyes landed on Catherine. "He's always getting himself in a pickle, but he won't carry a gun."

John Tupper's reaction to the tidings bemused Easy. The insurance adjuster had stopped swabbing and sweating. He stared, round-eyed, at Catherine's hands. A greenish tinge spread under the man's eyes. Easy feared John might lose his lunch.

Catherine noticed Tupper's stare. She drew herself into the corner.

"You're wearing Mother's ring." John's tone held indignation.

Catherine jerked her hands beneath the table. "Pardon?"

"That's Mother's ring. Jeffrey gave you my mother's ring?" John mopped furiously at his clammy brow.

Catherine slowly brought her left hand into the open. The big blue sapphire glittered and winked as if alive, surrounded by the fire of small diamonds. "No," she said. "You're mistaken. Jeffrey had this made for me."

John shook his head in firm denial. "That is my mother's ring! When she died, Roberta inherited it. She never took it off her hand. Never. It was all she had left of Mother."

Cringing even farther into the corner, Catherine stared at the ring. "He made it for me."

"Mother's initials are inside the band. *G-T-T,* for Gladys Tyler Tupper. My grandparents gave it to her the day I was born."

Looking a tad ill herself, Catherine worked the ring off her slender finger. She held the band to the light streaming in from the wide bank of windows. She squinted, bringing the ring closer and closer until it almost touched her nose. She gasped and dropped the ring.

Easy caught it before it struck the table. He, too, peered inside the band. There, carved in the gold in tiny elegant script, were the letters *GTT.*

Chapter Nine

Catherine had been wearing a dead woman's ring. A nasty taste filled her throat and mouth. Jeffrey lying about his age was silly and conceited. Knowing her own reluctance to speak of painful subjects, she understood his failure to mention a previous marriage.

The ring, however... She envisioned his face, candlelit and earnest, his eyes shining. How he assured her in proud sincerity that he had the ring made especially for her. To match her eyes—to play her for a fool.

She watched John take the ring from Easy. The man cradled the shining jewel in his palm, gently, reverently, his hands trembling. His lower lids reddened and turned wet. His Adam's apple bobbed in his thin neck.

"John." Trish rested a hand on his shoulder. "Are you okay?"

"Roberta was a good girl. She always had time to help out others. She never asked for much. When Mother died, I told her to keep the house, but she refused. She wanted my family to have it. It's a good place for children to grow up." He lifted his moist gaze to Catherine. "He didn't have to kill her."

This slim, nervous man wore a mantle of sorrow around his bony shoulders so heavy it seemed too much for any one man to bear. It shrouded Catherine, as well, casting a pall over her heart.

Catherine suffered through a miserable lunch. Unable to eat, she sipped a glass of iced tea. She choked down the cold, slightly bitter brew, and wished she could order something stronger, something powerful enough to blot out Easy's scent. His essence clung to her, rising with every minuscule movement. He crowded her in the booth. Her knee kept finding his beneath the table. She bumped his elbow. Each touch jolted her like a shot of static electricity.

John described Jeffrey's courtship of Roberta, how he'd swept her off her feet. Creepy claws trickled up and down Catherine's spine—Jeffrey had tried to rush her, too.

During a pause, Catherine asked, "How long did Roberta work for the mortgage company?"

"She started with them right out of college. She loved her job. She had trouble sometimes talking face-to-face with people, but she liked talking on the phone. That's where she did most of her business. She won some awards for productivity."

She did not want to ask the next question, but she had to know. "Did your sister have a drinking problem?"

John pulled an incredulous face. "She never had more than an occasional glass of wine." He thumped the center of his chest. "She had asthma. She avoided anything that depressed her ability to breathe."

Unable to meet his gaze, she toyed with a saltshaker. "Jeffrey claims she was intoxicated when she fell."

"He's a liar."

His cold statement said it all to Catherine. He'd loved Roberta, plain and simple. Her death had broken his heart. Her murder enraged his soul.

Catherine shifted her attention to Trish. Easy's sister had changed very little since high school. She still wore lots of makeup to enhance her striking face, and wore plenty of flashy jewelry. Like Easy, she was attractive, generous, quick-tempered, mouthy, witty and self-confident to the point of arrogance.

Now she wondered about the furtive little looks Trish kept darting her way. Trish seemed to know exactly what Catherine and Easy had been up to at his apartment.

Catherine wanted to be anywhere but here, with Easy, while this sad, sad man told her about his beloved sister.

That Easy could sit through the ordeal while eating a fish sandwich and french fries made her feel sick. Resentment mingled with longing. Surely every person at the table—every person in the restaurant!—knew what she and Easy had been up to. Everyone must know that her still-tingling cheeks had been reddened by his coarse beard stubble. Her lips felt five times too big from his kisses. If the people could not see, then surely they could smell the clinging aroma of lust and loving. She longed for a shower to wash away the last traces of his touch. How dare he sit there, chomping away, licking his lips and slurping iced tea, while she agonized in tormented silence.

"Jeffrey Livman is a creep," Trish said. "You aren't going to marry him, are you?"

"No." Under the table, Easy found Catherine's hand and squeezed her fingers. "We sort of broke up already."

"Help us catch him." Trish bobbed her head so that her dangling earrings danced against her cloud of black hair. "We know he did it. We just have to prove it."

"I don't know what I can do." Her guilt and shame deepened. Unwitting or not, she played a role in Jeffrey's game, which made her responsible for some of John's agony. "Jeffrey lied to me. About Roberta, about the ring. Even about where he works." Most likely he lied about loving her, too.

Trish glanced at her watch and groaned. She gulped the remains of her iced tea. "John and I have to get back to work." She shook a finger at Easy's face. "We still have a lot to talk about." She followed John out of the booth.

"Can we get together tonight? And you, too, Catherine. I'd really like a chance to talk to you. Not just about this. About…old times?"

She stared out the window at the parking lot. She didn't want anything to do with these people. "I'll have to let you know."

Alone with Easy, she wished he'd move around to the other side of the table. He draped an arm over the back of the bench seat. His dangling fingers brushed her shoulder.

"Are you sure you don't want something to eat?" His voice held a note of concern.

"No, thank you." The weight of the evidence against Jeffrey crushed her. Her now-bare left hand felt slimy and soiled from the purloined ring. "It's true. Jeffrey murdered her."

"Yep."

How, she wondered, had she fallen for Jeffrey's lies? They appeared so transparent now. She saw where he'd taken advantage of her unwillingness to delve too deeply into his life. She had little need or desire for socializing, so there were few opportunities for her to hear inconsistencies from his friends. What was it that Easy had said? Jeffrey had *played* her.

Even Jeffrey's angry, hurt silence fit in with the game. The silent treatment was supposed to frazzle her so much, she'd do anything to appease him.

"I don't understand why the police won't do anything."

He tapped a finger against his forehead as if dislodging thoughts. "*Just* because he was the only person present when she fell and *just* because he profited from her death, the state can't charge him. There isn't any hard evidence a crime was committed." His smile turned lopsided. "Truth is, that's the way it ought to work. I've been in countries where malicious prosecution is a fact of life. Not pretty." He wiped his mouth with a napkin then tossed the wilted paper on his plate.

She couldn't help laughing at her own gullibility. With the laughter came anger, deep and cold. "Jeffrey knows my financial situation. Grandma's estate was worth almost three hundred thousand dollars. I paid cash for my home and Blazer. I have a nice nest egg. I make a fairly steady income from royalties. Children's books don't make massive sales, but they stay in print a long time. Plus I'm in the middle of negotiating a contract worth more than a million dollars."

He made a sharp sound. "For drawing pictures?"

"Not just any pictures. I've been chosen to illustrate Doc Halladay's science book series."

"The Science Brain?" He whistled softly.

"You know about him?"

"His picture is everywhere and his shows are all over the cable stations. Not to mention aisles full of Science Brain crap in every store. A million bucks, huh." He grinned. "My lucky day. Beautiful and loaded. Want to take me shopping? I need new shoes."

She laughed, genuinely this time. "Get serious. Now you've got me all worked up and I'm mad. What are we going to do about Jeffrey?" Several ideas occurred to her: boiling in oil, hoisting on a petard, stranding him on a desert island.

He looked around the now-quiet restaurant. The majority of the lunch crowd had cleared out. Waitpersons clustered in a knot around the cash register while busboys cleaned tables. Easy lifted a strand of Catherine's hair and rubbed it idly between his forefinger and thumb.

"Can you think of anything you've seen in his house? Anything he might have said?"

Now her appetite made an appearance. A display of pies and cakes caught her attention. "He only tells me what I want to hear." She waved her hand to flag down a passing waitress. She ordered more iced tea and a salad. With some regret, she pushed thoughts of pie from mind. No matter how upset she was, she wasn't drifting back into old bad habits.

"We need a confession, Tink."

She used her elbow to make him move over and give her some breathing room. "Let me borrow your phone. I'll call him now." She mimed holding a phone to her ear. "Excuse me, Jeffrey, I was wondering if you killed your wife. You did? Thank you for sharing."

"Sarcasm doesn't become you, babe."

"Idiocy doesn't become you. Jeffrey won't even talk to me. He knows I know he lied."

"His motive goes a lot deeper than greed."

"What do you mean?"

"Maybe he believes he did it just for the money, but I think it goes back to when he was a kid. Talking to his mother gave me some insights."

Catherine groaned. Jeffrey had even lied about his family. As much as she disliked her own parents, she'd never told anyone they were dead. "I called Mrs. Livman. She sounds like a nice lady."

"Maybe, maybe not. His father died not long after Livman was born. He has five older sisters. I contacted some of them. They want nothing to do with their brother. One got angry at me. She thought I would give her phone number to Livman."

"What happened?"

"According to the mother, Livman could do no wrong. The sisters say he was a monster. He started fires, abused animals and lied for the hell of it." He gave her hair a light tug. "Get this, all his sisters are blue-eyed blondes. Does that suggest any possible neuroses to you?"

"You're scaring me."

"You should be scared. He has you locked in his radar. I don't think he'll give you up without a fight."

She stared incredulously at his face. "Are you saying he'll hurt me?"

"I told you about Melissa and Joan. Both of them claim he was a perfect gentleman, *until* he got into an argument he couldn't win. Then he turned violent."

She tried to shove down the fear he roused, but failed. The waitress brought the salad, and Catherine was glad for the distraction. She nibbled a piece of cucumber. "If it's so important for him to win, why is he giving me the cold shoulder? I've spoken to him once in the past four days. He acted as if I were trying to sell him something."

Easy played a rolling tattoo on the tabletop. "He could be buying time. He has to somehow explain the information he stole from your house."

She doubted if she'd ever be able to shower again without double-checking all the locks and barricading the doors.

"He's a sociopath, a man without a conscience. If he feels anything about killing Roberta, he feels smug. I'll bet that's the ego boost he's waited for all his life. Now he's targeted you. He won't let a little thing like the truth stand in his way." He dropped his hand onto her shoulder and his long fingers squeezed her flesh. "He's arrogant. He believes you'll fall for any line of bull he feeds you. He thinks I'll quit because of a couple of thugs. That's how we'll nab him. You can get him to confess."

She had to swallow hard several times before she could speak. "I don't know if I can even face him, much less talk to him."

"So he gets off scot-free because you're chicken." He leaned back and quirked a challenging eyebrow. "I guess I can wait until he picks out another victim. Maybe she'll help—if he doesn't kill her first."

She twisted on the seat to give him the full benefit of her glare. "You fight dirty."

He held up his hands as if to prove his innocence. "Hey, I learned from the best." A slow, wicked smile turned his face from gorgeous to breathtaking. Not even the blackened eye disguised the fact he was a beautiful man. "Remember what you used to tell me about being good? You said you didn't love me because I did good things. You loved me because I was good, period."

She rubbed absently at her throat. Easy had been good, along with generous, kind, warmhearted and full of spirit. He'd been so eager to please her back then, as she'd been eager to please him.

"I don't want you within fifty miles of that dirtbag. But you're the only one with a chance of getting to him." He leaned over until he nearly touched her ear with his lips. His warm breath ruffled her hair. "Catching him is the right thing for a good person to do."

"I hate you, Easy Martel," she said through gritted teeth.

"Yeah, yeah, that's what all the girls say." He snitched a crouton out of her salad bowl and popped it into his mouth. "Finish eating. We've got work to do."

"I didn't say yes!"

"You will."

CATHERINE PAUSED at her front door. Key in hand, she stared at the doorknob. Jeffrey had breached her home's safety. He'd betrayed her trust. For that reason alone she would force herself to confront him and make him confess.

The sound of Easy's car coming up the driveway reassured her. She unlocked the door.

Oscar and Bent greeted her with tail-wagging fawning, rubbing against her legs and showing her wide doggy grins. She petted them and cooed the baby talk they both loved. She allowed them outside, then stood on the deck, watching them give Easy a cursory inspection before loping off to do their business.

Holding her elbows, she studied the sky. A thunderstorm built to the south, rolling its slow way toward the city. She hoped the rain reached her place. The forest was unseasonably dry.

"Are you okay?" Easy touched her elbow.

"I feel like an idiot. He was so nice to me, so very charming. He always said the right things. I would get annoyed by some of the things he did, but then he'd be so attentive and sweet. I felt guilty about feeling bothered." She lowered her face so her hair offered some protection against Easy's gaze. Either he pitied her or he thought she was stupid. Neither sat well with her. "Looking back, I can see he's a lot like my father. He always has to be in charge. He has to make all the decisions."

"Don't beat yourself up. He made it his life's work to be your best friend."

"Don't try to make me feel better," she said wearily.

She called the dogs. Across the scrubby, wildflower-dotted clearing, they ran with the powerful grace of their breed. Paws pounding, they leaped onto the deck and crowded past her into the house.

"Those are cool dogs," Easy said.

"You can adopt one. Or two. Retired racers without breeding prospects are euthanized if they can't find families. They make nice house dogs." She paused inside her studio, seeking any sign of an intruder.

Easy touched her back and she jumped.

"Sorry." He held his hands high.

Between fear of Jeffrey and the instability of lingering sexual desire, she wondered if her nerves would ever calm. "Fix yourself a drink. I'll be right back." She hurried down the stairs.

In the bathroom, she avoided looking at the ruined towel bar and holes in the wall. She critically eyed her face in the mirror, seeking evidence of Easy's lovemaking on her features. Other than smudged cosmetics and tousled hair, she looked much the same as she had before she ended up in his bed.

She certainly felt different. Softer somehow, and off-balance. Definitely discombobulated and uncertain.

She felt ashamed. She'd made a promise to herself: she'd never, ever endanger another child. In one heated encounter, she'd broken that vow. She no longer felt certain of anything, most of all, not of herself.

She washed her face and brushed her hair. She opened the bathroom door. Easy stood next to her bed. He held the small silver frame containing the photograph of the faux Elizabeth.

Her insides shriveled. "What are you doing?"

His face revealed no trace of contrition or embarrassment. He held the frame so she could clearly see the smiling child in the photograph. "Who's this?"

"You have no right to be in my bedroom."

"I was worried about you."

"Put that down and get out of here."

He resumed his bland-faced study of the little girl's face. "This looks just like Trish when she was little. Did you cut it out of a magazine?"

"Easy, please..."

"This is supposed to be her, isn't it? Our Elizabeth."

Once again, he brought her near tears. She pinched the bridge of her nose.

He put the photograph back on the bedside table. "Tell me about it."

Unable to speak, she shook her head in firm refusal.

"I'm not trying to upset you. You've been carrying the load alone too long. This picture is her, right? You can tell me."

She stared in dumb misery at her toes. "It's just a picture. I don't know who it is."

"Do you think this is what she looks like? Uh-uh, she's probably a blonde like you. She's real smart, too. Even with half your brains, she's gotta be a genius."

She dashed angrily at her eyes. He had no right to speak so casually about their lost baby.

"I bet her parents are proud of her. They probably thank you every day for having the guts to give her up."

She lost it then. Grief, anger, fear and loss gushed from within her. Unable to control the tears no matter how hard she pressed the heels of her hands to her eyes, unable to control her sobs and the choking in her throat, she knew she was going mad.

Easy grasped her shoulders and guided her to the bed where he sat her down. "I hate it when you cry."

"I—I—so—sorry." She gulped air in a futile attempt to stop the tears, but all it did was make her hiccough. She accepted the box of tissues Easy thrust at her.

He dropped to a crouch before her and dangled his hands over his knees. "You know what hurts the most? Knowing you had to do all this alone. I can't ever make that up to you, babe. I know it, you know it. I have to live with it. I don't know how to make it right."

She scrubbed at her eyes, shredding a handful of tissues. "It hurt so much to give her up. It *physically* hurt. I ached for days and days. My stomach and my breasts and my arms. I was so empty. I loved her so much. I had twenty-four hours to decide. I wanted to run away with her and somehow make it on my own." She managed a ragged breath. "I wanted to die. If it wasn't for Grandma, I would have killed myself."

"Oh, God..." He dropped forward on his knees and rested both hands on her lap.

"I couldn't take care of her. My parents said if I didn't give her up, I could never come home. Grandma had arthritis real bad. She couldn't help with a baby. I would have had to drop out of school and get a job and leave Elizabeth with baby-sitters all the time. I couldn't do it to her. She needed parents. Giving her up was the only thing I could do for her." She tore another handful of tissues from the box. "I want to find her. I really do. I want to know I did the right thing for her, to make sure she's happy and healthy and loved."

"I'll find her for you." He nodded eagerly. "It won't take more than a few phone—"

"No! This can't be about me." She felt his shared pain. Temptation nibbled at her soul. They could find Elizabeth, be a family, erase the past and start over. "We can't," she added, more to herself than to Easy. "She isn't ours anymore. We're the ones who made the mistake, but if we interfere in her life, she's the one who will suffer."

He looked past her to the small silver-framed photograph. "So you settle for magazine pictures."

She nodded.

"We don't have to talk to her. We can just find her. You know, check to see if she's okay—"

"I'm not strong enough to do that. Honestly, I'm not. If I see her, I'll want her. I won't be able to walk away a second time." She covered his hands with her own. "It's so hard. I want to know how she is, what she looks like. I want to meet her parents and know they're good people. I want to assure her how much I love her, but I can't."

His shoulders raised then he exhaled slowly, powerfully. "You're a strong woman, Catherine St. Clair."

"I don't feel strong." She glanced at the telephone on the bedside table. "I can't call Jeffrey right now. My throat is sore. I'm too shaky to say the right things." She turned her head and blew her nose. She hadn't cried so much in years. It left her light-headed, empty and raw. Exhaustion made her slump.

"No problem. Lie down, kick off your shoes. I'll fix you some hot tea. With lemon and honey?"

It wasn't until she curled up on the bed that the vulnerability of her position struck her. She trusted Easy. She trusted him with her soul wounds, with her home and even inside the sanctuary of her bedroom.

A very strange thing.

"HEY. TINK, WAKE UP." Easy reached for Catherine's shoulder, but he hated waking her. She slept hard, completely silent and still. She looked like a little girl, all rosy cheeked and cute, her lips ruffling slightly with each exhalation.

Arousal hit him fast and hard. He tucked his hands beneath his armpits and stared helplessly at her sleeping form. Tangled emotions tightened his chest until each breath caused him pain. He loved her. It was as if he'd spent the past twelve years in a cocoon, shielded against any other woman, any other love. When she'd been in his arms, their bodies joined, their souls connected, he'd known she loved him, too.

Now he didn't feel so certain.

He glanced at the pitiful magazine photograph in the fancy frame. His uncertainty deepened. He liked to fix things, solve puzzles and problems, but he doubted his ability to fix this.

He breathed deeply, shoving down the erotic memories, and hardening his soul against her beauty. When he felt in command of himself, he shook her shoulder. Her eyelids fluttered.

"Dinner's ready. Come on, up and at 'em. You slept the whole day away."

She opened first one eye then the other. She peered unfocused at him and frowned. "What time is it?" Her words slurred.

He had swallowed the rising thickness in his throat. "Almost nine."

"At night?" She struggled into a sitting position and raked her hands through her tousled hair. "I can't believe I slept so long."

Her soft mouth and the tender curve of her cheek, the vulnerable line of her neck and sleepy eyes tormented him.

He picked invisible lint off his shirtsleeve. "I found some veggie pizza in your freezer and I made a salad."

She nodded and mumbled something about coming upstairs in a moment. He made himself turn away and went upstairs.

When she finally appeared, she'd exchanged her skirt for a pair of baggy, ragged denim shorts and had pulled her hair into a ponytail. Her eyes were puffy. Her face was pale. The dogs hopped off the sofa and silently flanked her, twining around her legs like a pair of cats. She petted them absently.

"Why are you still here?" she asked. "Weren't you supposed to meet Trish?"

"I didn't want to leave you. I talked to her on the telephone. She's rarin' to go after Livman." He grinned, tempted to recount the wild fantasies he'd been spinning—sexy fantasies that had nothing to do with a wife killer. "Besides, it took me most of the day to figure out how you organize the kitchen. Why do you keep coffee and tea in the freezer?"

"To keep them from going stale."

He pulled out a chair for her at the small round table now set for two. His hand brushed her shoulder—soft, so soft. He hurried around the table. "So when did you turn into a health nut? You've got tons of grains and beans and tofu crap in there. No secret goody stashes."

"Actually, it's because of Grandma. She had arthritis really bad. Her hands were curled up and she had a hard time walking. She didn't want to end up in a wheelchair. We started investigating alternative medicine. Massage, acupuncture, diet, exercise, vitamin therapy, prayer."

"Did it work?"

"I think so. She still had arthritis, but the pain wasn't so horrible and she didn't end up in a wheelchair. She got so she could walk at least a mile every day. Swimming was as close to a miracle cure as I've ever seen."

"I get it. You were her personal trainer."

She gave the question a moment of thought, then nodded. "I guess you could say that. Grandma didn't get discouraged if I exercised with her. Truth is, once I stopped eating meat and refined sugar, I felt a lot better." She grinned sheepishly. "And one day I noticed I had a real waistline. I didn't even realize I was getting in shape until I was almost there."

"Good for Grandma."

"I really miss her. I was a hundred times closer to her than I'll ever be to my parents."

He didn't doubt it for a second. "I take it they haven't changed."

She shook her head. "After Grandma died, I got homesick. I guess I thought with me grown-up, they'd like me better. I was wrong about that. I only see them when Mom insists I come to dinner."

"They're still toads."

A sparkle filled her beautiful eyes. "Dad wants me to quit fooling around and find a real career. And Mom..." She shrugged. "She's still Mom. Never a kind word to say about anything." She laughed. "I never did get around to introducing them to Jeffrey. Now they never have to know about that particular disaster."

Glad she still had a sense of humor, he served up the pizza and salad. She dug into her food. He noticed she still ate with nervous little bites as if afraid someone might see her. This, he knew with a certainty he'd never felt before in his entire life, was exactly what he wanted, exactly where he wanted to be. Right here, with Catherine, sharing meals and making small talk.

He itched to tell her what he was feeling right now. How he wanted them to start over, start fresh. They'd been perfect together twelve years ago; they were perfect together now. They had a deal, though. He consoled himself with the knowledge that she'd get around to renegotiating the terms.

"Do you feel strong enough to start working on Livman? I jotted down a script."

She froze with a fork full of salad halfway to her mouth. "I have to call him?"

He nodded.

"I don't know if I can. I'm scared of him."

"Don't be scared. You've got me."

Chapter Ten

Catherine studied the array of electronic equipment spread across Easy's coffee table. She could disassemble and reassemble an animal skeleton, and use clay to accurately rebuild the individual muscles. Anything mechanical, though, boggled her completely. The bits of wires, colorful connectors and metered boxes looked like so much junk to her.

She shifted her seat on the hard couch in Easy's apartment. A few days ago, she'd been loaded for bear where Jeffrey was concerned. He had lied to her, breached the safety of her home and played her for a fool. He had hired thugs to hurt Easy. He'd given her a dead woman's precious memento and dared to call it a custom-made engagement ring. Righteous indignation had bolstered her spirits and mustered her courage.

Righteous idiocy, she mused. She couldn't believe she'd allowed Easy to talk her into this nutty scheme. No way could she look into the eyes of a lying, manipulative, possibly homicidal con artist, and pretend to be his friend.

Easy slipped on a pair of headphones and fiddled with an electronic gadget. Trish bustled about her brother's apartment, freshening drinks and rummaging for snacks in the small kitchen. John Tupper sat rigidly on a chair, his feet together. He mopped at his damp face with a hand-

kerchief. Never in her life had Catherine ever known anyone who perspired as much as John did.

"Want a cookie?" Trish asked. She offered a bag of
chocolate chip cookies to Catherine.

"No, thank you."

"Are you nervous?" Trish munched a cookie, heedless
of the crumbs floating down the front of her shirt.

"Extremely." Catherine watched Easy. The swelling
had eased from his face, and the bruise had blackened so
it looked more like a bad makeup job than a wound. Being
with him was the most difficult part of this whole affair.
She didn't touch him, but she wanted to. She felt his desire
to touch her, too. They didn't talk about the past, but it
hovered in the air, crackling like ball lightning. Being in
this apartment, only a few feet away from where they'd
made love, tormented her.

"Jeffrey knows something is going on. He knows I
know he's a liar." She glanced at her watch. She was
meeting Jeffrey at the Grape and Olive in about an hour.

Easy slid the headphones off his head. "We know he
knows you know. That's why you aren't going to lie to
him."

She rubbed her throat. It ached as if encircled with tight,
cold bands of iron. Fear or not, she had to do this. She
couldn't work. She jumped at every noise. The realization
that she'd almost married a killer awakened her in the middle of the night with cold sweats and a pounding heart. If
she were ever to resume a normal life, she had to finish
her relationship with Jeffrey.

"You'll do fine. Trust me."

"I'd sooner trust my dogs with guarding a steak," she
muttered.

"I've dated guys like Livman," Trish said. "They think
they're smart and everyone else is stupid. One guy used
to pull the same stunt on me that Livman is pulling on
you. He'd get mad, then give me the silent treatment. I

was always apologizing. It drove me crazy until I realized he was acting like an immature brat.''

Catherine managed a wan smile, but wondered if Trish's ex-boyfriend's immaturity extended to homicide. When Easy beckoned her to rise, her smile faded. He gathered electronic gear and a roll of medical adhesive tape. He urged her to follow him into the bedroom.

He caught the edge of the door as if to close it, but paused. "I can suit you up out there. I thought you might want some privacy." He grinned, his eyes sparkling with good humor. "Want Trish to chaperon?"

He enjoyed this, she realized. All these I-spy shenanigans excited him. "That's quite all right." She lifted her chin and settled her sternest expression on her face. "We're adults."

He shut the door. "Some of us are. Take off your vest and blouse." He began tearing off strips of tape and hooked the ends over the dresser. "Excuse me in advance for getting personal."

Refusing to look at him, she removed the embroidered vest and unbuttoned her cotton blouse. Her fingers fumbled on the tiny wooden buttons. Her cheeks warmed as she slid off the blouse and stood facing him with only a filmy brassiere shielding her breasts. She braced for a smartaleck remark. Or worse, something sweet and sexy.

With the businesslike demeanor of a window dresser arranging a mannequin, he slid a dime-size microphone under her bra and between her breasts. He had her hold it in place while he affixed it to her skin with tape. After asking her to lift her arms, he snaked a wire around her rib cage to her back.

"Don't slap me. I have to put this where he won't feel it if he hugs you." He hooked his fingers in the elastic waistband of her skirt and tugged it down low on her hips. Her bikini panties seemed to shrink four sizes. She gritted her teeth, forcing herself to stay put. He placed a cigarette-package-size transmitter low against the small of her back, right above the cleft of her buttocks. When cold plastic touched her skin, gooseflesh prickled her back. He pulled her skirt back into place.

"How does that feel?"

"Fine," she said through gritted teeth. Her face burned.

"It's not bad for me either." He chuckled irreverently and used more strips of tape to make sure the wire lay flat against her skin. Every place his fingers smoothed tape, she burned and quivered.

His insolent grin irked her. "You're liking this far too much."

He lifted his eyebrows, but didn't deny the accusation. "Maybe you can pretend nothing happened between us, but I can't." He glanced at the bed. "You can put your blouse on."

She needed no urging to shove her arms in the sleeves and hastily button the front. She put on the vest. "You promised not to mention that."

"I didn't mention *that*." He planted his fists on his hips and glared down his nose at her. "It wasn't *that*, Tink. We made love. You and me, just like old times, but believe me, it was a helluva lot better than old times. You sent me flying, babe."

"Easy!"

"You seemed to be flying pretty high yourself. Why are you so embarrassed?"

Her face felt ready to burst into flame. She hugged herself and stared miserably at the floor. "This isn't the time or the place. We have a deal."

"You and your damned deals. You didn't mean it anymore than I did. I'm tired of dancing around you. Sick and tired of not touching you! Just looking at you is pure torture."

She turned her back on him, knowing if he glimpsed her eyes, they'd betray her longing for him. "What happened the other day was...temporary insanity! It won't happen again.''

''Want to bet?'' The smooth challenge in his voice rasped her nerves. ''You can't resist me any more than I can resist you.''

''And you call Jeffrey arrogant? There is nothing between us. Why can't you understand?''

''I'll tell you what I understand. You're bummed because you don't get your big wedding and two point two kids with Mr. All-American. You're scared because Livman turned out to be as bad I said. You're still mad at me about losing Elizabeth. Or you're mad at yourself. It doesn't matter which one. What matters is, you'll get over it. When you do, I'm right here.''

She couldn't help it, she had to look at his face. She had to witness with her own eyes that he truly believed his puffed-up, egotistical, arrogant, simplistic analysis. His sincerity beamed like a beacon. She opened her mouth for a snappy retort, but her mind went completely blank.

''The sooner you quit fighting it, the sooner we can get on with our lives.'' He rolled a hand imperiously. ''Turn around. Let me see if anything shows.''

Grumbling about his overinflated male ego, she executed a slow pirouette.

He waggled his fingers. ''Let me feel you up.''

She scrambled away from him. ''You stay away from me!''

''It's business, Tink. I don't want him feeling the wire. Hold your arms out.''

''If he touches me, I'll vomit.'' She knew that as certain as the mountains were high. She'd been kissing a killer.

She held out her arms and suffered him patting her sides and back for any sign of the wiring. He lingered under her breasts and she definitely knew he caressed rather than patted. He snaked his arms around her. She gasped, stiffening in his arms.

"Just checking to make sure he can't feel the transmitter if he hugs you."

He pressed the long, hard length of his body against her, belly to belly, thigh to thigh, and his hands slid sensuously down her back, teasingly close to her derriere. If Jeffrey had ever embraced her like this, nothing Easy Martel said or did could have made her give him up. She shoved at his arms.

He kissed her. Full on the lips, wet and lusty, all consuming, unmistakable in his demands. Her knees turned to water. Her belly softened and burned. She parted her lips and his tongue dueled tenderly with hers. He tasted so fine, so fresh and enigmatic. Arousal spread through her like the billowing clouds of an explosion, until even her hands and feet felt full, turgid with desire. She clutched the back of his shirt with both hands. Knowing he was aroused excited her and she pressed her body against his, feeling his hardness, feeling him tremble.

He broke the embrace with a suddenness that left her staggering. She groped blindly and found the edge of the dresser to hold on to for support. Breathing hard, she was glad for the vest that not only concealed the microphone and transmitter, but her hardened nipples now pressing painfully against the confines of her bra.

She glared at him, but his smile never faded and the word, *sorry* never passed his lips. His sheer irreverence struck a chord within her. No matter what happened, no matter the circumstances, Easy Martel remained Easy Martel. Brash, impudent...irresistible.

He shifted his stance and tugged at the waistband of his jeans. The effects of that kiss were obvious under the wear-softened denim. "Don't smile," he warned.

"You," she said, each word clipped, "are an egotistical buffoon."

"And you're the sexiest woman in the world. We're a perfect match."

Unbidden, unwanted, a smile blossomed before she could stop it. She turned her head and covered her mouth with a hand. "Leave me alone."

He poked her shoulder with his finger. "You don't mean that."

She slapped at his hand and skipped out of reach. "I do, too." His devilish smile and the unrepentant gleam in his eyes tickled her. A giggle rose and she tried to stop it, but it escaped. She wondered how she ever deluded herself into thinking she could remain angry at him.

"Hey!" Trish thumped noisily on the door before pushing it open. "What's going on? You're taking a long time in here."

"Ready for a sound check." He bowed graciously. "If you ladies will give me a moment, I want to check clarity. Stay here and chat."

Her skin itching where the tape pulled, Catherine watched him leave the room. He closed the door behind him. She hugged her elbows and smiled wanly at Trish.

Trish sidled across the room, her expression too carefully neutral. "So what's the deal with you and Easy? Are you guys getting together again?"

The bed behind her seemed to quiver with laughter. Catherine refused to glance over her shoulder; refused to face the object of her guilt. She meant to assert that she and Easy were definitely not now, not ever getting back together. Her throat refused to loosen enough for speech.

"I can see the chemistry is still there. He's never been serious about anyone else. You ought to at least give it a shot." She fluttered her eyelashes. "After all you guys have been through, it seems silly not to try."

Catherine sensed the meaning beneath the innocuous words. Her scalp prickled. "We dated in high school. Nothing more."

"Ah, come on, you did a lot more than just dating."

Catherine saw the knowledge in Trish's too-sweet smile

and wide eyes. Trish knew about Elizabeth. Which meant Easy had told her. He had probably told her everything.

Trish's smile faded. "I don't mean to make you mad." She twiddled with a long beaded necklace. "Maybe you could go over to the house. Mom and Dad would love to see you again. It would be like old times."

Feeling trapped, she hugged herself harder. Mr. and Mrs. Martel had been more like parents to her than her own parents had been. Kind, warm and affectionate, they'd always welcomed her into their home. News of a lost grandchild would hurt them. She wondered if Easy had told them, too.

"He told you," Catherine whispered. "You know why I left that year."

Trish stared at her feet. "Well...yeah." She jerked up her head and her dark eyes snapped. "Why did you do it? He would have married you. He loved you. I thought you loved him."

"I did." She almost added, *I do,* but caught herself in time. "I was scared, I was stupid. I thought I was alone."

Eyes downcast, the corners of her mouth turned down, Trish formed the very picture of dejection. "You weren't alone." An edge of anger crept into her voice. "It isn't fair. I'm a relative, too. I'd be a terrific aunt."

"I did what I thought was the best at the time."

"I don't know how you can say that. You really hurt Easy."

"That wasn't my intent."

"He had a right to know."

Catherine had no reply to that elemental truth. "I don't wish to discuss this," she said stiffly.

"If you'd discuss stuff with people maybe you wouldn't go around hurting everybody."

Catherine realized Trish hadn't changed much in the past twelve years. Still blunt and outspoken, she preferred to apologize rather than hold her tongue. "It's none of your business. Easy shouldn't have told you in the first place.''

''The baby is my blood, too. I have a right to know what happened to her. I have a right to know what's going on with you and my brother.'' She clamped her fists on her hips. ''So where is she? Are you going to get her back? Easy can find her with a couple of phone calls. Even I could do it. He can sue for custody, you know. You have no right to deny him his own baby—''

A knock on the door made both of them jump. ''Sound check!'' Easy called through the wood.

Catherine gasped and caught her throat with her hand. She'd forgotten about the wire. Cautiously, uncertain if he'd heard the argument, she asked, ''Can you hear me?''

''I can hear you,'' he called. ''Have Trish say something. I want to test the recorder.''

''We'll talk later,'' Trish mouthed. Then louder, she said, ''If Easy wasn't so mean and stingy, he'd let me borrow his motorcycle.''

''I heard that!'' he yelled.

His sister stuck out her tongue and made a rude noise. ''Did you hear that?''

Easy opened the door. ''Smart aleck.'' He pulled the headphones off his head and let them rest around his neck. ''Everything works fine. Are you ready, Tink?''

She slid a glare at Trish and Trish met it with heat of her own. One small consolation was that now instead of terror over facing Jeffrey, she had anger at Trish to distract her. ''I'm ready.''

IN THE PARKING LOT of the Grape and Olive restaurant, Easy parked near the exit. Catherine had set up a late-evening date, so darkness covered him. Even if Jeffrey came outside, his chances of spotting surveillance were minimal. Easy settled the earphones on his head.

Next to him, on the passenger seat, Trish folded her arms and sighed loudly. "Think she can pull this off?"

Easy clenched his jaw. If not for John Tupper in the back seat, he'd be blasting his little sister right about now. She had no right to grill Catherine about the baby. Or to make threats. His belly ached from pretending he hadn't heard what the women had been saying in his bedroom.

"Quiet," he growled. "I need to adjust this thing."

They'd selected the Grape and Olive because it was one of Jeffrey's favorite restaurants, but mostly because it didn't have a live band or music playing over speakers. Still, the sensitive microphone picked up every clatter, murmur and clank. A man greeted Catherine by name and told her Jeffrey was waiting.

"You don't have to bite my head off," Trish said. "Only a question."

"Keep your big mouth shut, okay? You've done enough damage already."

"What— Oh! You were listening." She tossed her head, setting her curls flying. "I only said what had to be said."

Even in the darkness, Easy could see John's wide interested eyes as he followed the conversation between the siblings. "Shut up, or I'm throwing you out of the car."

"She's still in love with you. I see how she looks at you. And you're still in love with her. Don't even try to deny it. The only thing holding her back is she feels guilty. Find out where the baby is. You'll both feel better."

"Get out of my car."

She huffed. "I'll shut up. But you know I'm right." She twisted on the seat so she faced John. "Don't you think people who are in love owe it to each other to be completely honest?"

Easy caught his inner cheek in his teeth. Once Trish was wound up, there was no stopping her. He regretted telling her about Catherine and the baby. He focused on the noise coming through the headphones.

"I know you're angry with me, Jeffrey," Catherine was saying. "I lied to you."

Easy waved frantically for silence. When Trish kept talking, he clamped a hand over her mouth. He hit the record start button on a cassette recorder. Sound from the headphones filtered through the speaker.

"Lied about what?" Jeffrey Livman sounded peevish and cold.

Easy mentally urged Catherine to keep her cool.

"About not knowing you were married. You see…a package came in the mail. It was full of information about you. And Roberta. I couldn't believe what I saw. I don't know why anyone sent it to me. I didn't know what to do."

"Package?" Livman's voice held a threatening note that lifted the short hairs on the nape of Easy's neck. "What do you mean, a package?"

"It came anonymously from some private security firm. Newspaper clippings and such. I gave it no real importance. I didn't even want it in my house. But it scared me. I can't imagine why anyone would send it." A long pause was punctuated by a male voice cheerfully describing the evening specials. Rustling noises crackled in the headphones and Easy winced. He imagined Catherine shifting around on the seat.

Easy listened to the change in Livman's voice while he spoke to the waiter. A casual observer would guess Livman hadn't a care in the world. Just a dope out on a date.

Finally the waiter left. Livman changed instantaneously; his voice turned to ice. "You have no idea who sent that…package?"

"Not a clue." Her voice broke. Easy winced again. The girl couldn't lie to save her soul. "Somebody is trying to break us up. I mean, I understand how very difficult it was for you to tell me about your wife. It makes me want to cry just thinking about it. Who would want to hurt you like that?''

''It is extremely painful,'' he said. ''So where's the package?''

''I must have thrown it away. Not that it contained anything important. Not really. Some newspaper articles and—and Roberta's death certificate. Why would anyone do that?'' She paused. Crystal clinked with a faint bell-like tone. ''There was a name on letterhead. A private security firm. I thought about calling them, but it all seems so—so—so dirty, somehow.''

''Why didn't you tell me?''

Catherine didn't answer for several seconds. Easy could picture her squirming, her face turning red. ''Come on, babe,'' he murmured. ''You can do this.''

''I didn't believe it.'' Her voice was surprisingly firm. ''I thought the names were mere coincidences or else somebody was playing a cruel joke.''

''What do you believe now?'' Livman asked.

''You've suffered a terrible tragedy. I also believe you have an enemy who wants to hurt you.'' She paused, her breathing audible. The microphone picked up the sound of her swallowing. ''It's working, isn't it? I haven't seen you in ages. You're angry with me. I don't blame you for not trusting me. I should have called you the second that package arrived.''

''You should feel terrible about your distrust. I'm the man you love.''

''I'm so sorry! Can you ever forgive me?''

''I don't know if I can, Catherine,'' he said.

Despite knowing Catherine merely acted as if she groveled, Easy seethed with disgusted anger.

''Let's put it all out in the open,'' Catherine said. ''Tell me what's going on, then we'll work it out. Is somebody trying to hurt you, Jeffrey?''

"Actually, yes. I have an enemy."

"Who is he? What does he want?"

"My wife's brother. His name is John Tupper. He's as sick as Roberta was."

John lurched forward and draped his elbows over the seat. He made an astonished noise, blowing hot breath across Easy's cheek. Trish patted his arm with a comforting hand.

"He's going around telling people I killed my wife."

"Why would he say such a horrid thing?" Catherine sounded genuinely appalled and Easy felt proud.

"Because he's sick. Not to mention greedy."

"Greedy? Whatever do you mean?"

The waiter returned, accompanied by loud clangs, bangs and thumps. Again, Livman's tone changed. He chatted pleasantly with the waiter, asking about his family and his college courses. Easy shook his head in wonder. The dirtbag was so good he ought to be in the movies.

"What's this crap about me being greedy?" John demanded.

"Hush." Easy waited for the waiter to leave and for the conversation to resume. He was dying to know how Livman justified calling John greedy, too.

Small crunches said Catherine ate something. Easy wished he could tell her to stop chewing.

"Roberta and her brother leached off each other. He's part of the reason she was in debt. He also had it in his head that she inherited a bunch of money and antiques when their mother died, but that was a crock. She hocked everything to pay for booze."

"I think I'm going to be sick," John murmured.

"Plus, she had a small insurance policy," Livman continued. "She must have told her brother about it."

"How much did the policy pay?"

"Barely enough to cover funeral costs. After the casket and grave site and everything, I had maybe two hundred dollars left over. I donated it to charity, in her name. It was the least I could do for her. Tupper seems to think I made a fortune. He tried to make trouble with the insurance company, but that didn't work. So now he's telling everyone I killed her. He wants the insurance.''

"That's awful. What are you going to do?"

"No, no,'' Easy muttered. "Make him talk about the policy. Come on!''

"I've thought about leaving town. Starting over somewhere else.''

"No, you have to stay and fight. You can't let him ruin you.''

"What can I do, darling? Even you, the woman I love, believed him over me.''

"No, I didn't! I swear. I was confused, yes, and curious, but now that I know the truth, I want to help you. Suppose I speak to her brother for you? I can show him the insurance policy and the funeral costs, and he'll have to understand you had no reason to hurt Roberta.''

"He's crazy. It won't work.''

"Then what about my father? He's a well-respected attorney. He handles civil cases similar to this all the time. Trust me, if he speaks to that man, that man will listen.''

"And have your father thinking his future son-in-law is a wimp?''

"Then we'll hire another attorney. We'll get a restraining order.''

"It won't work, Catherine. Don't you understand? Tupper would kill me if he had the guts.''

"It doesn't take guts to kill!'' John shook a fist at the tape recorder. "Liar!''

"Shh.'' Easy adjusted the volume. Catherine sounded as if she chewed gravel.

"It's okay, John.'' Trish kept patting his arm.

Easy regretted John's presence. The man kept a fairly cool head, considering the circumstances, but listening to his sister's killer twist the truth could very well push him over the edge.

Jeffrey spoke to another man. Easy shut off the recorder to conserve tape. He settled back to wait until Catherine began speaking again. When she did, he activated the tape recorder.

"Tell me exactly what happened. All the newspaper stories said is that she fell. Surely there was someone around who can say it was an accident."

"It was an accident. She was drunk and she slipped. End of story."

"Don't be angry, darling," Catherine soothed. "I'm trying to help. Unless some evidence actually exists, no one can hurt you. Are the police investigating?"

John flung himself back on the seat and the car rocked slightly with the force of his movement. "He'll never confess."

"Give her time," Easy said. "I can almost hear his gears grinding while he cooks up a way to use her. We've already caught him in about fifty lies."

"You don't understand how he operates. I wouldn't put it past him to bribe a witness to say I pushed her."

"Stop being so pessimistic. You're the one with the evidence. Surely Roberta had pawn-shop receipts to show she sold her mother's belongings. The insurance policy proves how much money you received. You have reports from the rehabilitation centers, right? Doctors or psychologists who can testify about her self-destructiveness?" Catherine said.

"I tried to get her into rehab," Livman replied testily. "I never said she actually went."

"What about her friends or former employers. Surely they—"

"Why are you going on and on about this? I thought you were on my side?"

Again, crackling pinged at Easy's ears. He wondered if she were scratching or fiddling with the microphone.

"I am on your side. All I'm saying is, if this Mr. Tupper is intent on doing you damage, then you must fight back."

"I won't lower myself to his level."

"What about me?" A long pause was punctuated by the waiter filling glasses and the sound of chewing. Finally, she continued. "What about me, Jeffrey? Our relationship looks bad. Roberta's accident happened only a month before we met. Does her brother believe you and I were involved while you were married?"

"So what if he does?"

"It's bad enough you concealed your past from me. Now you're—"

"Talk about something else."

"No. You're my fiancé. I have to right to know what's going on with you."

"Look how long it took you to admit you slept around and got yourself knocked up. You're a hypocrite. You'll have sex with every street-corner stud you find, but you barely kiss me. So if we're talking truth, why don't you tell me who you're whoring around with?"

Catherine gasped. Easy shifted uncomfortably on the seat. Glad the darkness hid his burning face, he avoided looking at Trish or John. He wondered when Catherine had told Livman about the baby, and why. In any case, Livman's vicious words weren't part of the plan.

"If you're going to speak that way to me, I'm leaving." Her voice cracked. Dishes clanked.

"You're the one so hot about the truth. So be honest, *darling*. Who's the lucky stiff getting the pieces of you that I'm not?"

"Let go of my hand. You're hurting me. Jeffrey!"

Easy cursed and clamped his hands on the headphones, prepared to rip them off and run to the rescue.

"What's he doing to her?" Trish cried. "Stop him, Easy. Make him quit."

"Shh! He won't hurt her in front of witnesses." Easy hoped.

"Where's the ring?"

"Jeffrey! Turn—loose!" A glass sounded as if it cracked. The murmuring of other diners hushed. The distinct sound of flesh slapping flesh snapped through the speaker.

"He's hitting her!" Trish yelled and pushed open the car door. The dome light flared on.

"Wait a minute," Easy called. "Hold on."

"Don't you ever put your hands on me like that again!" Catherine sounded more angry than afraid. "I'm leaving. We're finished." Rustling and squeaking announced her leaving the leather-covered booth.

An anxious voice asked Catherine a question. Restaurant noises marked her passage. Easy looked at the double doors in time to see them fly open as Catherine straight-armed her way out of the restaurant. She looked in the direction of Easy's car then lowered her chin.

"I can't do this, Easy," she said. "I won't! He's a monster." She dug through her purse while she stalked across the parking lot toward her Blazer.

Jeffrey Livman burst through the restaurant doors. He paused a scant second, his head swiveling. He lunged after Catherine.

"You have to stop this right now," Trish said. "If you don't, I will."

Easy hesitated. If Livman were angry enough, he might say something incriminating. Livman caught up to Catherine.

"Get away from me!" she snapped. Keys jangled.

"Nobody walks away from me," Livman said, his voice an icy growl. "Nobody. Do you hear me? Nothing is over until I say it's over."

Catherine's hair caught the parking lot lights, sparkling like gold as she tossed her head defiantly. "Then say it's over, Jeffrey. Because it is. You're a liar. You lied about everything. Roberta. Your own mother. Even your age. And you're cruel."

"You want cruel?" He shoved her against the Blazer.

She hit with a loud thump and a burst of static. The radio receiver went silent. Easy tore the headphones off his head. In unison, he, Trish and John scrambled out of the car.

"Stop it!" Catherine screamed.

"Hey!" Easy yelled. His boots crunched gravel. His vision filmed in furious red.

Livman sprang away from Catherine. She slumped against the Blazer, her beautiful face strained with pain and fear. Easy skidded to a stop between Livman and Catherine. Up close, he noted Livman was smaller than he appeared either in photographs or from a distance. Shadows cast his face into a furious mask. He appeared as dangerous as a rabid dog.

Easy raised his fists. He'd never in his life wanted to hit anybody as much as he wanted to hit Jeffrey Livman. "Back off."

"Who—?" Livman looked directly at John. Slowly, he straightened his back and lowered his shoulders. A thin, grim smile slashed his face. He looked between Catherine and John, then chuckled. "Oh, you bitch," he said, softly. "You're trying to set me up."

"Murderer." John advanced, his thin shoulders shaking. "You aren't getting away with killing her. I'll see you rot in prison the rest of your miserable life."

Easy knew the game was over. Livman had won on a TKO. Easy thrust out a hand, ready to hold John back before he committed assault and battery. With his other hand, he reached for Catherine. Her silence scared him, and he prayed it meant she was only scared and not hurt.

Chuckling, Livman tugged at his lapels and smoothed a hand over his hair. He smiled at Catherine with an intensity that turned Easy's blood cold. He nodded at his former brother-in-law. ''You'll never prove anything, John. Get over it.'' He sauntered away.

Chapter Eleven

"I'm sorry." Catherine slouched on a chair in Easy's apartment. She did not know what else to say. Jeffrey's attack had shocked her, shaken her. It confirmed that he was capable of murder. It also confirmed that Easy was right; she did not know Jeffrey at all.

Worst of all, she'd blown it. When she allowed Jeffrey to rattle her, she'd destroyed any chance of inducing him to confess to Roberta's murder. Heartsick, she watched Easy fiddle with the broken transmitter. When Jeffrey slammed her against the Blazer, the unit had cracked. Catherine could feel a bruise forming all the way to her tailbone. It seemed too small a price to pay for ruining John Tupper's chances of ever finding justice.

"I'm sorry," she repeated.

Easy shook his head. "Not your fault. I should have known he'd react like that."

"You couldn't have known," John said. He paced aimlessly around the crowded living room. "Nobody can predict what he'll do. He's insane."

Easy grunted. "He isn't insane. We underestimated him."

Trish came out of the kitchen. She bore a mug of steaming tea. She handed it to Catherine. "Are you sure you're okay?" she asked. Her dark eyes shone with concern.

Catherine accepted the tea. "He scared me, that's all." She inhaled the steam off the fruity tea. The moist fragrance of blackberry helped somewhat to soothe her tangled nerves. It did nothing for the guilt rampaging through her soul.

Lost in her own glum thoughts, she paid scant attention while Easy, John and Trish plotted new strategy. Their conversation led nowhere. Finally John said he had to leave. Trish left with him.

Catherine stood. The small of her back twinged. Grimacing, she rubbed it. "I better go home."

"You can stay." Easy canted his head toward the sofa. "I'll sleep out here. You'll be safe."

She shook her head. Easy Martel presented far too much temptation. In her vulnerable state, she doubted if she could resist him. "I'll be fine."

He caught both her hands and held her firmly. He leaned in until she finally looked up into his eyes. "Quit blaming yourself," he said. "If anybody is to blame, it's me. I should have prepared better."

She sighed heavily. "If you want to know the truth, I hoped you were wrong. I wanted him to say something to prove that he couldn't have hurt Roberta. I saw a side of him tonight that terrifies me. His eyes..." She closed her eyes against the memory. "I have never in my life seen anyone so cold, so—so—"

"Evil?"

"Evil," she repeated in full agreement. "What are you going to do?"

Without releasing her hands, he lifted his shoulders in a quick shrug. "Put the heat on him. Maybe if I squeeze hard enough, he'll squeak."

She wrinkled her nose and fixed her gaze on his wounded eye. "What about the men who hurt you?"

"They caught me off guard once. It won't happen again." He pointed his chin at the cassette recorder. "I'm taking the tape to the district attorney. Livman lied about the insurance policy and burying Roberta. He lied about her being drunk.''

''You don't sound hopeful.''

''It's a toughie, but not impossible.''

She gave his fingers a quick squeeze, then stepped away. She picked up her purse. ''I really should go home.'' She turned for the door.

''Hey, Tink.''

The way he used the nickname caused a strange sensation below her diaphragm. The very first time he'd ever asked her out, she'd been so flustered that the cutest, funniest, most popular boy in school spoke to her, she'd actually run away. Humiliated, she'd felt convinced he'd never speak to her again. Instead he'd cornered her the next day and tossed a handful of confetti at her. ''Fairy dust,'' he'd proclaimed. ''Now you can't fly away, Tinker Bell.'' She'd fallen in love with him at that very moment.

''How about dinner tomorrow night?'' He grinned mischievously. ''You're no longer attached.''

It bothered her how much she wanted to say yes when she'd proven she couldn't trust herself around him. Despite harsh experience, she'd taken a foolish chance and possibly risked the life of another child. ''I need some time alone. I need to sort this out, get my head on straight.''

His smile faded. ''I'll call you.''

''Give me some time, okay?'' She slipped out of the apartment before she lost her resolve and ended up in his arms.

HIS FIRST CALL CAME before Catherine reached home. Easy left a message on her answering machine. ''Let me know when you get home so I know you're safe.'' Weary and heartsick as she felt, she couldn't repress a smile.

She called the number he'd left. He answered on the

first ring, making her wonder if he'd been sitting by the telephone. "I'm safe," she said. "Good night, Easy."

He called the next day. He wanted to know how her back felt. If she thought the injury needed to be checked, he'd be glad to take her to the doctor. She told him it wasn't necessary.

The day after that, when the telephone rang, she rushed to answer, anticipating his sexy voice. She'd been sleeping poorly, tossing and turning and longing for Easy. They were grown-ups now. She could spend the night in his arms and not have to worry about the rising sun. Such thoughts disturbed her as much as they excited her. After what she'd been through, she ought to be swearing off men forever, not imagining life with Easy. She snatched up the handset and sang a cheery hello.

Jeffrey said, "Hello, darling."

She went dead cold. Her chest tightened up so much she couldn't breathe. Her legs trembled. "Jeffrey?"

"You sound surprised. You don't believe a little spat would break us up, do you? I love you, Catherine, and I miss you. I'm sick without you. I can't sleep or eat. Let's give ourselves another chance."

Incredulous, she pulled the handset away from her ear and stared at the mouthpiece as if it might offer a clue. She swiped her mouth with the back of her hand. "Don't call me anymore," she told him, and hated her weak voice. "We're finished. I never want to see or hear from you again."

"How can you say that? We're soul mates. I love you. I'm sorry I lost my temper. You did provoke me, but I can forgive you. Let's get together. I'll come to your place. I'll bring wine. We'll have a good talk and straighten this all out."

For a moment, she wanted to invite him over. She'd have a second chance to help John. She could wrest a confession from his lying mouth—no! He attempted to trick her. She'd proven how ill-equipped she was to challenge him.

"We're through," she said, this time strong. "Don't call me ever again." She killed the connection.

Within seconds, the telephone rang again. Hugging her elbows, she backed away and allowed the answering machine to pick up.

"Don't ever hang up on me!" Jeffrey spat the words. "We are not through! We're getting married, Catherine. You promised and I'll make you live up to that promise. Now quit acting like a baby and pick up the damned telephone!"

She touched the off button on the answering machine, cutting him off. She unplugged the telephone.

She debated calling Easy. She knew, though, he'd come charging to the rescue. With her emotions so frazzled and her nerves as brittle as late-spring ice, she knew it would take little more than a smile from him for her to throw caution to the wind. She draped a newspaper over the telephone so the sight of it wouldn't tempt her.

The next day she plugged the phone back in, but watching and waiting for it to ring made her so nervous she couldn't work. She unplugged it and buried it again under newspapers. The day after that, she felt so resentful about allowing Jeffrey to cut off her communication, she plugged it in and dared it to ring.

When the telephone did ring, she shoved away from her worktable and advanced on the machine. "Go ahead, Jeffrey. Say something nasty."

The answering machine activated. Margaret's peevish voice demanded Catherine pick up the phone.

Chuckling in relief, Catherine picked up the phone. "I'm here, Margaret. What's going on?"

"I've been trying to reach you for days! I couldn't even get your machine. What is going on?"

"I'm sorry. I—I— Remember my engagement? It's off.

Jeffrey and I broke up.'' She resisted filling in the agent on all the gory details. Margaret would want Catherine to turn the experience into a book or a screenplay or something.

"I'm sorry to hear that. Are you all right? I warned you about getting involved. How is your emotional state? Ready to go to work?"

Margaret's self-centered concern depressed Catherine. Her agent adored her because Catherine made lots of money. If the relationship ever turned unprofitable, it would end.

"I'm fine." She carried the telephone to the window. All her life she'd dreamed of living in the country. A place where she had enough room to ramble and keep any animal she pleased. Instead of peaceful solitude, she felt isolated, vulnerable. Alone... Unloved... Unlovable. "Is everything going okay with the contract?"

"The attorneys are fighting over reproduction rights for your original paintings. It's half a percentage point, for goodness' sake!" Margaret wailed. "I'm going to kill all the lawyers!"

"Tell our man to give it up. I just put the spider book in the mail, so I'm out of contract. I need the work." Catherine slumped on a chair. She wanted to whine about how having nothing to do gave her too much time to worry about Jeffrey Livman and Easy Martel. Finding herself perilously close to tears, she pinched hard on the bridge of her nose. "I'm perfectly happy with the money situation. Honest."

"Halladay and his publisher are going to make a fortune on this and you're getting a mere pittance."

Catherine lifted her eyebrows. Even if she never earned out a penny in royalties beyond the advance, a million bucks qualified as a lot more than a mere pittance.

"In any case, free up your calendar. Doc Halladay has a two-day break in his schedule one month from today.

His publicity agent is making arrangements for the taping.''

Catherine looked around the studio. A month might give her enough time to make the house look presentable. If the dry weather held, she might even manage to have the driveway graded and graveled. In any case, she'd have so much to do she wouldn't have time to sit around and feel sorry for herself.

After the call ended, she wandered around the main floor. Considering its age, the house was in excellent shape, but sorely outdated. When she moved in, she'd ripped out the avocado green shag carpeting, exposing oak flooring. Gouges and stains marred the wood, however, and the finish had worn through in places. The dogs followed her, making anxious little noises, and tried to herd her toward the door. She'd been too nervous to make her usual morning runs; the dogs were restless.

The walls needed painting. The upstairs bath had green fixtures and lime green-checked floor tile. The kitchen needed a complete makeover. She found a notepad and began making a to-do list. Every time she turned around, she tripped over one of the dogs.

"Why can't you guys grow thumbs? You could help me instead of getting in the way." She shifted her glower from Oscar to Bent. They wagged their skinny tails and pleaded with their soft eyes. Her sternness faded under the onslaught of their optimism. "All right, all right. Want to chase the ball? Where's the ball?"

The greyhounds scrambled to race each other into the studio. They bounced on the sofa and dug under the cushions. Oscar pounced, coming up with a well-chewed softball. Catherine opened the door and scooted out of the way before the dogs bowled her over.

She stepped out on the deck. Sun glare made her squint. Silence pummeled her ears. She looked around the property, seeking any signs of life. The curve of the driveway concealed the road from her view. Tall trees ringing the property made it seem as if she were in the middle of a wilderness. Resentment filled her—she hated being afraid. Shoving down the fear, she marched across the deck and called for the dogs.

Bent had stolen the ball away from Oscar. With the large ball straining her narrow jaws, she ran with that peculiarly beautiful, humpbacked run of her breed, her powerful haunches thrusting her forward at blinding speed. Catherine prepared to jump out of the way. The dogs were a lot better at starting than stopping. As Bent ran past, Catherine shouted, "Drop it!"

Bent circled, dancing away from Oscar, clearly unwilling to give up the prize.

Catherine held out a hand. "Drop it."

Bent growled at Oscar, then dropped the ball. Catherine scooped it up. "Ready?" The dogs followed the ball with hypnotic intensity. They were sight-hounds, relying not on their noses or ears, but their eyes. Catherine threw the ball with all her might, sending it sailing over the scrub grass. The dogs lunged after it, leaving trails of floating dust.

Enjoying the sunshine and the dogs at play, Catherine threw the ball until her arm was tired. She chased the dogs and let them chase her. Then Oscar ran straight at her. She tried to dodge him, but he hit the back of her knees. She pinwheeled her arms for balance, but fell heavily to the ground. Unhurt, she laughed while both dogs fawned over her, licking her face in apology.

The sound of a car coming up the drive dried up the laughter. She leaped to her feet. The trees were closer, but the telephone was inside the house. She'd make for the house, she determined, if it were Jeffrey.

A white car came around the bend. *Easy.* Panting as much in relief as weariness, she leaned over and grasped her knees. When the car stopped, she straightened. She tried not to feel so happy about seeing him. She warned herself that jumping into a relationship with him right now would be the second biggest mistake of her life. She had her career; she had her own home; she was vulnerable after the mess with Jeffrey.

Still, the sight of his shiny black hair and broad shoulders sent a thrill of pure delight coursing through her midsection.

"Hey, Tink," he called. He sauntered across the grass, his loose-limbed walk radiating pure male sexuality. A black T-shirt with a Harley-Davidson logo printed on the front stretched alluringly across his chest. A pulse down deep in her midsection shook her to her toes.

Bent took advantage of the distraction to snatch the ball away from Oscar. She took off with Oscar in hot pursuit.

Settling her face into a neutral expression, she folded her arms over her breasts. "What are you doing here?"

"You didn't answer the telephone." He watched the dogs chase each other.

"You drove twenty-five miles because I didn't answer the phone? Tell me the truth."

"That is the truth. I worry about you." He boldly looked her up and down, making her self-conscious about her paint-smudged T-shirt and ragged denim shorts. "You're looking good."

"Your taste is appalling." She reveled in the compliment anyway. "As long as you're here, want something to drink?"

"Sure. So why didn't you answer the phone? I can't even get your machine."

She whistled for the dogs. "Jeffrey called. I didn't want to deal with him, so I unplugged the telephone."

She headed toward the house. When Easy demanded to know what Jeffrey had said, she regretted telling him anything. "He wants to talk to me." She laughed wryly. "He says he forgives me and we should put all this nastiness behind us. *Right.*"

"Did he threaten you?"

"He still wants to get married." She looked him straight in the eyes. "I cannot for the life of me imagine what I ever saw in him."

Inside the house, she glanced at the answering machine and was relieved to see a steady red light instead of a flashing message indicator. She offered Easy iced tea.

"I think I might have a break in the case," he said.

"Really?" She used a paper towel to wipe her sweaty face. Twin thumps marked the dogs flopping onto the wood floor to cool off. "What kind of break?"

"The last time John spoke to Roberta, he came away with the impression she was afraid of Livman." He perched on a stool and accepted the tall glass of tea.

"I thought that was a given." Catherine sipped her tea, wondering where this might lead.

"Livman abused her. Maybe it was verbal or emotional abuse. Maybe it was physical. We'll never know for sure. I can understand why she wouldn't want to rile the waters by telling her brother. But if she thought Livman meant to kill her, that's a different story."

Catherine mulled over her father's vile temper and the rages that had sometimes turned physical. He'd never actually beaten her, but he had lashed out, striking her with a fist or slamming her against a wall. Easy had been the only person she'd ever told about the physical abuse. Each admission had been accompanied by heart-wrenching shame. She'd always blamed herself for her father's temper. If she were a good girl, he wouldn't get so angry.

"She may have been ashamed. Or she couldn't believe he would want to kill her."

"How could she ignore the insurance policy? No matter how embarrassed she felt, half a million must have made her nervous. Unless she didn't know."

Catherine pulled a face. "Impossible. A man can't insure his wife without her knowledge."

"Exactly. So I talked to Livman's insurance agent. He gave me all kinds of goodies."

Remembering her father's furious frustration whenever he had to deal with insurance companies, she was impressed. "Is that legal?"

"I didn't ask him for details about the policy. I showed him photographs of Roberta. He isn't sure she's the woman who purchased the policy. So he let slip the name of the nurse who gave Roberta her physical. She isn't positive about the ID either."

As his meaning sank in, Catherine scowled. "Jeffrey used an impostor to fool the insurance company?"

"A *healthy* impostor. There's no mention of Roberta's asthma in the physical report."

She chewed over the implications. "Could Roberta have concealed her condition?"

"The nurse claims she always checks for chronic, potentially lethal diseases. She doesn't think she'd have missed the asthma. Besides, John says his sister would never falsify that kind of information." He waggled his eyebrows and saluted her with his iced tea glass. "If I'm right, then this proves premeditation. He took out the policy only three months before she died."

"How in the world could he get someone to pose as Roberta?"

"How did he get you to agree to marry him?"

She clamped her arms over her chest and threw him a dark look. "Okay, fine, he's persuasive." So was Easy, she mused, if he'd convinced the insurance company employees to concede they may have royally screwed up.

"Romoco Insurance is reopening an investigation. They'll bring in big guns from the national fraud bureau. If we can prove Livman used a ringer, it ought to be enough for the district attorney to rethink the coroner's findings." He reached into his back pocket and brought out a clumsily folded envelope. He gave it to her. "In the meantime, check this out."

Catherine pulled a Polaroid photograph from the envelope. It pictured children swinging in a park. On the white border below the picture, someone had scrawled, "Any time, anywhere."

"What does this mean? Who are these children?"

Easy pointed out two little girls. "Those are John's kids. The picture was stuck in his door."

Queasiness rolled her stomach. "Did Jeffrey send this?"

"I imagine so."

"This is so sick! How can he threaten children? Did John go to the police?"

"They can't prove anything. We have to catch Livman in the act before we can press charges. So if he calls you, or sends you any messages, save them. Document whatever he says. Can you record calls on your answering machine while you're talking?"

She nodded affirmatively. She touched Easy's eye. The stitches were gone, but yellowish remnants remained of the bruise. "What happens if he sends those men around again? Or if he sends them after John or his family?"

"John is sending his wife and kids to visit his in-laws out of state. Neither of us think Livman will try anything outright. He likes his victims meek and mild." He held up his right hand, his forefinger and middle finger crossed. "I think the fraud investigation with the insurance company is going to pan out." He waggled his eyebrows. "I have a hunch whoever the impostor is, it's bugging her. She shouldn't—"

Catherine jolted as if hit with an electric spark. "Noreen."

"What?"

She held a hand level with her head. "She's about my height, but much thinner. She's blond." She thumped her head with the heel of her hand, seeking solid memories. "She's a very strange woman."

"Who is she?"

"She's a closer at the title company where we signed all the papers for buying this house. Jeffrey appeared to know her very well. He was teasing and joking with her, but she seemed very uncomfortable. I remember wondering, why doesn't he notice how much she dislikes him? She was at the Grape and Olive when Jeffrey proposed. She seemed upset. I thought maybe she had a thing for him. But after you gave me all that stuff about Jeffrey, I called her at work. She hung up on me."

"That is strange. And it sounds guilty. Where does she work?"

"Downtown at Morgan Title. But why would she pose as Roberta? She has to know it's illegal."

"Why don't we ask her?"

"We, *kemo sabe?*" She shook her head emphatically. "I've had all the spy snoop nonsense I can stomach."

"Seeing you might push her over the edge."

"She won't talk to me. She hung up on me."

Easy made spaniel eyes, batting his lashes and turning up the wattage on his smile. "Please?"

She made as if to throw her iced tea on him. "Stop it. I don't want to get involved. My life is already a total mess. Look at this place. I have a ton of things to do."

He picked up the photograph of John's children. He gazed sorrowfully at it and clucked his tongue. "I guess I can *try* to talk to her. I *might* get lucky—"

She slammed down her glass. "You are shameless. You don't need me and you know it. You're just jerking me around."

He sniffed as if offended. "I do, too, need you. If Noreen is our girl, then she's feeling guilty as hell. If she thinks you know what she did, then she'll crack. I'm sure of it." He smiled sweetly.

Her stony glare didn't affect his smile one little bit. Truth was, Catherine's curiosity about Noreen nagged at her. If the woman knew about Roberta's murder, then quite possibly she knew about Jeffrey's plans for a second marriage and a second victim. Anger at Jeffrey returned full force.

"Well?" Easy asked.

Catherine turned her gaze on the notepad containing her extensive to-do list. Doc Halladay and his camera crew and the book contract suddenly seemed paltry. An image of John's stricken face flashed through her mind. "All right. I'll go with you."

Easy's smile rivaled the glory of the morning sun. "We'll nail him, Tink. I know it."

CATHERINE TAPPED her knuckles lightly on the open office door. She prayed she didn't look as nervous as she felt. Before Easy confronted Noreen Dawson, he had checked around and gathered some information. It looked damning. The woman behind the desk lifted her head and smiled. Recognition lit the woman's eyes and the smile turned frozen.

"Hello, Noreen," Catherine said. "Do you remember me?"

"Umm, yes, Ms. St. Clair, isn't it?" Noreen's voice quavered.

Easy stepped into view. He put a hand in the small of Catherine's back and urged her to step into the tiny office. He closed the door. Noreen's face paled to the color of ash.

"Miss Noreen Dawson, I'm Earl Z. Martel, private investigator. I'm looking into the death of Roberta Livman. I understand you're a friend of Jeffrey Livman's." Without awaiting her reply or invitation, he pulled a chair around for Catherine. Easy remained standing.

"I, umm, I really don't know Jeff all that well."

"According to brokers I've talked to, Mr. Livman uses Morgan Title almost exclusively for his real-estate transactions. He's used you as a closer for several years."

Noreen pressed a hand over her eyes. "It's only business," she whispered.

Catherine leaned forward. As gently as possible, she said, "We talked to Howard Greer, Jeffrey's old boss. He said you and Jeffrey were very close. Were you having an affair with him?"

Easy placed a wallet-size portrait of Roberta on the desk in front of Noreen. "You and Mrs. Livman resemble each other. You could be sisters."

Tears welled in Noreen's eyes. Her chin quivered.

Nausea rose in Catherine's throat. Everything Easy suspected was true. She glanced at him; he nodded slightly. Catherine cleared her throat. "You know Jeffrey murdered Roberta, don't you? And you know why. You helped him purchase the insurance policy from Romoco."

"Both the insurance agent and the nurse who conducted the physical are willing to identify you, Miss Dawson." Easy leaned both hands on the desk, looming over the tearful woman. "What did Livman promise you for helping him kill his wife?"

"I didn't know!" Noreen wailed. She shoved away from the desk and jumped to her feet. The chair skittered across the floor. She pressed her back against the wall and grabbed her pale hair in both hands. "I didn't know he was going to kill her!"

Chapter Twelve

Noreen Dawson blew her nose. With cosmetics washed away by tears, and her cheeks and forehead blotched with heat, she'd lost her prettiness.

Instead of pity, Catherine seethed with gelid anger. How, she wondered, *why* had the woman done what she had? Money? Noreen wore a chic, peach-colored suit that probably came from a fine boutique. Layers of gold necklaces encircled her throat and her fingers glittered with jeweled rings. Catherine guessed the woman's fingernails were acrylic, and expensive to maintain. The thought of Noreen's frivolity being paid for by Roberta's death made Catherine feel sick.

Easy rested a hip on the corner of Noreen's desk. "Were you and Livman having an affair?"

Noreen pulled another tissue out of a box. She scrubbed at her eyes. "No. We were friends, just friends, nothing more. I only saw him at work. It's always business."

"Did you know Roberta?"

"I met her a few times. She was nice."

Catherine pressed a fist against her mouth to stop a disgusted groan. Unable to contain herself, she cried, "So nice you helped him murder her?"

The woman blanched, cringing. "I didn't know that's what he meant to do. I didn't know anything about it."

Avoiding Catherine, she beseeched Easy with her eyes. "He never said he wanted to kill his wife. And—and—and the newspapers called it an accident! It was an accident. He didn't kill her."

"You know better," Easy said, while taking notes in a small spiral-bound pad. "You knew better when it happened. Did he pay you, Noreen?"

"No!"

"So you committed fraud for the fun of it."

Noreen doubled over and clutched at her belly. "No, no, no!" She dragged in a long, snuffling breath. "You don't understand. I thought I was doing him a favor. Roberta was sick. She had a condition. They'd been turned down by insurance companies. It was all her idea anyway."

Catherine leaned back on the chair. "Roberta's idea?"

"Yeah." Noreen nodded eagerly. "She was scared she'd end up sticking Jeff with big medical bills. She's the—"

"Noreen," Easy interrupted, "are you claiming Roberta told you, face-to-face, she wanted you to impersonate her?"

"Not exactly. But Jeff said—"

"I can't listen to this." Catherine pushed off the chair. Unable to look at the woman, she hung her head. "Roberta Livman is dead. You helped Jeffrey make killing her profitable. Now you want to act like a victim? You're the one with the cast-iron stomach, Easy, you talk to her. She's making me sick."

He waggled a hand at her. "Hold on a sec, Tink. It sounds like Noreen is a victim."

"Just like every other criminal is a victim." She whirled on the woman and leaned over the desk. Her purse hit the desktop with a thud. "You know what he did, but you never warned me. When I turned up dead, were you going to call that an accident, too?"

Easy rested a hand on Catherine's shoulder. "Chill. We need to hear Noreen's side of the story." He jotted a few notes in his book. In a casual tone, he added, "I find it hard to swallow that she's an accessory to murder."

"Accessory? No!"

"That's what the cops will think." He clucked his tongue. His brow twisted in an expression of bemused concern.

Smooth, Easy Martel, Catherine thought, backing away to give him room to work.

"Look at it from their point of view. There's no question you committed fraud. Witnesses can identify you. The question the cops will ask is, why? If you and Livman were lovers, that would be one thing. But you say it's nothing like that. Which leaves only monetary gain. You can get the death penalty."

"Oh God, oh God," Noreen whispered.

A knock on the door was followed by an older woman poking her head inside the office. "Excuse me. Noreen, your two-o'clock closing people are waiting."

Noreen covered her face with a tissue. Nodding, she waved at the woman to indicate understanding. "Be right there."

"Uh, okay." After giving Easy and Catherine wondering looks, the woman backed out, closing the door behind her.

"The law treats accomplices as culpable as the perps," Easy said. "That means the way things stand, you're as guilty as Livman. But if you confess to the insurance fraud, and cooperate in his prosecution, they'll probably go easy on you."

"I can't," she whispered. "I'll lose my job." She blinked rapidly. "I'll go to jail."

"If you make them come after you, you'll definitely go to jail. Right now it looks like Livman paid you to help him murder his wife."

"It does?"

"That's how it looks to me."

"He didn't give me any money!"

Catherine gritted her teeth. "Then what did he give you?"

"Nothing! It was a favor. Just a favor!" She popped to her feet and gripped the edge of the desk with both hands. "Get out of my office. I have clients waiting. Get out!"

"Are you afraid of Livman?" Easy asked gently. "Did he threaten you?"

The woman scowled stubbornly at her desk.

"This isn't over, Noreen." Easy closed his notebook. "If I were you, I'd hire the best attorney I could find."

Catherine managed to hold her peace until they left Morgan Title. At the elevator, awaiting a car, she could stand it no more. "She's a liar!"

"I know." He draped a comforting arm around her shoulders. "But it doesn't matter. We have her dead to rights."

"She'll never talk."

"Care to make a small wager? We have witnesses and physical evidence that she committed fraud. It's a baby step from there to a murder investigation." He winked. "Noreen won't go down alone."

His smug self-confidence irked her. "What if she leaves town? Runs away?"

"She has family here. Friends. A good job. She owns a condo. She won't run, trust me. Bury her head in the sand and hope we go away, yes. Run, no."

"You're sure of that?"

"I have to be. I can't lock her in the trunk of my car until the cops finish the paperwork." He chuckled and pressed the already lit down button. "Don't worry. It won't take much for her to realize she has no choice except to spill her guts."

The elevator arrived. Easy guided her inside and turned,

never releasing his hold of her shoulders. Despite her frazzled, anger over Noreen, Catherine liked the safe feeling—the comfortable familiarity—of his arm.

"I believe her when she says she didn't know he meant murder."

"I don't." Catherine concentrated on recalling every word the woman had spoken. And, the way she'd spoken. "I think she knew what he intended to do the minute he asked her to impersonate his wife."

He cocked his head and frowned. "Why do you say that?"

"Call it intuition."

The car stopped, the doors slid open. Jeffrey Livman stared directly into her eyes.

The three of them stood for so long, the doors began to slide closed. Jeffrey shot out a hand and blocked the door. "Well, darling, fancy meeting you here." He glanced at the directory of businesses hanging on the wall next to the elevators.

His smile chilled Catherine's blood. Had she actually kissed him? Imagined she could love him? Wanted to bear his children? Looking at him now, she could not conceive of ever missing the emptiness in his eyes.

Easy urged her to move, but he never loosened his hold on her shoulders. On wooden legs, with her heart pounding so fiercely it battered her chest, she walked out of the elevator. She knew if Jeffrey touched her, she'd scream.

He shook a finger in the air. "And you, sir, you're the private eye. I've heard you guys move fast, but this must be a record. Catherine, do you think you can tear yourself away from lover boy long enough to have a little chat with me?"

"No."

Jeffrey's smile remained, but his eyes narrowed. A vein pulsed in his forehead. "I'm not finished with you, Catherine."

"Stay away from her, Livman." Easy placed himself between Jeffrey and Catherine.

"She's my fiancée, Martel. I'll thank you to take your hands off her."

The lobby doors opened and a knot of people in business attire walked inside. Catherine murmured, "Let's go." Jeffrey frightened her, but at the moment, Easy made her nervous. Cords stood out on his neck. Jeffrey would love nothing more than for Easy to take a swing at him. She nudged Easy's hip, hard.

To her relief, he headed for the door.

"Catherine St. Clair!" Jeffrey yelled. "It's bad enough you have to sleep around with every guy you pick up off the street, but at least you could give me the ring back!"

Catherine gasped. Heads swiveled in her direction. Her face burned. She stumbled and would have fallen, but for Easy's strong arm. He hustled her out the door and onto the street.

She looked back, her horror rising. "He knows we talked to Noreen."

"Relax, that's a big building. Besides, I doubt even Livman can convince Noreen to go to prison while he gets off clean."

EASY PARKED HIS CAR in Catherine's driveway. Still shaken by the encounter with Jeffrey, she licked her lips and played her fingers over the door handle.

"Are you all right?" he asked.

"I don't know if I'll ever be all right again. Did you see his face? He's going to get me."

"Relax. By Monday, it'll all be over. He'll be arrested, charged and locked away."

She graced him with a baleful look. "And what do I do in the meantime?"

He gave it a moment of thought. "The Sky Sox are playing Saturday. Want to go?"

One more second of his sexy smile and sparkling eyes, and she'd agree to ride a soapbox racer to the moon with him. The scent of him filling the car interior tormented her soul. "I hate baseball, Easy. That much hasn't changed."

"You still love popcorn, don't you? My treat, all the popcorn you can eat. I'll throw in a hat, too. An official Sky Sox baseball cap. What do you say?"

A strange dilemma, she mused. Hang around the house and worry about Jeffrey, or run around with Easy and worry about him. She opened the car door. Heat slapped her face. A storm was building, making the air feel heavy. "I have stuff to do."

"What stuff? What's so important?"

She explained about Doc Halladay wanting to do a piece for his show about her. She swept out an arm, indicating the property. "I have to clean the house from top to bottom. There's painting. The deck is a mess, and I have to do something about the driveway." With so much physical labor to occupy her, she could keep her mind off Jeffrey— and keep her traitorous body away from Easy.

"I'll paint your deck."

"That's all right. I'll hire someone. I know you have a lot to do, too."

"You can hire me."

She laughed.

"I'm serious. You wouldn't believe how much the payments are on my motorcycle. I can use all the cash I can scrape together."

She knew darned well his offer had nothing to do with earning money. "Stop pressuring me. I'm not ready for a relationship." Her cheeks began to warm. Making love with him had been heaven and hell rolled into one. "I appreciate all you've done for me, but it's over."

His sunniness cooled and his gaze went distant. "You don't mean that."

"Give me a break." She bit back a complaint about how

easily she'd fallen into Easy's bed, and in the process turned upside down everything she thought she knew about herself. "I don't even know how I feel right now."

"Yeah, sure."

His hurt burned through her heart, aching like an open wound. "We have a deal." She hated the uncertainty in her own voice. "I cooperate, you leave me alone."

He swung about, his expression raw with emotion. "Come on, you know I didn't mean it. Neither did you. We're meant to be together."

The truth cut her to the quick. She'd probably go to her grave loving him and only him. As a boy he'd ripped apart her life; as a man he was doing it again. Yet, he pleaded with her as if shredding her life were the sign of ultimate affection. Her heart yearned toward him; her body ached for his touch; only her mind rebelled.

"That's why you blabbed to your sister?" She regretted the accusation as soon as it emerged, but refused to stop. "You had to go and tell her about Elizabeth. She thinks I'm hard-hearted and you're the poor victim whose little baby was stolen away."

He flinched as if she'd slapped him. Some of the color faded from his dusky cheeks. "Because you want to act like Elizabeth is a nasty little secret doesn't mean I have to."

Touché. She lashed him; he slashed her. As far as Catherine was concerned, they were even. Biting her lower lip to keep from crying, she lifted her chin. "Goodbye." She stepped out of the car.

"That's your answer to everything, isn't it, Tink? Batten down the hatches and run like hell."

THE THROATY GROWL of the Harley-Davidson rumbled through the trees.

On the deck, Catherine straightened too fast and a rush of dizziness made her vision swim. She dropped the scraper she'd been using and leaned heavily against the deck railing. She blinked rapidly and gulped air. "Ought to wear a hat," she muttered to the dogs. Storms had raged through the Front Range, but this morning the sky gleamed like turquoise enamel and the temperature soared into the nineties. Summer had officially arrived. She wiped clammy sweat off her face.

She watched Easy guide the motorcycle around potholes. He'd called her several times. The calls had been chatty, filling her in about what was going on with Noreen and the insurance company, but cautious, as if he feared she might hang up on him. She dreaded him finding out how much she looked forward to the sound of his voice. Or how much she missed him.

She picked up the scraper. Easy Martel was a man she needed to get over, not encourage. Still, her heart leaped with joy at the sight of him. Her body tingled with remembered passion.

He parked the bike and turned off the engine. The sudden silence made even the birds seem hushed. With greedy anticipation, she watched him pull off the helmet, freeing his hair. His smile held the power to melt her knees.

"Hey, Tink. What are you doing?"

"Cleaning the deck. What are you doing?" Beside her, the dogs rose and stretched, yawning to show all their teeth. They wagged their tails in a lazy greeting.

He hopped lithely onto the deck and caught both her hands. She dropped the scraper for the second time and it bounced, clattering on the wood. "I'm celebrating," he announced.

His happiness made her wary. Their last argument had been nasty, and neither had apologized yet. She refused to believe he'd merely forgotten. She certainly hadn't. "Celebrating what?"

"Toni Johnson finally called me."

"Who's he?"

"She. Assistant district attorney. She's opening an investigation."

Eager for details, Catherine nodded in encouragement.

"Romoco Insurance backtracked over what I dug up. John provided enough handwriting samples for Romoco to say, without a doubt, that Roberta's signature on the insurance papers is a forgery. Romoco's employees will testify that Roberta isn't the woman who applied for the insurance."

"Jeffrey will be arrested?"

"Eventually. Toni doesn't want him on fraud alone, she wants him for murder. We won, Tink. Livman is going down."

Catherine squeezed his fingers. "He's finally going to pay for what he did."

"It won't be easy, but it'll happen. That's why you need to go to the D.A.'s office on Monday."

"Why me?"

"Right now, the fraud case is airtight, but the homicide case is shaky. Motive isn't enough to prove murder and Toni isn't sure Noreen will give up Livman all the way to murder. Toni needs every scrap of evidence she can find. She's afraid if she arrests Livman on the fraud charge, he'll make bail and skip."

"He won't run. He thinks he can win."

"Toni won't take the chance. Livman has plenty of liquid assets. He can cash out and be gone within hours."

It finally struck her how very close she'd come to marrying a murderer. The queasy, light-headedness returned. Catherine had to sit down.

Easy dropped to one knee before her. "Are you okay? Your face went dead white."

She used her wrist to wipe clammy sweat off her brow. "I'm okay." She drew in several deep, calming breaths. She blinked moisture from her eyes and her vision cleared. "Jeffrey and I were always running in secluded areas. We did some rock climbing.'' She turned her gaze on her house. ''He could have pushed me down the stairs.''

He patted her knee. ''You're safe now.''

''What if he tries to shut me up? Or you?''

''Won't do him a bit of good. If he wanted to shut up witnesses, he should have shut his own mouth. He told different stories to the paramedics and to the police. Then he changed his story again to you and everyone else. We have some of his lies on tape.''

''What about Noreen? If she doesn't testify, is there a case?''

''She'll testify. She has no other option. We've got her cold.'' He threw back his head and laughed at the sky. ''And get this! If Romoco recovers their half a million, they'll pay a reward.''

''That's wonderful,'' she said unenthusiastically.

''Half of it is yours. You gave me the lead on Noreen.''

Shuddering in distaste, she hugged her elbows and grimaced. ''You're unbelievable!''

''I know. Let's go celebrate.''

''Poor taste, Easy. I can't celebrate the fact that he murdered his wife.''

He leaned an elbow on the railing. ''I always celebrate when the dirtbags get theirs.''

''Is life that black-and-white for you?''

He gave her question visible consideration. He frowned at a bird feeder. ''Yep,'' he finally said. ''It's definitely a no-brainer. The good guys win and the bad guys suffer retribution.'' He poked her shoulder with a finger. ''Don't tell me after all you've been through that you have feelings for the guy.''

An undertone of worry in his voice alerted her senses. ''Looking back I can see how he hustled me. He knew where I was vulnerable. And I'm angry.'' She clasped her hands. ''I'm embarrassed.''

''Why?''

"Because every time I get involved with a man, I mess up." She shoved out of the chair and retrieved the scraper. "You, Jeffrey. Maybe I'm too stupid for love."

He placed a hand on her shoulder. She twisted away. "Come on, Tink. It isn't your fault. He's an operator. He preys on women. He messed with your head, but it's over." He caught her shoulder again, and this time she let him gently turn her about. He touched a finger to her chin, lifting her face. His intense gaze touched her soul.

"This isn't about Livman. It's about me. How many apologies will it take until you know how sorry I am about Elizabeth?"

"I don't know." Her throat tightened.

"If there was anything I could do to make things better for you, I would."

She wanted to believe him. She wanted to love him…and that frightened her.

An approaching mail truck saved her from herself. She pulled away from Easy and watched the driver negotiate the driveway up to the house. The mail carrier brought an overnight package that Catherine had to sign for. She noted it was from her agent's New York office.

"Good news?" Easy asked after the mail truck trundled away.

Catherine opened the bulky package. She pulled out a copy of the Doc Halladay contract. She hefted it in her hand, amazed at how it was at least three times thicker than any other contract she'd ever received. A knot tightened in her belly. Fulfilling this contract would have an indelible effect on her career. Either she'd be a wild success or a total failure, with no in-between measures possible. "Ever seen paper worth a million bucks?"

Wide-eyed and openly impressed, Easy assured her he hadn't. She handed him a copy and pulled another from the envelope.

Easy whistled in appreciation as he leafed through the

contract. His thick eyebrows knit into a puzzled frown. "All this for some pictures?"

"For twenty books worth of pictures." She trailed her fingers over the bright white cover page marked with Tabor Publishing's logo. Now the deal was real.

Easy laughed as he handed her back the contract. "Congratulations, Tink. It's cool knowing somebody famous."

"I'm not famous." Feeling suddenly shy, she examined her grimy fingernails. A major sore spot in her life was that she had so few people to be happy about her successes. Grandma had been her biggest supporter, but Grandma was gone. Her parents were singularly unimpressed by her artistic endeavors. Her friends lived far away, with families and jobs to occupy them. Easy sounded genuinely pleased and happy for her. She remembered how in school he'd never been intimidated by her intellect or threatened by her academic successes. He was as self-contained and self-confident as a cat. He didn't have a selfish bone in his beautiful body.

"I've worked hard for this." She studied his reaction. "I'm going to paint my brains out."

"If anybody can do it, you can. I'm really proud of you." He puffed his chest and hooked his thumbs in his belt loops. "Your name on all those books. Wow, I don't know what to say."

The knot in her belly melted. He said everything perfectly, without even trying. "About the other day," she said, softly, hesitantly. "I'm sorry. I shouldn't have said what I did."

He waved off the apology. "Don't sweat it. I'm the one who should apologize. You want to be friends and nothing more, I can respect it. I don't have to like it, but I respect it." He extended his right hand in a gesture of peace. "Are we friends?"

For a long moment she stared at his hand. She lifted her gaze to his eyes, seeking any insincerity or hint of a trick.

He gazed back at her with the solemnity of a preacher. She shook his hand. "We're friends."

His smile rivaled sunshine. "Then how about a friendly lunch to celebrate? You'll love riding my bike. I guarantee it."

"I don't know...."

"Come on! I just broke the biggest case of my life and you're a millionaire. If that doesn't call for celebration, I don't know what does." He leaned in like a conspirator and waggled his eyebrows. "I brought an extra helmet, just in case."

She'd been scraping dirt and old paint off the deck all morning, and had made precious little progress. She hadn't been off the property for days. She was suddenly sick of the house. "I'm filthy."

"I don't mind waiting while you clean up."

Clean... She slid a look at the door. "The house is a mess."

He showed his empty hands. "No white-glove inspection. Promise."

Sighing, she invited him inside. When he took in the havoc she'd wrought while stripping down her studio, he lifted his eyebrows, but made no comment.

She showered and dressed in record time. Garbed in jeans, boots and a T-shirt, she skipped upstairs. Easy lounged on a chair, leafing through a magazine. He wore a funny little smile, one of pure orneriness.

On the way out the door, she glimpsed the dry-erase board she used for reminders. In the center of it, a bright red heart surrounded by lacy frills enclosed the declaration: *Easy + Catherine 4ever.* She opened her mouth to protest, then decided, what the heck, let him have his little joke.

A joke that made sitting behind him and wrapping her arms around his lean waist all the sweeter.

As he'd promised, she loved riding on the motorcycle. With the roar of the powerful engine, Easy swept her back to sweeter times. The speed and sensation of flying over the road exhilarated her. She outran her worries, leaving them far behind. The world looked fresh and bright; anything was possible.

Easy drove a meandering route, with no apparent destination. On open rural roads, he cranked up the speed. Catherine alternated between whooping in joy and yelling at him to slow down. When they reached the city limits, he drove as if the traffic laws were burned into his brain. His concern made her feel like a girl again.

Easy bought her lunch in a charming café in Old Colorado City. He reduced her to helpless giggles with stories about his army days. He rode her up and down the downtown streets, and she knew he remembered she loved the old Victorian-era houses. When they stopped at a light and a car full of teenagers practically drooled over the sight of the monster bike, she grinned. She felt with-it and too cool for words.

By the time they finally returned to her home, the sun had reached the mountaintops. Wispy clouds made a light show of orange, pink and purple. At the sight of her driveway she almost cried out in relief. She ached to her bones and her arms were chilled. The thought of a hot cup of tea and a soft, unmoving chair almost made her salivate.

Easy slowed the motorcycle. Catherine relaxed to follow him into the turn. He suddenly gunned the engine and sped down the road. Catherine clutched him.

"What are you doing?" she cried. It took several seconds to realize he couldn't hear her through the helmet face plate and over the engine noise. He turned left on the next street and her confusion grew complete.

He drove about a quarter mile then stopped. With one foot on the ground for balance, he idled the bike. He used his thumb to flip up his face plate.

Catherine struggled with her face plate. It stuck and she envisioned a deep-sea diver yelling soundlessly, trapped in the murky deep. Finally she managed to lift it. "What are you doing? You can't be lost."

Eyebrows lowered in a scowl, he stared in the direction of the main road. "Did you see the brown car?"

She saw only a layer of dust in their back trail. "What are you talking about?"

"There's a car parked across the road from your driveway. No-neck is sitting behind the wheel."

"Who?"

"The dirtbag who sucker punched me. He's watching your driveway."

Chapter Thirteen

Catherine crouched next to the fence post. She peered cautiously up the road to where the brown car was parked beneath a stand of cottonwood trees. Enough dusky light remained for her to make out the shape of the car, but she couldn't see the driver. "Are you positive it's the man who hit you?"

Easy fingered the healing scar in his eyebrow. "Positive."

"What is he doing?"

"Either waiting for you to come home, or waiting for you to leave." He turned a narrow-eyed gaze west to the mountains, where the sun had vanished behind the peaks. "Or maybe he's waiting for dark."

Catherine scrubbed at the creepy-crawly flesh on her arms. "Don't tell me that! Call the police. I know you have a cell phone."

He chucked her chin lightly with a knuckle. "You're so cute. What do I tell the cops? There's a bad guy parked on a public road?"

She harrumphed. "What do you suggest, smart guy? It's getting kind of cold." She shifted uncomfortably. "A bathroom would be nice, too."

He straightened and extended a hand for her. "Let's go talk to him."

She clamped her arms over her chest and pressed her back to the fence post. "Not on your life! What if he has a gun? What if he hits you again? Or me? No!"

"He won't hurt you. I promise."

"I promise," she mocked. "You're insane and I'm crazy for having anything to do with you."

"I know you want to know what he's up to."

Even in the gloomy light, his eyes sparkled, radiating self-confidence and pure devilment. The awful part was, she did want to know what Jeffrey and his minions were up to. He'd humiliated her the other day downtown by yelling insults in public. He was a coward, as well, sending bully boys to do his dirty work. She pushed away from the fence post. "All right. What are we doing?"

"I've got a plan."

A plan—Catherine remembered his plans. During the homecoming game, he'd talked the cheerleaders into wearing glow-in-the-dark bloomers. At halftime, he arranged for a friend to cut the football field lights, treating the spectators to a show of bobbing, glowing butts. Another time, he'd created an official-looking memo with the president of the school board's signature forged on the bottom. It declared caffeine a dangerous drug which would no longer be allowed on school grounds—which meant getting rid of the coffeemaker in the teachers' lounge. The teachers had almost gone on strike.

"Your plans are dangerous."

"Yeah, but they're fun." He stared thoughtfully at the brown car, now nearly invisible in the shadows. "Walk up to the car. Go around the front, and keep the driver's door between you. Talk to him."

"That's it? That's the plan? What do I say?"

"Ask him why he's so ugly." He shrugged. "Just catch his attention and keep it. See if you can get him out of the car, but behind the door. If he makes a move toward you, run like hell."

Before she had time to reconsider, Catherine marched down the road. "Run like hell," she muttered. "Good plan, Easy. Terrific." Despite her misgivings, curiosity and anger kept her walking.

Several cars passed. Their bright lights illuminated the interior of the parked car. Catherine finally understood what Easy meant by calling the thug No-neck. Even seated inside the car, he looked as bulky as a gorilla. The temperature had cooled dramatically with the setting of the sun, but sweat trickled down the nape of her neck and between her breasts. Her leg muscles ached to run. Across the road from the car, she paused, sizing up her escape routes. A barbed wire fence enclosed the land next to the car. Her best bet would be to dart back across the road and into the forest. If she didn't kill herself by running into a tree, she could make her way to the house. She shoved a hand in her pocket and made sure her keys were accessible.

Another car approached. While waiting for it to pass, she noticed No-neck noticing her. His bullet-shaped head turned, following her progress. She sauntered across the road, attempting a nonchalance she didn't feel. Moving around the front of the car, she stopped before the side mirror. No-neck had the window down.

"Uh...hello," she said. "What are you doing?"

He leaned an arm on the window well. What an arm, she thought in amazement. It had to be as thick as her leg. She swallowed hard. Talk to him, she thought in dumb dismay. Her ability to make coherent speech fled.

He had beady eyes, which appeared even smaller because his muscle-bound jaw flared into cartoonish proportions. Stupid eyes, she surmised. He stared at her as if she had horns. His expression almost made her laugh.

A faint crunch of gravel startled her. She remembered in time to not jump. She forced a broad smile. "Why are you watching my driveway? I'm calling the police."

He started the engine. The headlights flared.

Easy suddenly loomed out of the darkness behind the car. He jerked open the driver's door. "Hey, No-neck, the lady asked you a question!"

The huge man roared in fury and burst from the car with the speed of a striking snake. Too surprised to scream, Catherine froze with her mouth hanging open. *Run,* her rational brain said, but her feet remained rooted as she stared in awe at the sheer amount of man flooding from the car.

Easy punched him. The blow sounded like a hammer hitting a sack of cement. In the wan light from the car interior, the big man stood stock-still. Catherine pressed her hands to her mouth. She was about to witness Easy's murder by pummeling, and there wasn't a thing in the world she could do about it. Easy drew back for another punch. No-neck crumpled in almost graceful slow motion to the ground.

Catherine gingerly grasped the top of the door and peered over it. The giant stretched out on the gravel. Easy shook his right hand, then rubbed the knuckles.

Her gorge rose. "You killed him."

"I only hit him once."

"See if he's breathing."

Easy backed a step, pulling a face. "You see if he's breathing."

"Easy! Maybe he had a heart attack."

He drew his hand closer to his face, peering intently as he formed a fist. "I have been working the bag at the gym. Must have paid off."

She clamped her hands on her hips. "Earl Zebulon Martel! If you killed this man, I'll never forgive you. Or myself!"

"He hit me first." Easy reached out with the toe of his boot and lightly touched the huge man's shoulder. "He's breathing."

Frightened by the idea of No-neck playing possum,

Catherine swallowed several times, working up her nerve. Finally she sidled as close to him as she dared and reached out with her fingertips. She touched his neck. It was as solid as an oak block. Below his ear, she found a pulse, steady and strong.

She scrambled out of possible reach. "Okay, he's alive. Now what? Should we call an ambulance?"

Easy grabbed her arm and jerked her to the side. He dropped to a crouch behind the car, pulling her with him. She opened her mouth to protest, but he clamped a hand over her mouth. "Somebody's coming," he whispered in her ear. He scooted toward the trees, away from the circle of light coming from the car.

Catherine heard male voices and footfalls on the road. She scrambled after Easy, trying to be quiet as she wriggled her way into concealment. The two of them crept behind the thick trunk of a cottonwood, and scooched down into a hollow formed by the roots. Tall grass and brush offered some cover, but not much.

Catherine recognized Jeffrey's voice. Her heart nearly stopped.

Jeffrey and a taller man walked across the road. Jeffrey broke into a run, calling, "T.J.! What—?"

Both men skidded to a stop, looking down at their fallen companion. Catherine recognized the tall man. He did odd jobs for Jeffrey, cleaning up and doing repairs on rental properties. Jeffrey had never introduced her to him, but she had waited in the car a few times while Jeffrey and the handyman discussed business.

Easy rested a steadying hand on her back. The huge man finally began to rouse. A string of cars passed by. Easy and Catherine pressed closer to the tree trunk, trying to make themselves small. Catherine noticed Jeffrey ducking away from the car lights as well. She didn't want to think about what he'd been doing at her house.

Jeffrey and the handyman helped the groggy T.J. into

the car's back seat. The handyman slid behind the wheel. Jeffrey hurried around to the passenger side. They drove off, spewing gravel and skidding when the wheels touched blacktop.

Catherine stood to watch the receding taillights. "What was he doing in my house, Easy? Oh, the dogs!" She pushed her way through the brush and ran across the road. Heedless of ruts and potholes, she raced up the driveway. The security light next to the garage lit the front of the house.

She stopped at the base of the porch. "Oscar? Bent?" She tried to whistle, but her dry mouth foiled the attempt.

Easy ran up behind her. "Damn, Tink, you really did get in shape." He huffed a few hard breaths, then asked for her keys.

"My dogs. Do you think he hurt my dogs?"

"I'll check. Stay here." Keys in hand, he jumped up on the deck and went to the front door. "It's locked," he called. He fumbled a moment with the key, then opened the door.

Oscar and Bent streaked past him. Catherine could have wept to find them safe and sound. She opened her arms to the greyhounds and let them fawn and lick her face. She hugged them tightly and kissed them in return. Easy turned on lights inside the house.

"How am I supposed to tell if he did anything?"

Feeling a bit testy over his reference to her trashed house, she said, "If the doors were locked, he didn't get in. He must have been waiting for me to come home."

She glumly eyed the night sky and wondered how much harassment she'd be able to take from Jeffrey. She prayed the district attorney arrested him soon.

"Tink?"

"What?"

"He got inside." He beckoned with his fingertips. His grim expression frightened her.

Reluctantly, she edged her way back inside the house. She followed his pointing finger. On the dry-erase board, *Easy + Catherine 4ever* had been slashed through by two, angry red lines.

"LUCKY FOR YOU the hardware store stays open late on Saturday," Easy said. He tightened a screw on the new dead bolt he installed on the door leading to the deck.

"If you say one more word," Catherine warned, "about me not changing the locks before, I will drill a hole in your head." To give meat to her threat, she depressed the trigger on the electric drill. The motor whirred. "You're just mad because I won't call the cops." She glanced at the clock. After midnight, she noted with an inner groan.

"That and you insist on putting yourself in danger. He's not playing games with you, Tink." He shook the screwdriver at her. "He means business."

"Other than him crossing out your little note, there's no sign he was in the house. What there is evidence of is you nearly killing No-neck. If I call the police about Jeffrey, he'll call about you. And you're the one who'll get in trouble."

He smiled sweetly at her and batted his lashes. "I have a witness who says that dirtbag swung first."

"I can't lie to the police." She began coiling an extension cord. "We checked this house from top to bottom. He didn't steal anything, he didn't vandalize anything. He didn't hurt the dogs." Venting anger on Easy was much, much better than brooding over what exactly Jeffrey had been doing in her house.

"Let me think. If I wanted to get even with an ex-fiancée, what kind of mischief could I pull?" He tapped his chin with the screwdriver and rolled his eyes heavenward. "Hmm, I could go through her files and pull utility-company account numbers so I can turn off her water and electricity. Lift her credit card numbers and run up big bills. Go through her address book and find out all the names and numbers of her friends so I can send them nasty notes. I could—''

''Shut up!'' She scrubbed at her upper arms.

''I've seen it done, Tink. With your name, birth date and social security number, he can ruin your credit and even get you in trouble with the law. You can find yourself flooded with pornography or have your mail forwarded to another address. You might end up as the pen pal for half the prison population in Canon City.''

Unable to bear it, she rushed into the back room she used for an office. She jerked open the top drawer of a file cabinet. Being a self-employed artist, her taxes were a nightmare. She saved every receipt and billing statement. The file drawers were crammed full of folders, stuffed to overflowing with bits of paper.

She slammed the drawer shut. Easy leaned a shoulder against the doorjamb. His somber expression upset her as much as his words. ''What if he did get all my account numbers? What do I do?''

''We can take some preventive measures. It'll be a pain in the butt, but it's better than doing nothing. Cancel the credit cards. Contact your bank. Utilities. Credit bureaus. Change your telephone number.''

Catherine sagged against the wall and covered her eyes with a hand. ''I don't have time for this. My first deadline for the Science Brain books is in four months. I have a ton of research to do. Doc Halladay's film crew will be here in less than a month.'' Emotion rose, choking her throat. Appalled by her weakness, she pushed away from the wall.

''The first thing you need is sleep,'' Easy said, his voice turned gentle. ''You don't look so good.''

''I don't feel so good.'' At the moment she felt as if a giant vacuum cleaner had sucked all the strength from her bones. She wanted nothing more than to crawl into bed, pull the covers over her head and shut out the world.

"Got an extra pillow? I'll sack out on your sofa."

She opened her mouth to tell him, in no uncertain terms, that there was no way, no how, he was spending the night at her house. Gratefulness rose instead. She fetched a pillow and a blanket. She made up the camelback sofa in the parlor, knowing it was too small for him, and the cushion was hard, but his only other choice was the dog's sofa.

He caught her arm before she could turn away. "Chances are," he said, "when he's arrested, he'll have so many legal problems he won't have time to harass you."

"He's going to blame me for those legal problems."

"There isn't much he can do to you from prison." His hold on her arm transformed into a caress that made its lazy way over her shoulder to her neck. He placed a hand flat against her cheek. "I'll take care of you." His promise caressed her, too, enveloping her in warmth.

She knew he shouldn't kiss her, but could not resist. She lifted her face to his, her eyelids drifted closed. In his arms, protected by his embrace, she felt whole and strong again. He kissed her sweetly, the pressure of his lips tender. She sensed his tenuous control, knowing he wanted more.

So did she.

She turned her face away. He pressed hot kisses over her cheek and brow. She clutched his biceps, wanting to cling to him, but needing to drive him away.

"I'll be careful, Tink," he said. "We don't have to do anything. I just want to hold you. Kiss you."

Mustering every ounce of strength she possessed, she stepped out of his arms. She hugged herself, squeezing her own arms painfully. "No."

"I'll keep my pants on."

She loosed a dry, weary laugh. "As if I can resist you? Get real."

He offered a hand, palm up. "If you want me, and I want you, then what's stopping you? We're not kids anymore. We're grown-ups, we can do what we want. We belong together."

Torture couldn't have made her refute his words. They did belong together. Why or how, she hadn't a clue, but in her heart, she knew he was the only man she'd ever love. She cleared her aching throat. "I made a promise."

"To whom?" The struggle to control his anger, or frustration, showed clearly on his expressive face.

"To myself...to Elizabeth. I promised I will never, under any circumstances play Russian roulette with a child's life again. I will not risk having another baby unless I am in a solid, committed, stable marriage. Two parents, loving home and the means and time to be a good mother. Nothing less. I don't know what happened to me before, but I won't do it again."

"I'm committed to you."

She shook her head hard. "You're horny. There's a difference."

"You're horny, too."

"So?" She backed away. "Like you said, we're grown-ups. We can control ourselves." One more second of his beautiful eyes boring into hers, and she'd lose what little control she had. She spun about and fled.

CATHERINE SAT on the edge of the tub. Bent over, with her elbows on her knees, she waited for the nausea to pass. She reminded herself that she'd always had a queasy stomach. Part of her weight problem as a child had been because she overate to soothe chronic stomach aches. Whenever she was upset or stressed, she felt it first in her stomach. Jeffrey breaking into her house was enough to upset anybody. Besides, she rationalized, she hadn't eaten since lunch yesterday.

Liar, said a quiet little voice in her mind. *You're late.*

She walked out of the bathroom and straight to the rain forest-animals calendar hanging on the wall next to the bedroom door. She stared at the numbered squares, hoping a clue would occur to her. Hard as she tried, she could not recall the date of her last menstrual period. She padded back to the bathroom and peered closely at her reflection in the mirror. Every month, like a little cuckoo bird announcing the hormonal shift, a pimple popped up in the middle of her chin. She searched her chin carefully. She poked and prodded with a fingertip for any sign of an impending skin eruption.

Except for bruised-looking smudges under her eyes, her complexion had never looked better.

"I am not pregnant," she told her reflection. "It's stress. I haven't been eating right."

Tapping on her bedroom door made her jump. She caught the sink with both hands and moved only her eyes. The doorknob rattled. She'd locked the door last night.

"Tink?" Easy called softly. "Are you awake?"

She pressed a hand to her flat belly. "Just a minute!" She grabbed her robe off the back of the bathroom door and shoved her arms into the sleeves.

"Your dogs want out."

She tied the terry-cloth robe shut. She opened the door. Tousle-haired and sleepy-eyed, Easy stood bare-footed before her door. Her joints did a slow melt. Even needing a shave, he was beautiful.

"Are you okay?" He cocked his head and peered at her with suspicion.

"I didn't sleep well." She wasn't that late, she assured herself. No more than a week at most. Her periods glitched on occasion. She only noticed because she felt guilty about having sex.

"Is it okay to let the dogs out?"

"I'll do it." Head down, she eased around him, taking care not to touch him.

"Tink?"

His worried note drove home how well he did know her. She clutched her throat. He touched her back.

"What's the matter?"

The past flashed before her eyes. All the fear, the shame, and the heartache felt as real now as it had been twelve years ago. The agony of her empty arms and empty soul after she signed the papers and knew she'd never see Elizabeth again. Weeping every night, grieving for her baby, missing Easy…hating herself. Never again. She turned around slowly. The past became the present and the future. She heard herself telling Easy she was pregnant. He'd be noble, insisting on marrying her. How well did they know each other, really? The foundation of their relationship had been laid when they were little more than children. So much had changed since then. She needed more than a shotgun marriage, more than a father for her child—she needed love, true commitment and stability. She needed to know her husband married her because he wanted to, not because of guilt.

She forced a smile. "I'm so hungry I'm about to die. I can't go that long without eating." She rubbed her now-grumbling belly. "We skipped dinner."

The tension eased from his brow. "I could do with some bacon and eggs."

"How about an omelette and oatmeal?"

"Omelette, yes, oatmeal, not on your life."

"It's good for your heart."

He tweaked a strand of her hair. "You're good for my heart." He kept up the teasing banter while they went upstairs. His good mood relaxed her.

That the nausea didn't return while she tended the dogs and prepared breakfast, relaxed her even more. Perhaps she wasn't late after all. Between the spider book deadline, Doc Halladay negotiations, Jeffrey and Easy, she'd been a mental space case. She pushed thoughts of pregnancy out of her mind—for now.

Over breakfast, Catherine asked, if they successfully prosecuted Jeffrey for fraud, would that prove he'd pushed Roberta off the rocks? Easy's optimism flagged.

"I don't know," he said. "A good defense attorney will argue that Roberta was part of the fraud. She knew she couldn't get a policy because of her asthma. That she died was merely a tragic coincidence."

"What about Jeffrey's lies? His conflicting stories? If he isn't guilty, why all the subterfuge?"

"Could be a character issue. He's a compulsive liar. Lots of people will testify Livman lies for the sake of lying."

"We know he did it."

"Knowing it and proving it to a jury are two different things." He drank coffee. "Toni is a good prosecutor. If she thinks she can win, then we have to trust her. In any case, he's for sure going to jail on the fraud charge, and he'll have to reimburse Romoco."

She looked around the studio, seeking clues as to why Jeffrey had broken into her home. The sight of shiny new locks on the doors made her angry. He'd coldly, in a calculating manner, kept a set of keys to her home. Which could only mean that months ago, he'd targeted her. Jeffrey had no right to disrupt her life and attempt to victimize her. "I wish he'd confessed to me."

"So do I." He patted her hand. "But hey, you gave it your best shot."

She began clearing the table. She carried dirty dishes to the kitchen sink. "At least I have so much to do, I don't have time to worry about him. I'm sure you have plenty to do, as well."

"Are you throwing me out?" He put away honey, milk and jelly.

"I appreciate you keeping an eye on me last night. I appreciate you putting new locks on the doors."

He cocked an eyebrow. "But you're throwing me out."

"I don't need a bodyguard."

He huffed a martyred-sounding sigh. "If Livman turns up, you won't—"

"Do anything stupid," she finished for him. "I won't talk to him or let him in the house. I'll call the police. You're the one who needs to be careful. I bet No-neck is really mad at you."

He chuckled wickedly, his eyes gleaming. He ground a fist against his palm. "The bigger they are…"

"You got in a lucky shot. I doubt if he'll let you get lucky again." She shooed him with both hands. "Now go on. I have a million things to do."

"All right, all right, I'm going." He took a step, then paused. "I'm supposed to go to my folks' house tonight for dinner. Come with me. They'd love to see you again."

It felt as though a great fist squeezed her heart. Over the years, she'd sometimes found herself missing Mr. and Mrs. Martel almost as much as she missed Easy. The Martels had always represented the ideal family to her, a close-knit, warmhearted group who stuck together through thick and thin.

"Call me later. If I've made enough progress, I'll go."

"Great." He took another step, again paused, then swooped in a graceful turn and caught her around the waist with one powerful arm.

Too surprised to protest, she stared wide-eyed at his endearing face. He kissed her, quick and hard and deep. When he released her, she staggered in a daze, her mouth burning and her blood pulsing like lava through her veins. He tossed her a wink and sauntered out of her house.

Later that day, Easy called to ask her about dinner with

his parents. Time alone had given her the chance to worry about being pregnant. She couldn't face Easy or his parents. He tried to wheedle her into changing her mind, but she stood her ground. He sounded disappointed, but promised to call her tomorrow with news about Jeffrey.

The next day she refused to think about Easy, except to follow his advice. She contacted the utility companies and told them she had a problem with a stalker. Under no circumstances were her accounts to be altered unless she made the request in person. She canceled her credit cards and contacted credit bureaus. Dealing with endless voice mail and bureaucrats exhausted her. It had never occurred to her before how very vulnerable a person was when almost every transaction could be completed on the telephone. All any crook needed was a name, birth date and social security number.

Mail delivery drove that point home in spades. Her mailbox was full of offers from credit card companies, mortgage companies, book clubs and catalogs. Jeffrey could amuse himself with filling out applications and ordering merchandise by phone—all in her name.

She wrote a note reminding herself to ask Easy what else she could do to protect herself, then tackled the house cleaning. She decided the best way to present her studio would be to strip it down to bare essentials. She'd turn the parlor into a gallery to display her best work. She spent most of the day carrying boxes of supplies to the garage.

Easy called her late in the afternoon. At the sound of his voice, she beamed in relief. Jeffrey must be in custody.

"Are your doors locked?" he asked.

"What's the matter? What's going on?"

"Noreen Dawson disappeared. No one can find her anyplace."

Chapter Fourteen

Easy watched Catherine pace. She hugged her elbows and muttered to herself. Her complexion looked sallow under her suntan. Even her hair seemed to have lost some of its shine. He felt rather sick himself.

Catherine whirled on him. "They have to arrest him! Jeffrey kidnapped Noreen. Maybe he's killed her. Why won't the police do anything?"

"What do you expect them to do? Pick him up off a street corner and beat him with rubber hoses until he confesses? Noreen is gone, but it doesn't mean Livman took her. None of her neighbors heard anything. Nobody called the cops. Her car is missing. For all we know, she got scared and took off on her own."

"You said she wouldn't run! Did the police talk to Jeffrey?"

Easy rubbed his eyelids with the pads of his fingers. He'd blown this case. In hindsight, he saw he was not only the wrong man for the job, but the worst man. He'd let his emotions rule his actions and he'd consistently underestimated Livman. Because of him, Livman knew Catherine had helped John Tupper. Because he couldn't bear staying away from Catherine, he'd probably tipped off Livman about Noreen's involvement.

"Well? Did they?" Catherine stalked to the door and

pulled back the curtain over the window. She glared at the darkness beyond the house.

"He declined to talk to them."

"What is that supposed to mean? He can't decline."

"He has rights, Tink. The police can ask questions, but he doesn't have to answer. So he didn't. The man knows the law."

"So why don't they arrest him? They know he committed fraud."

He knew her anger had less to do with him than with her own fear. If Livman could make Noreen disappear, he could do the same thing to Catherine. "Without Noreen, the insurance fraud case falls apart. Livman can argue that Noreen didn't impersonate Roberta. He'll say Romoco is pursuing a vendetta against him in order to recoup the claim. The only witnesses are Romoco employees, who stand to gain if the company wins. Without the fraud to prove premeditation, there is no murder case."

"They have to find Noreen."

"She's over twenty-one, and there's no sign of foul play. The best the cops can do is treat her as a missing person."

Her eyes reddened. Tears glimmered on her lower lids. Unable to bear her pain any longer, Easy went to her. For a moment she resisted his embrace, but then sagged in his arms and pressed her head against his shoulder. He stroked her soft hair and gently kissed her forehead.

The telephone rang. Catherine stiffened in his arms and pressed her cheek hard against his shoulder.

"Answer," Easy said.

"What if it's him."

"I want it to be him. Answer the phone."

Dry-eyed, but paler than before, Catherine reached for the telephone. "Hello?" Her eyes widened. "Jeffrey."

Catherine's heart thumped painfully against her chest

wall. Bile rose in her throat, filling her mouth with the taste of pennies.

"You sound surprised to hear from me, darling. What's the matter?"

Easy hurried to the answering machine. His facial contortions and wild hand gestures told her to keep talking. He studied the answering machine, hesitated with his hand over the bank of buttons, then finally pushed the memo button. A loud beep announced the action. The recording indicator began to flash.

"What's that noise?" Jeffrey asked.

"What noise?" Catherine asked. "I didn't hear anything."

"Are you taping this call?"

"No, I'm hanging up on this call. Goodbye—"

"Don't you dare hang up on me. We have matters to discuss."

Easy grabbed an envelope and scribbled on the back. He showed her the message: *Ask him why he broke into your house.*

Flustered, wishing she'd had time to prepare for this, she decided blunt truthfulness was her only option. "Okay, let's discuss why you broke into my house. You kept a set of house keys."

"Whatever are you talking about, darling? I never go where I'm not invited."

"Liar! I know you broke in here. I saw you. I saw your friends, too."

"You creative types, such imagination. The matter I wish to discuss is the engagement ring. I'd like it returned, please."

Easy wrote again: *Is he threatening you?*

Catherine made a negative gesture. "I don't have the ring. I gave it to John Tupper. It belongs to him, not you."

"The ring belongs to me. If you don't return it, I will

have no choice except to file a lawsuit. Let's not get ugly, darling. Not after all we've been through.''

She gasped in indignation. ''You go ahead and try!'' She snatched the pencil from Easy's hand and wrote, *now he's threatening!*

''Before it gets out of hand, let's get together and talk. Your place?''

''If you come anywhere near my house, I will call the police.''

Jeffrey laughed, the notes flat, lacking emotion. Yet, she sensed, he was enjoying himself immensely. She struggled for control, to calm her pulse and even the tones of her voice.

''Just what do you think the police will do?'' he asked. ''Until you return the ring, we're engaged. I have every right to visit you whenever I wish.''

The oily threat behind the words made her flesh crawl. She watched Easy's increasingly frantic efforts to get her to tell him what Jeffrey was saying. ''I'll tell you what, Jeffrey,'' she said. ''You tell me what you did with Noreen, and I'll give you the ring.''

Easy's eyes widened and his mouth dropped open. *No!* he mouthed emphatically.

''I know you kidnapped her to keep her from testifying against you. Did you murder her?''

A long pause made her wonder if he'd hung up on her. Holding her breath, she waited for the effects of her taunts.

''I have no idea what you're talking about, darling. Noreen who?''

''Noreen Dawson. Did you kill her to shut her up?''

Easy threw his hands in the air and rolled his eyes as if beseeching the gods to save him from her foolishness. Catherine heard a slight catch, a subtle difference in Jeffrey's breathing. She prayed he confessed before the minicassette in the answering machine ran out.

''Oh, yes, that Noreen,'' he said. ''Charming lady. But

I fear I haven't seen her in ages. Such a funny woman. Always getting herself into little pickles. Forget Noreen. I'm talking about you and me. When can I see you, darling? Tonight?''

"You come anywhere near me and I'll—I'll—"

"You'll what, darling? Are you making threats?" He tsked. "It isn't nice to make threats to the man who can have such a powerful influence over your career."

Dread crawled through her like a cold, primeval beast. She held the telephone so tightly, her hand began to ache.

"Your new boyfriend is bad for your career as well. Such a small world, isn't it? Your high school sweetheart is now a private eye working for my former brother-in-law. What do you guess the odds are about such a coincidence occurring? A *million* to one?''

She spun about, her gaze finding the package containing the signed contracts, ready for mailing back to New York. "What are you talking—"

"I sense this is an inconvenient time. I'll get back to you." A click, and the connection severed.

She pulled the phone away from her ear and glared at the mouthpiece. "I hate him!" Dry laughter husked from her throat. "He's acting like the aggrieved party."

Easy replayed the conversation on the answering machine. Catherine despaired over how she squeaked and stammered as if she bordered on a nervous breakdown, while Jeffrey came across as perfectly calm and in control. He sounded like an ex-fiancé who wanted the engagement ring returned, and expected his former girlfriend to be reasonable about it.

"Did you hear that?" She rushed to the contract package and snatched it off the table. "He saw this. He's going to do something horrible." She returned to the door and her unhappy perusal of the night. "Is it too late to call the police about him breaking in? He all but confessed."

Easy looked around the studio where Catherine had

made remarkable progress in cleaning and organizing. She had scrubbed clean the dry-erase board. "Even if the cops find Livman's fingerprints, it proves nothing. He had legitimate reasons to be in this house before."

"He still has my keys," she said. "That proves—"

"Nothing," he interrupted. "It's your word against his that you didn't give him a set of keys. You can't stay here, babe." Faced with her hollow eyes and fearfulness, he felt helpless.

"Where am I supposed to go?"

"Your parents?"

"So I can listen to my father's lectures about my deplorable taste in men and how I'm too stupid to live on my own? Besides, Mother will never allow the dogs in her house. Or even in the yard. You know how she is."

Easy meant to rebut that her safety took precedence over her discomfort with her parents, but he remembered too well what her home had been like. The St. Clairs could make the pope wish he'd never been born. "You can stay at my place then. The dogs, too."

"I can't!" She swept her arms wide, indicating the studio. "I don't have time to hide out from Jeffrey. I have to get this place in shape. I have a deadline. Besides, who's to say your apartment is any safer than this house? Jeffrey knows all about you. He knows about us!" She sagged with her forehead against the door.

"Be reasonable."

"I am reasonable!" She clenched her fists and let her head fall back. Her entire body went rigid in a silent scream. "He's going to tell Doc Halladay about Elizabeth. Everyone will know what I did. They'll know I have low morals—"

"Stop it!"

Startled, she hugged her elbows and stared at him.

"So what if Livman tells the publisher about Elizabeth?

If anything, giving up the baby shows you have courage and character.''

She peered suspiciously at him.

''It's true,'' he said, and realized he meant it with all his heart. ''What you did was incredibly brave. You could have taken the easy way out and had an abortion. You could have kept her and ruined her chances for a stable family. Instead, you made a sacrifice. You put her needs above your own. There's nothing immoral about what you did. You have nothing to be ashamed of.''

Some of the tension faded from her shoulders. Her hands relaxed. She cocked her head, her eyes gone soft. ''Do you mean that? Really?''

Without hesitation, he nodded. ''I still wish I could have been there for you. I wish you'd told me. But you did the right thing and I admire you for it. You saved our daughter's life.''

Pressing knuckles against her mouth, she turned away. Her back hitched.

''Doc Halladay loves kids. He's all about kids. He'll understand you did the right thing because you love kids, too.'' Rather than go to her, he shoved his hands in his pockets. ''You look worn-out. Get some sleep. The dogs and I will stand watch to make sure Livman doesn't try anything funny.''

JEFFREY DIDN'T TRY anything funny the next day. Catherine received several phone calls where the caller hung up when the answering machine activated. She guessed Jeffrey tried to call her. She attempted to call her agent, but Margaret had gone to Los Angeles and wouldn't return until Friday. She prayed she'd misinterpreted Jeffrey's threat and he wouldn't try to sabotage her work for Doc Halladay.

Easy hung around. He left once after arguing with her to accompany him to his home and office. She pointed out the shiny new locks on the doors, and promised if she even suspected Jeffrey was in the neighborhood, she'd call 911. While he was gone, she found herself pacing restlessly, unable to concentrate or settle on any task. Without Easy, the house felt empty, lonesome and incomplete. She brooded over what he'd said about Elizabeth. No matter how she examined his words, his tone of voice and his body language, she came to the same conclusion. He meant exactly what he'd said.

When he returned, he defiantly displayed a suitcase. He appeared ready to battle her to the death over his right to protect her in her home. When she graciously invited him to make himself at home, his surprise amused her.

In the days that followed, Catherine saw no sign of Jeffrey. She mailed the signed contracts. She worked on the house.

She worried about being pregnant. As fear of Jeffrey faded, her fear of another irresponsible pregnancy grew. She wanted to run into town and buy a home-pregnancy test, but Easy refused to leave her side. Over and over, she practiced in her head how to tell him. Each time the voice of reason told her to wait, see if her fears were true.

She painted the parlor. She and Easy had moved all the furniture to the family room downstairs. While she rolled white paint onto the wall, Easy wandered into the room. He carried the telephone.

He examined her work. "I told you that primer would cover the wallpaper. It's looking good."

She used the back of her hand to swipe tendrils of hair off her hot face. Even with all the windows open, the room was so humid she felt slightly ill. Sweat dampened her T-shirt and made her hands slimy. "Who were you talking to?"

"Toni Johnson. There's still no sign of Noreen. She's talked to Lou Palmer and T. J. Whitehead, though."

"Who are they?"

"The handyman and No-neck. They, of course, deny any involvement with Livman other than maintaining some rental properties." His eyes crinkled in good humor. "She asked No-neck about the knot on his jaw. Turns out he had some wisdom teeth removed the same day I decked him. No wonder he went down so fast."

"What about Jeffrey?"

"His attorney said Livman will grant no interviews, period."

She loaded the roller with paint. She rolled paint on the wall until nothing came off the roller. Noreen's anguished face flashed through her mind. She remembered Jeffrey's strange comment about the woman always getting herself into pickles. He'd sounded so flippant, so uncaring about Noreen, the woman who could send him to prison for a long, long time.

"Tink?" He touched her shoulder.

"Jeffrey doesn't have to kidnap Noreen, because he knows she'll never testify against him."

"Because she's dead."

She laid the roller on the pan. She paced to the window, and inhaled deeply of the fresh air. "She assured us over and over that she and Jeffrey weren't having an affair. She swears she didn't do it for money. What does that leave?"

He pulled at his chin, his expression thoughtful, but skeptical. "Getting herself in a pickle?"

"Exactly. Do you honestly think he'll allow her, or anyone, to hold anything over his head?"

"She could go to jail for her role in the fraud."

"Ha! He must know if Noreen squeals, Romoco will be far more interested in hanging him and getting their money back than in prosecuting her. It strikes me as really odd that she keeps doing business with him. I've seen how much she dislikes him. If she had any say in the matter, she wouldn't have anything to do with him. And if she has the power to hang him, why does he keep putting himself in a position to remind her? She's hiding something and it isn't insurance fraud.''

"I'm biting, Tink.''

She lifted her chin, invigorated by the chance to do something other than hide from Jeffrey Livman. "I bet he didn't have to go to her. She went to him and he's helping her run. Let's find her.''

"You'd make a great P.I., Tink.'' Smiling, he picked up one of her paint-splattered hands. "It's late. How about we finish up here, then first thing tomorrow, we'll start looking.''

Having finished painting the deck, Easy joined Catherine in the parlor-turned-gallery. She liked working with him. He was quick, efficient and cheerful. He sang along to the music playing on the radio and teased her about nonsense. Together they finished with the first coat of paint in less than an hour. Working with him, having had him in her house for several days, also made her see how good they were together. They balanced each other. She was quiet, he was noisy. She appreciated his often raucous good cheer; he liked her usually dry humor. He had an energizing effect on her; she suspected she soothed him.

While cleaning up, the telephone rang. "I should sign up for caller ID,'' Catherine said. "Isn't there a way to block certain numbers?''

"Yep,'' Easy replied.

The answering machine activated. After Catherine's short message, Margaret's excited voice boomed over the speaker. "You better be home, Catherine! The fan has been hit and you're directly in the path of—''

Catherine snatched up the telephone. "I'm here. What's going on, Margaret?''

"You tell me! Tabor Publishing and Doc Halladay are going ballistic. I don't know what kind of crap you're involved in, but I thought you had enough sense to keep it to yourself!''

Catherine had heard her agent angry before, but the anger had never been directed her way. Too flustered to reply, she huffed and picked at paint speckles on her arm while Margaret stormed about the deal falling through. When the agent finally paused to take a breath, Catherine found her voice.

"I don't know what you're talking about."

"Tabor and Doc Halladay both received faxes. Twenty-five-page-long faxes. They contain your entire sexual history, including the bits about illegitimate children and abortions, and the names of men who are suing you for infecting them with diseases. There are grotesque photographs of you with your current boyfriend. It's disgusting! How could you?"

Catherine nearly dropped the telephone. She grasped the cordless unit with both hands and staggered to a chair. "How could I do what, Margaret? I haven't done anything."

"It's all there in black and white. To sweeten the deal, the man who sent the fax claims he's contacted every tabloid in the country. They're panting to run stories about Doc Halladay's book illustrator!"

Blinking rapidly, certain this must be a nightmare, Catherine gazed into space. "Jeffrey did this."

If Margaret heard, she gave no indication. She ranted about Doc Halladay refusing to sign the contract and Tabor Publishing talking about filing a lawsuit and how all this might affect Margaret's reputation and her other clients.

During another pause, Catherine said, "It's all a lie, Margaret. Jeffrey Livman did this. He's trying to ruin me."

"Well, he's done it!"

"But it's all lies! Nobody is suing me. I haven't had any abortions. Nobody could possibly have any disgusting photographs of me. I don't do anything disgusting!"

"I've got another call. Goodbye." The agent abruptly severed the connection.

Easy gently tugged the telephone from her hand. "What happened?"

"Nothing much. Jeffrey just trashed my career, that's all." Dizzy, she pressed the heels of her hands against her eyelids. "He sent faxes to Doc Halladay and the publisher. He even included photographs of me doing disgusting things."

He jumped upright. "Where do you keep your photo albums?"

Realizing exactly what he meant, she pushed off the chair and hurried to the back bedroom she used as an office. She kept old yearbooks, albums and journals on a small shelf near the door. She glanced at the computer atop a desk. She didn't use the computer much, but she'd taken classes in computer graphics and art. She knew how easily photographs could be scanned into a graphics program and manipulated.

She leafed through an album. Though her research photographs were meticulously organized, her personal albums were filled randomly. What she did do, though, was fill every space. She discovered several pages where photographs were missing.

"What did he take?" Easy asked.

"I don't know exactly, but he obviously took enough." She glumly studied a page where two photographs had been removed. She envisioned a sickening composition with her face transposed onto a pornographic scene. Returning her attention to the bookshelf, she noticed two yearbooks were missing. The book from her junior year in Colorado, and her senior college yearbook from Arizona State. Jeffrey could have pulled the names of any number of young men she'd gone to school with. If Tabor investigated they'd find people who knew her, but denied involvement. Denials which would sound suspicious. She slammed the album shut. "I'm going to kill him."

"Livman lied and you can prove—"

"Prove what?" she interrupted. "If Doc Halladay chooses to believe me, then Jeffrey will sell the story to the tabloids. Do you think they care about the truth? It'll make their year to use me to bring down Doc Halladay's media empire."

"You have a contract."

"I'm the first to sign. Nobody else has." She shoved the album back on the shelf and scrambled to her feet.

He reached for her. She slapped his hands away. "This is all your fault! If you'd kept your big nose out of my business, Jeffrey never would have resorted to these tactics."

He gave a start. His eyes flashed black fire. "You'd have your million-dollar contract, but you'd be dead."

"You never proved Jeffrey killed Roberta. You never proved anything!" She shoved past him and all but ran into the studio. Now stripped down to its bare essentials, it looked professional and efficient. "This is my life!" she yelled, spreading her arms. "Don't you understand? I don't have anything except my work. Nobody will ever hire me again."

"Tink, be reason—"

"Publishing is a small business. Everybody knows everybody else. Word of this will be all over New York within days."

"You've always got me."

"Right! Mr. Trouble with a capital *T!* You waltz into my life, destroy everything and I'm supposed to be thankful?" She grasped her belly with both hands. "For your information, hotshot, you've done it again."

"Done what?"

"Knocked me up. I—" She clamped her mouth shut. Too late. She saw in his startled expression that he'd not only heard her hasty confession, but understood exactly what she meant. She stared at him; he stared back. A wide range of emotions swept over his expressive face: disbelief, amazement and concern.

"You're pregnant?"

Anger disappeared as if she'd pulled a plug. Without the fire to sustain her, she felt suddenly empty and weak. Realizing she continued holding her belly in a protective grasp, she dropped her hands to her sides. "I don't—I'm not... I don't know."

He loosed a long breath. "When were you going to tell me?"

Now ashamed, both of her irresponsibility and for taking out her anger on him, she hung her head. "When I was sure."

"I see." He sounded hurt.

"It could be a false alarm. I'm under a lot of stress. I swear, Easy, I meant to tell you. I've been trying for days to work up the nerve."

He nodded. His calm dismayed her, as did his shuttered expression and the way he half turned so he didn't face her directly. "Days. You'll never trust me, will you?"

His flat statement—flat truth—shamed her more than anything else. She saw herself through his eyes: a whiny, self-pitying baby who didn't need anyone victimizing her, because she was too busy victimizing herself.

"All these years," he said. "I never stopped loving you. In the back of my mind, I always hoped for a second chance. I knew I'd do things right the second time around. But it doesn't matter what I do."

"Easy, I..."

He waited for several moments, expectant, leaning forward in encouragement. Catherine found nothing to say.

Chapter Fifteen

Easy hurried down the stairs. Catherine's bedroom door was closed. Despite his urgency, he hesitated about knocking. After blurting out the news about being pregnant, she'd gone to her room. She hadn't been out since. He feared seeing her face. Feared the blame in her beautiful eyes. Feared the guilt. His wounds were still raw from yesterday.

He raised a fist to knock, but couldn't make himself complete the act. Okay, he thought. She didn't love him, she didn't trust him, but that's life. He couldn't always get what he wanted. If she was pregnant, he'd be a grown-up about it and take full responsibility. Even if she couldn't love him, he wouldn't let his child suffer for it. Nor did he intend to make her suffer.

He knocked on the door.

She opened the door a few inches. Her eyes were swollen and red. Her face was pale. She looked as if she hadn't gotten any sleep at all. "You're still here," she said.

Seeing her in pain roused all his protective instincts. He wanted to hold her and soothe her and assure her he'd never, ever stop loving her—no matter what. "The cops found Noreen."

She flung the door wide. "She'll testify? Jeffrey's been arrested? Is—?"

"She's dead."

She pressed both hands to her mouth. Tears welled, hovering on her lower lids.

"They found her in a motel room. It looks like an overdose on sleeping pills and vodka."

Shaking her head, Catherine backed away. She whispered, "No," over and over. She reached the foot of the bed and sat down hard. The greyhounds rushed past Easy and jumped onto the bed beside her. They nuzzled her and whined.

"She left a suicide note. In it she claimed responsibility for the death of Charles Newland. She also said she can't live with the lies she told about Livman. She said she blamed him for insurance fraud because he dumped her and she wanted to get even."

Her continuing silence alarmed him. He went to her side and nudged Oscar out of the way. He draped an arm around her shoulders. She shivered.

"You were right. Livman had the goods on her. Noreen lived with Charles Newland for several years. Newland slipped in the bathtub, knocked himself out and drowned. The death was ruled accidental. I'm betting it wasn't, and Livman knows it."

"He killed her," Catherine whispered. "Jeffrey murdered Noreen to shut her up."

"Looks like it. With any luck, the cops will prove he had something to do with her death."

"If they don't, then he gets away with it again." She leaned forward, her face on her hands. Her shoulders trembled.

Easy searched for words to soothe her, but his own conscience screamed at him. He should have been more careful with Noreen. He should have made sure she was protected from the moment he contacted her.

Through her fingers, her voice firm and cold, she said, "We have to stop him, Easy." She straightened and shifted on the mattress so she faced him. "He must feel like a god. He plays with people's lives. He rains down destruction on a whim. We have to stop him."

"We, Tink?" He searched her now-angry eyes, excited and dismayed by their sapphire fieriness.

"What I said yesterday…I was wrong. You're not to blame for what Jeffrey has done. Please forgive me."

He wanted to rush in with acceptance of her apology. He wanted to kiss her and assure her that all was well and he'd forget it. Images of her anguished face as she blurted out the news of her pregnancy haunted him. She did not trust him. She did not love him. Common sense said that now was the time to walk away, to encase his feelings for her inside a shell and tuck them permanently away.

"Forget it," he managed. He rose and shoved his hands in his pockets. He noticed the silver-framed photograph of Elizabeth's stand-in was missing. That hurt, too, in ways he couldn't quite define. "I have a meeting with Toni this afternoon. There might be something I can do."

"What about me?"

"I'll make sure Livman doesn't hurt—"

"That isn't what I mean! If not for me, Noreen would still be alive. Jeffrey has ruined my career. I stayed awake half the night trying to figure out what I can do to salvage the contract, and there is nothing." She lowered her gaze. Her chin quivered. "Look what he's done to us." She swiped the back of her hand across her nose and snuffled loudly. Her breast heaved in agitated breaths. "What happened between us, that wasn't your fault. Blaming you is cruel and stupid and I don't know if you'll ever forgive me. I don't know if I'll ever forgive myself."

He touched her chin with his fingertips, urging her to look at him.

"I wanted it, Easy. I wanted it as much as you did. When you showed up on my deck, I…I wanted you then. All those feelings, all those thoughts I imagined I'd outgrown, I haven't. You are so very right in calling me chicken. I'm so scared by how much I feel. I'm scared of losing you again. I'm scared of being pregnant, of losing another child. I'm even more scared of *not* being pregnant. I want a baby so much. I want *your* baby!'' She groaned, fraught with frustration. ''I don't know how you can stand being around me. I'm obviously insane.''

He slid his hand across her cheek, cupping her beloved face. She closed her eyes and leaned into his caress, sighing. He thought his chest might explode with the outpouring of affection and love he felt for her. He wanted to tell her he loved her and he understood. Except, he feared that tomorrow she might change her mind and take back her words. Tomorrow, she wouldn't want his baby at all. He backed away.

''I have coffee made.'' He hurried out of her bedroom and up the stairs.

She took the time to dress in shorts and a T-shirt before joining him in the kitchen. Easy caught himself several times staring at her flat belly. He handed her a cup of coffee.

''I meant what I said about going after Jeffrey.''

''There isn't anything you can do. I doubt there's much I can do.''

''You're going to quit? The man who always has a plan, is giving up?'' She laughed. ''I don't believe it. You want Jeffrey to pay. I know you do.''

''He's a killer. He's dangerous. I can't take the chance of him hurting you.''

''Ha!'' She picked up an artist's magazine, made a face at it, then tossed it across the counter. ''He's already hurt me. Even if I can salvage my career, the deal with Tabor is dead. And he isn't finished with me. We can use that. Somehow.''

He eyed her warily. ''When I talked to Toni this morning, she told me explicitly to turn over everything I've found to her office, and back off. She told John the same thing. All we can do is hurt the investigation.''

''Since when do you let anybody tell you what to do?'' She arched her eyebrows in unmistakable challenge.

He crossed his arms over his chest and glared down his nose at her. She took a step closer, meeting his heat with her own.

''Only one thing rattles Jeffrey,'' she said. ''In all the time I knew him, nothing shook him. Except when I told him no. The cops can't rattle him. Toni Johnson can't rattle him. But you heard what happened in the Grape and Olive. You know what he's like when he loses his temper. We can use that, Easy. You know we can.''

''He's dangerous.''

''Right at this moment, so am I. I'm too angry to be scared of him. I want his hide nailed to my wall. Are you with me, or do I have to do this myself?''

He threw back his head and laughed. The laughter came straight from the belly—for the first time in days, he felt alive. He felt good.

''Are you laughing at me or with me?''

''With you, babe. I'm with you all the way.''

CATHERINE PROWLED like a tigress. Each time she passed the telephone she glared at it. ''Why doesn't he call?'' she asked, for the umpteenth time. ''He calls ten million times when I don't want to talk to him, and now he won't call. What's wrong with him?''

Easy felt on edge himself. Catherine had left a message on Livman's voice mail. Plaintive, pitiful and whipped, the message should have had him flying to her home. ''Maybe he suspects a trick?''

She huffed her displeasure. Carrying a battered, well-chewed softball, Oscar followed Catherine around the room. He whined piteously. Except to let them out to relieve themselves, she hadn't taken the dogs outside in days. Bent was acting like a greyhound rug, barely moving on the sofa. Oscar paced and prowled, never more than a few inches from Catherine's heels. Easy sympathized with the dogs.

His cellular phone rang. Easy made a mental note. When Livman showed up, turn off the phone. He answered.

"Where are you?" Trish asked.

"I'm at Catherine's place. What's up?"

"What are you doing there?"

"I'll fill you in later. I'm waiting for an important call."

"Does this have to do with Jeffrey Livman?"

He wished his sister would spring for a decent cell phone; she sounded strange and the static made the connection almost painful. "I can barely hear you. Call me later when you're on a real phone. Talk to you later. Bye."

"Easy, don't—"

He disconnected.

"Wish I had a sister," Catherine said, her expression glum.

"I'll give you Trish. Cheap."

His telephone rang again. He answered with an exasperated, "Hello?"

"Easy Martel?" a woman asked.

He recognized the voice. "This is Easy. Toni?"

"It's me."

He flopped onto a chair and stretched out his legs. The day promised blistering heat. Despite open windows, the house was stuffy and warm. He wished he'd brought along a pair of shorts. "What's up, Toni?"

"I thought you might want to hear some good news. We've picked up Lou Palmer in connection with Noreen Dawson's death."

"What?" He gestured wildly for Catherine.

"We found his prints all over Dawson's car and inside the motel room. He isn't talking, yet, but he will."

"He didn't do it alone, Toni. You know Livman is involved."

"Oh, yes, indeed. When we searched Palmer's car, we found a prescription bottle for tranquilizers made out to Jeffrey Livman. I'm issuing an arrest warrant."

"You can make it stick?"

"You betcha. If the pills match what we found in Dawson's blood, then we're charging Palmer with first-degree murder. Trust me, he will not go down alone."

"What about his buddy No-neck? Where one goes, the other follows."

"We found some prints we can't identify. If they turn out to belong to T. J. Whitehead, then we'll pick him up too."

"What about Livman's prints?"

"Nothing in connection with Dawson. But get this, I went back to the case of Dawson's dead boyfriend. The investigating officers had run some latent prints from the house, but the case was closed as accidental, so the file went nowhere. I ran the prints."

"Livman."

"A direct hit. Our boy has a curious habit of being around when people die 'accidentally.' If this keeps up, I may end up solving every suspicious death from the past ten years." Toni laughed at her own joke, then rang off.

Springing off the chair, Easy loosed a rebel yell. He grabbed Catherine around the waist and swung her about. She demanded to know what Toni had said. "We did it!" he exclaimed. "Livman did himself in! He's going down!"

Laughing, feeling a hundred pounds lighter, he told Catherine everything Toni had told him. Her smile appeared, at first tentative and strained, then it blossomed gloriously. She hugged him, squeezing his ribs. "When will they arrest him?"

"As soon as they get the warrant. By close of business

today, he ought to be in an interrogation room, trying real hard to explain what happened.'' He caught her shoulders, holding her fast. Where only moments ago, her face had been drawn and wan, she now sparkled, her color high. His elation shifted to a warmer, more tender emotion as he studied the curve of her cheek and the shape of her eyes. Life, he decided, was too short for shielding his heart. ''I love you, Tink.''

Her smile faded, grew troubled.

''You love me, too. You know it and I know it. Why are we fighting it?''

''I don't know.''

He rubbed her arms, up and down. ''Let's do what we should have done twelve years ago. Let's get married.''

''Excuse me?'' She dropped a hand protectively to her belly.

''It doesn't matter if you're pregnant or not. If you are, fine, we'll have a baby. If you're not, fine, too. We'll get to work on making one. You need me, I need you, we're in love. Let's do it.''

''Good grief,'' she whispered. ''You actually mean it.''

''Hell, yes, I mean it. So what do you say? The weather's great. Let's hop on the bike and ride to Vegas. We'll get married, play a few slot machines, make love until our legs fall off, then live happily ever after. It's a great plan.''

''I—I—I don't want a shotgun wedding.''

His thoughts raced, whirling, seeking arguments and solutions. ''Okay! Let's get married, wait a week, then do a pregnancy test. Positive or negative, we'll never know for certain if we had to get married or not.''

She chuckled. The chuckle turned into a laugh. Suddenly she hugged him again. ''You're crazy, Easy Martel. Out of your mind.''

Bent hopped off the sofa. Oscar trotted to the door and stood on his hind legs to look outside.

"Somebody's coming." Catherine pushed away from his embrace. "What if it's Jeffrey?"

Easy and Catherine went to the door. Catherine pushed the greyhounds out of the way. Easy recognized the red Mustang coming up the driveway. "It's Trish. What the hell is she doing?" A sick feeling gripped him. Trish had been obsessing about Elizabeth. He wondered if she'd traced the adoption without him. She'd aided him often enough in running computer database searches, she knew the procedure. She also knew enough to contact private investigators in Arizona for help.

He pulled Catherine away from the door. "I know why she's here." He lifted his gaze to the ceiling. "She must have found Elizabeth."

She shoved his hand off her arm. "How? Why?"

"Because she's Trish! I didn't ask her to do it. I told her it was none of her business and she should leave it alone. I don't want this. Believe me."

The Mustang's horn honked.

"I swear, Tink. I didn't have anything to do with it. Even if she's found Elizabeth, it doesn't matter. I won't use the information. I promise. I'll let everything be. Say you believe me."

An odd, tightness blanked her expression. "You better go see what Trish wants."

"I swear, I haven't been trying to find Elizabeth. I won't disrupt her life. I promise."

The honking turned frantic. Assuring himself that Catherine understood, even if she were too shocked for speech, he hurried outside. "I'm going to kill you, Trish," he muttered.

His sister sat in the car, with both hands on the wheel. She watched his approach from the corner of her eye. He'd almost reached the car before her sallow complexion, tight mouth and sweat-shiny cheeks made an impact on his brain. He skidded to a stop. "Trish?"

"I'm sorry," she whispered. A single tear tracked her cheek.

Jeffrey Livman sat upright on the passenger seat. Smiling, he pressed the business end of a pistol against Trish's neck. "Greetings, Mr. Martel. Your sister is such a charming girl. I'd hate to blow her head off."

CATHERINE WATCHED Jeffrey leave the Mustang. Hands in the air, Easy marched around to the passenger side and slid in. Jeffrey handed him something shiny, but Catherine couldn't see what Trish or Easy did inside the car. Her fear deepened when Jeffrey herded Trish out of the car and made her climb into the trunk. He slammed the trunk shut. Jeffrey hoisted Easy's cellular telephone, then spun about and threw it with all his might. It sailed over the grass and landed with a puff of dust.

Catherine threw the dead bolt and ran to the telephone. Excited by her agitation, the dogs jumped on and off the sofa and ran around the studio.

Praying Jeffrey didn't start shooting, she pressed 911. Nothing. Not a ring, not a sound. Her heart began pounding. Her stomach clenched. She tried the telephone several times before the realization came home—the phone was dead.

"Catherine?" Jeffrey knocked on the door.

She ran into the kitchen. Peering around the corner of the doorway, she watched his shadow appear at the window. He tore off the screen and shoved aside the curtains. "Hello, darling, I'm home."

"I called the police! They're on the way!"

"Liar. I cut the telephone line. Now come unlock the door. You don't want a nasty old hole in lover boy's belly, do you? Don't make me hop through the window. It's undignified."

She didn't harbor a single doubt that he'd hurt Easy and Trish. Or kill them. She watched the dogs. They had moved to the window where they peered up at Jeffrey. If she survived, she determined, she was adopting the biggest, meanest, ugliest, noisiest dogs she could find.

On leaden legs, she trudged to the door and unlocked it. Tensing her muscles to keep from trembling, she backed away from the man she once believed she could love. His blue eyes looked like shards of flint—hard and emotionless. She tried not to look at the gun he held with such easy confidence. "You've already ruined me, Jeffrey," she said. "You destroyed my contract with Doc Halladay. You've sullied my professional name. My agent won't take my calls. What more do you want?"

"First things first, darling. I know you and lover boy cooked up a little trap for me." He gestured with the gun. "So, be a good girl and uncover all the microphones and recorders you've planted."

"No."

"How about I just burn down the house? Wood-frame construction. Dry roof. Shouldn't take more than a few minutes."

"It's over, Jeffrey! The police are looking for you. They arrested Lou Palmer. They know you murdered Noreen."

His pale eyebrows lifted, but he continued to smile. "Is that so? She killed herself." His teeth glinted wetly. "Despair is a terrible emotion, isn't it?"

She shook her head. "You'll never get away with it."

"Won't I? It's the oldest story in the book, darling. Kill your lover, then in despair, turn the gun on yourself." He raised the pistol, aiming directly at her face. "We had such a wonderful future ahead of us. Why did you betray me, Catherine? Why did you have to cheat and lie and treat me like a fool?"

Her dry mouth refused to cooperate by forming words.

"I loved you. I was ready to give you the world. Then you had to go and blow it." A flicker of emotion tightened his forehead and narrowed his eyes. "I thought you were different. I thought you and I were perfect. What happened?''

''You're a killer.''

He laughed softly. ''Where are they? Cameras? Microphones? How about I bring your boyfriend in here to find his toys? I bet if I blow off your kneecaps, he'll be real cooperative.''

''All right, all right.'' Wondering how in the world she and Easy were to escape this madman, she turned to a file box where a video recorder taped the proceedings.

''EASY?'' TRISH'S FEAR came through clearly despite her voice being muffled by the trunk. She thumped on the trunk, rocking the car. ''Easy?''

''I'm here, sweet pea. Relax. Don't panic. I'll get us out of this.'' He tried the trunk-release button, but it was jammed.

''I'm sorry,'' she called.

''Don't sweat it. Keep your cool.'' He jangled the handcuff binding his wrist to the steering wheel. Keeping an eye on the house, Easy dug in his pocket for his keys. He hoped that the handcuffs binding him were a standard model. The small car, tight jeans and his awkward position made retrieving his keys difficult, but he did it.

One-handed, he worked through the keys. The cuff on his left wrist was so tight, his fingers had gone numb and were turning an interesting shade of purple. He made a mental note to not be so rough with the cuffs in the future. It hurt. He fit the small cylindrical key into the keyhole. It stuck, and he feared Livman had specially ordered the cuffs so that a universal key wouldn't work.

''Easy?'' Trish thumped on the trunk again. ''What are you doing?''

He forced the key. The cuff released. Breathing a prayer of thanks, he rubbed his wrist briskly.

He shifted his attention between the house and the wide

field. Recent rains had caused a growth explosion of grass and weeds. If he searched for his telephone, Livman would see him. He didn't care about himself, but flying bullets could pierce the Mustang's trunk.

"Trish? Can you hear me?"

"I hear you."

"I can't open the trunk. You'll have to wait this out."

"What are you going to do?"

"I'll think of something. Stay quiet and quit pounding on the trunk." He opened the passenger door as quietly as he could and pushed it open. He crawled out of the car.

"Damn you, Martel!" Livman strode onto the deck. Catherine stumbled along behind him. He held her by the arm and cruelly jerked her in front of him. He shoved the pistol bore against her neck. "You have to make this hard, don't you? Step out with your hands up."

"No, Easy! Don't do it!" Catherine yelled. She yelped in pain.

Easy peered under the low-slung chassis, trying to gauge how far it was to the house. If he could get under the deck, he might be able to shake up Livman enough for Catherine to escape. He breathed hard, reminding himself that Livman had no military record, he didn't own a gun permit, he wasn't a hunter and he didn't belong to any sporting clubs. So the chances of him being able to hit a fast-moving target were slim.

"You have to the count of three, Martel! One—two—"

Easy burst from cover. Sprinting, his body remembering the fast moves from his high school football days, he zigged and zagged, churning gravel.

He didn't hear the shot. He didn't feel the blow. All he knew was that, somehow, he was staring at the sky, listening to a woman scream.

CATHERINE SCREAMED. A scream that was cut short when Jeffrey ran to the railing, jerking her along behind him.

She stumbled to one knee. Her fall pulled Jeffrey off-balance. His grasp loosened enough for her to twist away. She fell back, sitting hard on the deck. He reached for her. She kicked him with all her might.

Her left foot connected with a satisfying crunch on his thigh. Jeffrey yowled and hopped on his good leg. He hit the deck railing and nearly tumbled over. Catherine rolled, sprang to her feet and ran. She jumped down the steps, straight to Easy's side.

"Run," Easy croaked. He lay on his back, his arms and legs sprawled. Blood turned the front of his T-shirt black. His eyes blazed. "Run, damn it!"

Catherine looked over her shoulder, spotted Jeffrey recovering his balance. She ran.

A shot rang out. Running on instinct, she swerved, aiming for the closest trees. Jeffrey shouted at her. She ran faster. Thistles snagged at her skin. Spear grass whipped her bare legs. Wrong, she knew. Her direction took her away from the road and away from neighbors, toward a wild patch of forest. Another gunshot shoved reason from her mind.

She reached the trees and darted around the trunk of a pine. Panting, she peered back at the house. Jeffrey ran after her. Sobbing, she pushed away from the tree and ran again. Pine straw, pinecones, loose branches and snapped-off stumps made the path treacherous. She changed direction, scrambling up a hill. Rocks and brush oaks slowed her, but they offered cover, too.

She heard Jeffrey pounding behind her. She sucked wind into her burning lungs. She caught a boulder and climbed, banging her knees and shins on the rock, but not caring as she flailed about for foot- and handholds.

Half a mile, she told herself. Half a mile and she reached a road. A road with houses. Houses with people. Run! Over the hill, she slipped and skidded from rock to rock. An arroyo yawned before her. Though neither deep nor wide, it was full of rocks and broken logs. Unable to stop her wild downhill run, she jumped. She hit a narrow flat patch on the other side. The dirt crumbled beneath her feet.

She fell hard, flat on her belly. Unable to breathe or even think, she grabbed instinctively, her hands finding a rock to hold on to. The ground broke away from beneath her legs. Dirt and gravel poured into the arroyo, rattling and surrounding her in a cloud of choking dust.

"Stop!" Jeffrey ordered. "I have a dead-on shot. I will kill you."

She listened to him coming down the hill. His descent was reasonable and measured, marked by soft thumps and rustling foliage. She blinked back the urge to cry. An image of Easy, still and bleeding filled her head. If he died, she didn't want to live.

"Get up," Jeffrey ordered. "Slowly. If you try to run, I will kill you."

"You'll kill me anyway. Just like you killed Roberta and Noreen." She dug her feet into the sides of the crumbling arroyo, found a solid place and pushed herself forward. Rocks grating across the belly made her groan. The baby. She had to save her baby. She sat up, facing Jeffrey.

His face was red from exertion, but his demeanor was as calm as if they'd taken a pleasant jog. "You should be so lucky, darling. Roberta never saw me coming. I doubt if she felt a thing. And Noreen? Well, don't feel sorry for her. She was sick of living with the guilt of killing Charlie anyway." He laughed. "Do you know what the funny part is? She didn't kill him. Oh yeah, he had a nasty bump, maybe a concussion. But he was alive when I put him in the bathtub. So, even if she'd known I'd drugged the booze, she'd have drank it anyway. She wanted to die." He pointed the gun at her belly. "Now you on the other hand, you insist on making this as messy as possible." He gestured for her to jump back over the arroyo. "Get back over here. I can kill you now. I don't mind dragging you back—''

A large body crashing through brush cut off his words. He whirled about in time to see Oscar come over the top of the hill. The greyhound raced flat-out, ears flat against his skull, his eyes bright with lust for the hunt. He flew over an outcrop of boulders, hit the narrow path with his forepaws then sprang into a leap. Unable to speak or move, Catherine watched the dog hit the ground again. He seemed to fly. Jeffrey shouted at the dog to stop. He aimed the pistol. Catherine recognized joy in Oscar's eyes. The joy of the run, the joy of catching her in this wild game.

Realization struck. ''Jeffrey! Watch—!''

Eighty pounds of greyhound moving at top speed struck Jeffrey squarely in the legs. Man and dog tumbled into the arroyo. Oscar screamed in pain. Jeffrey made no sound at all.

''HEY, TINK,'' EASY SAID. He smiled groggily, floating in the warm woolly shroud of painkillers.

Catherine touched his face, rubbing her knuckles lightly over his cheek. Her beautiful eyes smiled warmly at him. ''Good morning. How do you feel?''

He gave her question serious thought. He'd spent three hours in surgery yesterday. Despite a broken clavicle, punctured lung and ripped muscles, the doctors assured him he was a lucky man. Lucky, he knew, as long as they kept providing painkillers.

Luckier by far than Jeffrey Livman. His fall into the arroyo had broken his neck. Toni Johnson had visited Easy last night, and if he remembered correctly, she'd told him Livman was now paralyzed from the shoulders down. Even if, the assistant district attorney had assured him, the confession Catherine had taped on the hidden wire she'd been wearing didn't earn him a prison sentence for three murders, he'd be imprisoned in a wheelchair for the rest of his life.

"I feel better than Oscar, I bet. How is he?"

"You're sweet to ask. He's still at the vet's. He broke both of his front legs. He'll never outrun Bent again, but he'll be okay. He saved my life." She rose from the chair and touched his lips with a tender kiss. "So did you." She snuffled and backed away. Her shoulders hitched; her eyes brightened. "Idiot! You're no smarter than that dumb dog."

"Yeah, but you love me."

Her fire faded and her smile returned. "God help me, but I do."

With great effort, he lifted a hand, urging her closer. She resumed her seat by the bed. "Where are my folks?"

"Your parents and Trish went to breakfast. I'll go tell them you're awake—"

"That's okay. Stay with me. Have you been here all night? How come they let you stay?"

"I told them I'm your fiancée."

He clucked his tongue. "You lied?"

She shrugged. "Is it a lie?"

"Not if you don't want it to be. Spring me out of this joint, and we're on the first plane to Vegas."

"No Vegas. If I marry you, it'll be a real wedding. Okay?"

He lifted his head and peered in the direction of her abdomen. "Can you make arrangements that quick?"

She rested her chin on her arms folded atop the bed. Her heavy sigh and sad eyes warned him. "I'm not pregnant." Her chin trembled. She blinked rapidly. "I didn't want to be pregnant, but now that I'm not, I feel awful."

He caressed her hair. "Me, too. Marry me, anyway. Let's do everything right this time. A ring, wedding, carrying you over the threshold. A honeymoon. The works."

"Ask me again when you aren't all doped up."

He searched her face. "Why wait? You know you don't stand a chance against me."

She laughed, sweet music in his ears. "I never did, Earl Zebulon Martel. Not once."